The Legend of the

ULTIMATE
TREASU

Alexander Way B
and
Daisy B

ISBN 978-1-7398885-1-0
Published in the UK by

Louannvee Publishing
www.louannveepublishing.co.uk

Dedicated to my
Auntie Ida,
who lived with us, throughout
most of my childhood
and was like my third parent.

To my wonderful,
supportive wife Akiko!

A big thankyou to Daisy-B
(Aged 10) for enthusiastically
drawing some of the illustrations
and covering herself in charcoal!

READER REVIEWS

"A roller coaster ride of a story, for young readers of any age, with some excellent themes and wholesome adventure"
Revd AJ Bawtree

"Fantastic story captures the imagination of both young and old. I couldn't put it down. Brings the fun back into story time with the kids. Highly recommend."
Leslie Mum of 14-year-old

"Fantastic and captivating for adults and children alike!" Lisa mum of 11-year-old.

"Magnetic adventure story, which gathers speed and excitement as the plot progresses. Strong characters and excellent links to conservation."
AFB teacher and lecturer

"A piratical adventure suitable for all ages: a real treasure of a tale."
Thomas

CONTENTS

1: A STORY FROM THE PAST p1

2: SOMETHING FISHY p12

3: THE TANGLED GARDEN p18

4: REBEL SCHOOL UNIFORM p22

5: IT'S ALL IN THE ENTRANCE! p28

6: IT'S A JUNGLE OUT THERE! p33

7: DISCOVERY IN THE LOFT p37

8: WHO IS C.C? p42

9: ON THE WRONG SIDE OF THE ROAD! p48

10: PIRATE's REUNION p54

11: THE FALL p59

12: A MESSAGE FROM THE PAST p64

13: RETURN TO BASE p72

14: A HIDING PLACE p76

15: GIANTS? p82

16: THE MIRROR p89

17: GREEN LIGHT p94

18: WHAT IS MY NAME? p102

19: THE MUSEUM p106

20: THE CLOCKMAKER p113

21: EYE PATCHES p119

22: THE PAINTING p124

23: THE HOUND p133

24: FAR REACHING HAND OF THE HOUND p139

25: THE EMPTY SEA p144

26: DEADLY BEAUTY p150

27: TIME TO SHARE! p159

28: IRRESISTIBLE p163

29: SHIPWRECKS p171

30: AN UNLIKELY ALLY! p176

31: CECILE's TALE p183

32: THE MIST DISAPPEARS p186

33: SITTING DUCKS! p192

34: S.O.S p197

35: RESCUE p203

36: THE BOAR p208

37: DELICIOUS p214

38: A KIND OFFER p221

39: FOR THE COLLECTION p226

40: THE MIST's ROOM p234

41: GLUTTONY AND
EXTINCTION p245

42: THE LAST OF THEIR KIND p249

43: A FAMILIAR FACE p254

44: AN OLD FRIEND p259

45: WAS IT ALL A DREAM? p264

46: ECO WARRIORS p268

47: DRAGON'S DESPAIR p274

48: A WEEK LATER! p280

49: DRIFTING p287

50: AN AGE-OLD GUARDIAN p296

51: A TEA PARTY p304

52: WOUNDED p310

53: SWAGGER OF A PIRATE p316

54: THE GREAT JOURNEY TO
AQUASENTIA p325

55: KINGDOM OF OLD p330

56: GREED p335

57: DON'T TOUCH THE
WATER p341

58: THE PRICE OF FREEDOM p349

59: IT BEGINS p357

60: RISK AND RUMBLE p362

61: CRYSTAL WATERS p368

EPILOGUE p376

Why is plastic a problem? p381
Here are some ideas p381
About the Authors and Illustrators p384
Acknowledgements p385

CHAPTER ONE

A STORY FROM THE PAST

It was *that* morning. The day that Jack and Suzan had been counting down to, even dreading. The children sat in an almost empty room swimming in fond memories. Sitting with their backs against a pile of cardboard boxes that contained their everything.

Jack the younger of the two, a boy with scraggly untidy brown hair, a tatty pair of jeans that looked like they had seen one too many adventures and a baggy shirt that was about five sizes too big. Suzan, his sister, slightly taller and older by a year, had long untidy brown hair and a determined tough looking face. She too was dressed in an old pair of jeans, which, if possible, seemed even more adventure scarred than Jacks.

She was wearing an equally distressed jean jacket, one she refused to take off, and even slept in sometimes. It was once black, but years of climbing trees, rolling in the garden play fighting and constant use had faded it to a washed out grey. On the back were hand drawn pictures she had done of various pirate flags using marker pens.

1

Jack and Suzan were like two peas in a pod. Best friends and inseparable.

Jack looked over to Suzan with a tear in his eye. 'Do we really have to go?' he grumbled.

Suzan mustered a brave smile and said: 'Yes, you know we do. Dad's lost his job and we can't stay in our city anymore.'

Jack's head slowly dropped in sadness.

Suzan shuffled a little closer to Jack and ruffled his hair. 'Come on, buck up Jack. As long as we are together, we'll be fine,' she said.

Jack managed a smile at Suzan. 'Thanks sis, you're always the strong one,' he said. 'Hey, tell me that story again sis. You know the one mum always told us when we were small,' he said.

'Oh, alright Jack,' Suzan replied. In a gravelly low tone, with a pirate twang, Suzan began:

'Imagine a time before electricity, before the internet, and before cars. A time when the world was full of mystery and many of the areas of the world were still uncharted! A time of great unrest between countries. It was a time when pirates ruled the seas! Blood thirsty, treasure lusting, immoral pirates! And most built their riches and reputations on their strength and their violent deeds. But not all...

'There was one infamous pirate who sailed the seas, who was a menace to so many ships, and known in every corner of the globe, surrounded by stories, yet none of them of violence, and blood! He was known by many a name, to some as the sly old cat, to others as the blunt blade, and to some as the phantom, but most called this cunning pirate the Mist. Very few had seen him, or his ship: the *Beluga*, but it was said that if you had, you were already a fortune worse off! How they did it no one knew.

'It was a mystery. Like the time a Spanish ship was sailing back home, laden with gold and one morning the crew awoke to find themselves vastly off course, drifting. Every man had strangely been asleep for days, including the night watch! And what was more, their ship was vastly lighter. Down in the hold a note saying: *Thanks,* and signed the *Mist,* was left alongside a single gold coin, like a token of good manners. The rest of the gold was stolen – gone, vanished! There was not a trace of anyone boarding their ship in the night, and none of the crew could explain how they had been relieved of the riches onboard.

'There are so many legends surrounding the captain, and his ship, but of them all, the biggest mystery was their final disappearance.'

Jack sat up; he was grinning, as he listened to his sister tell that favourite tale. Suzan was also grinning. Her voice seemed to get even more gravelly and pirate like, for the next part, as she continued:

'It was said that they were a menace to countries all over the world, but especially to three countries in Europe. The three European countries had lost so much treasure to the Mist, year after year, month after month, that they decided to try to join forces for one special mission. This was a thing that at the time was unimaginable, for the three countries were locked in a great feud with each other, competing for trade routes, riches, and ownership of faraway lands.

'The kings of all three countries had a vast and deep despising for each other, yet there was one thing that they hated more, the *Mist*! So, in a time of great conflict, they

3

called a meeting to attempt to put aside their differences and create a truce, a cooperation to capture and kill the Mist. Each country chose their best man…

'One winter's night, in an undisclosed secret location, the ancient oak door of a small, smoky pub, creaked open on its iron hinges. A man dressed in rich emerald-green, stepped through the doorway, wearing ornate high leather boots. He had a well-kept beard, a wide brimmed hat, with a feather and one of his hands firmly attached to the handle of his sword. His eyes shifted around the pub, scanning all the time. He continued walking towards the bar.

'The grubby bartender, with long brown hair, fumbled around nervously as he poured an ale. Too frightened to make eye contact, the bar man slowly lifted the drink and placed it in front of the emerald man. It was served in a beautifully ornate silver tankard. The sharply dressed man picked it up and wandered over to a table, in a dark, secluded corner. While he was sitting sipping his silken ale, the door creaked open a second time…

'A tall thin man, dressed in rich velvet blue, stepped in, out of the cold night. His hand also firmly on the handle of his sword. He too approached the bar and was served a silken ale, in a silver ornate tankard, by a doubly nervous bartender. He proceeded very cautiously as he approached the round table. Like a lion approaching a rival lion.

'Both knew that one wrong move and it could come to blows. The tall thin man sat on a chair, on the opposite side to the man in green.

'Just then the door opened a third time and in stepped another man; this time dressed in red velvet.

4

CAW-B

'His hand, sword and eyes poised; he moved towards the bar. The bar keeper seemed to be more and more nervous each minute. He fumbled around and just managed to serve that last silver tankard of silken ale. The man in red strolled over to the table and sat down.

'The bar keeper could not handle it anymore. He dropped down and crawled behind the casks and tanks, at the back of the bar. Like a rat scurrying away, when the cat gets home.

'The silence could be cut. The tension great as the three men, all lords, looked left and right at each other – their fingers and hands poised above their swords. They knew the last man, in that moment, to draw his sword, would pay the ultimate price.

'These men represented three kings - who despised each other deeply. That despising ran deep in each lord's veins too. Yet here they were together, sitting around a secluded table, in the corner of an unknown undisclosed bar.

'Finally, after several nail-biting minutes of intense tension, the lord dressed in green removed his wide brimmed hat, very delicately from his head. He placed the hat on the table, to the right of his silver mug that bore the emblem of his country, the crest of his king.

'Whilst still maintaining an alternating glare, between the left and the right of him, he slowly moved his hand away from his sword hilt and lay it next to his mug. In the corner of his mouth, the beginning of a grin appeared. The other two lords glanced briefly at each other, as if looking for some agreement, and removed their hands from their sword hilts. They placed their hands on the table.

6

A W-B

7

'The three lords sipped their silken ale and let out a short sigh. No one knows quite the details of their discussion that night, but certainly what we do know is that they agreed to put a stop to the ongoing conflict between their countries, or rather a pause! Instead, they turned their attention to the capture of the Mist. For each lord not only represented their king that night, but also represented the total naval force of their countries.

'Several weeks later an armada appeared in the channel. An armada that consisted of ships from three countries. Each ship sailed under its own flag. The fleet patrolled the coasts, waiting, watching, biding its time for the right moment and a chance to rid the waters of the Mist for good. The Mist, that cunning pirate and his crew, who had outsmarted them so many times. This time they would not get away! For this time three whole countries were working in unison, with one goal only.

'Day after day, and night after night they patrolled, determined! And their dedication finally paid off - several months later, in the summertime, during a horrific storm that was battling the coast and surging through the channel, a lone ship sailed its way through the waves. It cut through the stormy waves, almost as if it was a normality, as if it was strolling in the park.

'Not far off in the distance, struggling in the waves and the wind was the large armada and, in the lead, at the top of the crow's nest, was a man with a glint in his eye, dressed in green holding onto that fancy hat of his, as he scanned the horizon, taking advantage of every flash of lightning, to try to find that legendary ship, *The Beluga*. To his eye he had an ornate leather-bound golden telescope, as he perched himself to steady against the sway. Just then, in the glint of a flash of lightning, he recognized something on the horizon – something he had never seen before, but nevertheless he knew - *The Beluga*! The armada of ships signaled with each other and began to move in to surround that lone ship.

'Step by step they came closer, gauging their distance and their direction by the flashes of lightning. Between each flash, total pitch blackness and the raging wind and waves. They were almost there! The trap was sprung, and the Mist was theirs!

'Suddenly, just when they were readying the boarding planks, grappling hooks and arming up to the teeth, after one space of darkness, the next flash revealed an empty horizon. Where had that ship gone? How had it evaded them when it was surrounded? The conclusion they drew that night, was that it had to have gone down in the storm.

'When they reached the place where it had been, there was just debris floating on the violent waves. And that was the last that the legendary ship, *The Beluga*, was ever seen or heard of.

'Most people say that, that night she was destroyed by the storm, spared the fate of being caught by the angry naval forces. Instead, smashed to pieces, she was lying at the bottom of the sea, along with the remains all the great treasures and riches collected throughout the Mist's career, including the ultimate treasure: a legendary treasure he was said to have found.

'Yet there was a whisper, among certain pirates and those *in the know*, a murmur, no more, that the Mist had sailed right past them, up the river Seine, into enemy land, towards Paris. He was spotted, along with crew, drinking a pint in the underground pub, notorious for pirates, at the top of the hill in Argenteuil.

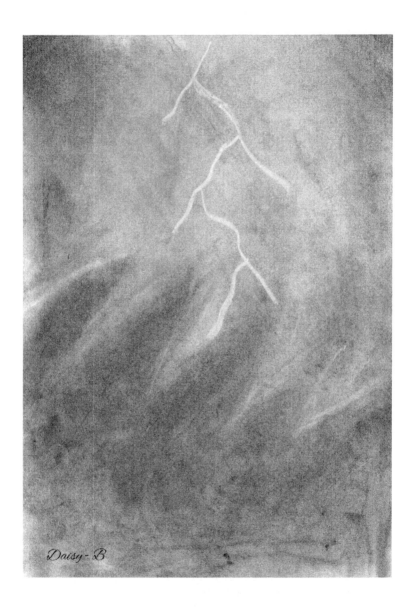

Daisy-B

But when push came to shove, no one would swear to it and the rumours faded like echoes on the wind. All trails of him went cold…' Suzan had a glint in her eye as she finished the last part of that very well practiced story.

Jack was smiling from ear to ear. It was his favourite story ever and his sis told it so well. For a moment they had forgotten where they were and why they were sitting with a pile of cardboard boxes. They had been carried away, as if by the sea itself.

All of a sudden, the magical moment was broken, as footsteps signalled that *it was time*! The door swung gently open and in walked their father. He looked tired, and probably was. The last few months had taken their toll on him, especially losing his job and now the worry of packing up and moving to the coast. He missed their mum too, they saw it in his eyes, but he always put on a brave face.

The children knew it was time. Getting to their feet, they took one last glance around the room, and followed him down to the car. They waited in the back while their dad met the removals people. Swiftly he jumped in the car, started the engine and they were off.

Suzan and Jack waved goodbye to that familiar street and soon found themselves speeding along the motorway. Both children sat in the back of the car, silently watching the cars flicker by. It was a long, long way to Dover, a town on the South Coast, with a busy ferry port. Silently lulled by the flashes of towns, rivers, and hills, they drifted off into thoughts, imagining what Dover would be like. Little by little they closed their tired eyes and drifted off to sleep.

CHAPTER 2

SOMETHING FISHY

Suddenly, the children were awoken by a jolt. It was evening, quite dark and the moon was out. They pulled into a small road, slowed down as their father looked for the house and eventually slipped into a parking space, outside an old, dilapidated building.

It was small, terraced and its front door almost opened onto the street. One old, chipped terracotta plant pot and two disgustingly dirty dustbins fought for space beneath the front window. Their new home looked like it was the only house left in the street, to have its original wooden windows and doors.

They clambered out of the car and stretched out the stiffness, from a long journey sitting. Then their father led them to the front door. It was very old and had an ornate brass handle on the front. He rummaged in his pocket for the key and struggled to turn the lock.

The door looked as though it had not been opened for a long time. Vine had wound its way across the front of the house and halfway over the roof. Eventually, with much jiggling, rattling and strategic bashing, their father turned the key and opened the door.

The door creaked open and stopped halfway, due to what looked like a large pile of junk mail that had accumulated over who knows how long. He found an old-fashioned Bakelite light switch and turned it on. They pulled the pile of letters out of the way and fully opened the door.

Finally, they stepped inside. The front door led into a small hallway, that led to stairs. Beside the stairs, the tiny hall opened into a long lounge, with an ornate fireplace.

At the far end of the lounge there was a low door, leading to a kitchen with uneven red stone floor-tiles. The walls had old floral wallpaper, that looked as though it was hanging on by its last few inches.

The hall and lounge had bare floorboards that were worn and rounded through age. And the internal doors were old, worn wood, along with equally worn skirting boards. It was very dusty too, as if it had been decades since their grandad had last lived there. Jack and even Suzan looked unhappy.

'I am so sorry kids,' said their father in a soft and sad voice. 'But, if it wasn't for your grandfather letting us live here, we would actually be homeless. I know it's old, but we'll soon fix it up and make it our home.'

Suzan smiled, 'Of course we will Dad!' she said and turned to Jack. He looked back. A small smile appeared, in the corner of Suzan's mouth and she said, 'Last one upstairs is a soggy poor excuse for a pirate!'

The three of them darted and jostled towards the stairs. Jack tried to stop Suzan, but she was too quick. The neighbours must have thought that elephants were running up the stairs, that evening, it was all so loud.

Suzan reached the top first, followed by Jack and last of all their dad. The two kids called him a soggy pirate and they all laughed!

Upstairs was also very old and tired looking. Their father said that their grandad had not lived there for a long time and had always been stubborn about not wanting to decorate, or update anything. He had insisted on keeping it just as it had always been, since his father once owned it. In fact, the house had been owned by many generations of their family, for well over two hundred years.

There were two small rooms upstairs and a small bathroom. Their father took the smaller of the two, leaving them the larger, front bedroom.

'Right, you two, I'll need your help, quite soon, when the removal van arrives, but for now you can both look round your room and decide where your beds will go, while I check out the kitchen,' said their dad, disappearing downstairs.

Floorboards creaked as Susan and Jack explored their new room.

'Look,' called Susan, suddenly spying an old, rather ornate, wooden window seat. 'We can sit and munch biscuits, as we watch the world go by. I've always wanted a real window seat!'

'Not much to see out there now,' said Jack, 'It's all dark and really quiet and...' before he could say any more, Susan had grabbed his hand and dragged him to the old wooden seat.

'It's got a lid – the bit you sit on – look,' she said excitedly.

'Yeah, probably nothing in there, just spiders and...' retorted Jack, pausing suddenly as Suzan lifted the heavy old wooden lid, with some difficulty.

'Help me Jack,' she yelled impatiently.

Jack lent a hand, to push the lid back towards the window, where it rested happily, supported by the windowsill. Both children peered inside the ancient window seat, wrinkling their noses, at the musty smell.

'Just some horrid old blankets,' said Suzan, disappointedly.

'And a rather unhappy spider,' said Jack, as he watched a fat, black spider scurry from the light and disappear beneath the old blanket. 'Hmm, I think I can see something, poking out, at the edge of the blankets.'

Susan followed his gaze, 'You're right,' she said, whisking the blanket away, sending clouds of dust, cobwebs and possibly a few spiders, into the air. 'Just an old book.'

'It's an old photo album, bet it's got pictures of our grandad and everyone in it,' said Jack, lifting and opening the leather-bound album, cautiously - for fear of damaging it.

'Put it on the floor, for a second, let's close the window-seat first,' said Suzan.

Soon, they were huddled together, on the window seat - the old album balanced carefully between them - both lost in the world of yesterday. 'Look how thick and brown looking these photos are,' remarked Suzan.

'That's because they're very old. Wonder who they were. He looks rather fierce, look at that thick beard and those bushy eyebrows,' said Jack, pointing to a photo of a middle-aged gentleman.

'That's strange,' said Suzan, suddenly. 'I'm sure I can smell the sea and the windows are closed.'

'I can too,' said Jack. 'But we're too far from the docks, to smell it from here, even if the window was open. It's weird.'

'I'm sure it's coming from the album.'

'Not possible, it's made from leather, not seaweed,' replied Jack, with a cheeky grin. 'Anyway, let's finish looking at it.'

'Oh look, I think that's grandad, when he was young, that's probably our gran beside him,' said Suzan, pointing to a faded black and white picture of a handsome man, arm in arm with a beautiful lady. 'Jack, that sea smell's getting stronger. Could someone have sprayed the room in sea smelling air freshener?'

'Maybe,' said Jack, doubtfully. 'But why is it getting stronger, the further we go in the book? Still, we're nearly at the end now, just this page then we're done,' he said, turning the final page.

'Not so fast, Jack, look…' Suzan pointed to an ancient looking photo, on the final page. 'Isn't that a strange rock, almost a mini mountain, all jagged and…'

'Sis,' yelled Jack, suddenly, 'the sea smell, it's overpowering, it's that photo that smells – I'm sure it is. It's…'

'You're right,' interrupted Suzan, 'almost as if it's drifting directly from the picture. It's quite overpowering, but somehow beautiful.'

'There's words, on the label, beside the photo,' said Jack. 'It says *Elgor's Rock*. Never heard of *Elgor's Rock*, wonder where it is. It could be…' Abruptly, Jack's words were drowned, by the sound of a heavy-handed knock on the front door. And the children's thoughts were forced sharply back to the present.

'Right, let's go. Dad's downstairs, checking out the kitchen. Guess he thinks we'll get the door for the removal people,' said Suzan zapping downstairs, calling her brother a sea slug!

CHAPTER 3

THE
TANGLED
GARDEN

A rather burly man appeared at the door, with arms full of boxes. 'Where do you want these li…' He was about to say *little girl* when he saw the pirate flag on Suzan's jacket and a stern look in her eye.

Just then, their dad arrived and took over organising where the boxes should go. The three of them and the men, worked hard to get the truck unloaded and the boxes and few pieces of furniture in.

Soon they said goodbye to the removal people and closed the front door. It was late, so their father unpacked some of the tinned food, a loaf of bread and the toaster. He made them all a late-night feast of beans on toast and a cuppa. They sat around using boxes as tables, tucking into the hot food.

'Dad,' said Suzan suddenly, 'we found an old photo album, in the window seat, upstairs. One of the really old photos had a strange sea like smell to it. Like strong sea breeze. What could cause that?'

'I can't think of anything that would cause that,' replied their dad, 'but, when we have a bit more time, we can all take another look at it, together, if you like.'

After they had eaten, they collected their sleeping bags from the car. Too tired even to sweep the dusty floor, they decided to camp out together, in their new house, for the first night. Soon they were all lying next to each other, wrapped up in their sleeping bags, taking it in turns to tell stories, until they drifted off to sleep.

The next day they were awoken by the sun, streaming through the curtainless windows. Suzan opened her eyes first, as the light cascaded over the new landscape of the lounge. She had that rare and strange feeling, of not knowing where she was, for a moment.

Her eyes scanned around the room, for a few seconds, before the events of the day before came flooding back to her. As she lay there, she had a mixture of sadness from the move, but also a strange glimmer of excitement too. She remembered the old album with its strange, sea-smelling photo and she started to imagine what stories the old house might have. It had obviously been standing there for a long time. But that thought was interrupted by her brother and father getting up.

The three of them washed and prepared for a new day. The house looked even more dilapidated and uninhabited in the daylight.

Suzan went into the kitchen to make some toast and tea. The old red tiles were cracked and worn, and at the end of the kitchen was a wooden door that she guessed led to a garden. Despite having a window, very little light was coming in.

She rubbed some of the dust from the inside and peered through her clean spyhole. She was looking through a bramble bush, which had grown directly in front of the door. From what she could make out, in fact, the whole back garden was a tangled mess.

Suzan tried the door, but even the handle wouldn't turn. She gave up and decided to go back to making breakfast, noticing that her dad had already unpacked the kitchen stuff.

Opening the old-fashioned cupboards, she took out a loaf of bread and looked at the mixture of plates that they had brought, alongside those that her Grandad had left behind. Susan chose three of the most interesting plates, belonging to her grandfather. Then she opened the cutlery drawer to find some butter knives for the toast and found an even more eclectic mixture of objects, cutlery and miscellaneous items. Some she recognised; some must have been left by their grandad.

As she was rummaging through the disorganised drawer, she came across an old magnifying glass. Susan peered through it, expecting to see the jam label in super, double large writing, but it just seemed blurry. She tossed the old thing back in the drawer and went back to looking for the knives, as her stomach reminded her that breakfast was well overdue!

After breakfast, the three of them began work to unpack the things, hoover the floors, and clean the thick dust that seemed to be everywhere. It seemed to take forever.

They woke up early every day that week and worked well into the evenings. Bit by bit they managed to clean and tidy the house. They put together the few pieces of furniture that they had brought – Suzan's bed and Jack's bed, a tiny coffee table, that they could perch around for dinner and that was about it. Most of the furniture, in their last place, came with the house they rented, so they had left it.

They knew difficult times were ahead, but they had each other, and the house was now organised and exceptionally clean. There was electricity and hot water and plenty of food. And they had the old album, with its mysterious rock photo to think about! Jack had looked up Elgor's Rock, on his dad's computer, but hadn't been able to find anywhere with that name.

CHAPTER 4

REBEL
SCHOOL
UNIFORM

It was Friday morning - almost a week since they had arrived, and Suzan was already up. She peered out of the old bay window, at the tiny front path. Gazing and waiting.

A flash of red and then the old brass letterbox flap creaked open and in dropped a post card. 'YES!' shouted Suzan, as she punched the air. In a flash she scooped it up and belted upstairs. The wooden banisters rattled as she went. She dashed into the bedroom and grabbed Jack's shoulder, which was attached to a sleeping Jack! She shook him, shouting: 'It's here, It's here!'

Jack, was just in the middle of a particularly fantastic pirate dream, fighting a ferocious captain on the deck of a ship, when he was abruptly awoken by his over excited big sis. 'EEEEEERRRRRRR,' he managed to say.

'It's HERE! Look!' yelled Suzan, refusing to stop shaking him, despite the fact he was very clearly awake.

He caught sight of the post card, she was waving around, in her other hand. He too, suddenly felt excited and jumped out of bed. The two of sat side by side staring at the picture on the front of the card. The wording said "*Beijing*". The two gazed at the images of buildings, on the front.

'You read this time Jack,' said Suzan, handing him the card.

Jack scanned the card and began to read the tiny writing:

"My Dear darlings, you must be in grandad's house now. I know it's probably old and tatty inside, but dad will fix it up. I'm in Beijing this week working on a huge deal with a company here for my boss, I won't bore you with the details. The food is really nice and the weather too. I'll be off to the next country in a few days for another business meeting. You will be starting school soon and dad will start his new job too. I have sent your dad a little money so he can get your school uniforms. I will be thinking of you both. Look after dad for me, he isn't as tough as he makes out. Loads of love, mum."

Jack looked a little upset. Suzan gave him a hug. 'Don't worry we should see her later this year.'

'Why can't she just come home and get a new job here?' Jack asked.

'You know that she'd love to Jack, but lots of people rely on her in her company and she can't let them all down.'

Soon, the smells of breakfast drifted up. Suzan lifted her head and sniffed the air, 'Pancakes!' she shouted. They jumped to their feet.

'Last one down does the washing up and mops the decks!' yelled Jack. At that he shot out of the room and darted downstairs. At the bottom of the stairs, he stopped suddenly, realizing that there was an old dining table sitting in the middle of the room and pancakes were served.

Their dad smiled. 'Do you like it? I got it from a second-hand shop for a couple of pounds. It needs varnishing.'

There were three chairs around it and a fourth one leaning against the wall in bits. Bare footed, they sat down and tucked into fresh breakfast.

Just as they finished the last drop of tea and drizzle of maple syrup their father stood up and said: 'Right, you lot, get ready for a trip down to town. It's not far, and we need to buy you some cheap school clothes. You start on Monday! Mum sent me some money. Let's leave the washing up, we can do that later.'

Suzan gave Jack a cheeky smile as if to say: *I got out of that.* Swiftly the three of them washed, put on socks, and left the house.

Their father led them down the old narrow streets, around a corner and into a little alleyway that had a fence and then a high wall on the left. A beautiful mural - depicting happy children and adults, and a little river with fish – transformed the ordinary wall. 'Look, at the plaque here,' said their dad. 'It's called: *The Happy River Mural, Barton Path* and it's designed by three local schools.'

'That's cool,' said Suzan.

'Yeh, but look here,' said Jack pointing to a trickling river on the right. There were flowers growing along the banks and ducks bobbing along. Sunshine glistened on the water.

The warm sunshine was a change after having been in the house, unpacking, for the last few days.

They followed the path as it meandered alongside the river.

'I think this is called the *River Dour,*' said their dad.

'It's pretty, but these won't help the wildlife,' said Suzan as she bent down and fished two empty beer cans, from the water.

Daisy - B

Soon they came out onto a road, crossed over, cut through another alley to finally come out close to a large supermarket. Grabbing a trolley, they went straight to the clothing section.

Jack was only too happy to find some black trousers, a white shirt, and a pair of cheap black shoes. He came out of the changing room and did a twirl! Then Suzan went to change into the white shirt and the trousers that she had chosen, but came out with her jacket on top of it all.

'You do know you can't wear that old jacket to school, don't you?' said her dad.

'Then I'm not going to school!' she replied.

'Oh dear,' answered her dad, 'looks like the school are in for a challenge!'

After that they ambled around the shops, and eventually meandered back home. The old house was now beginning to look and feel like their home.

A W-B

27

CHAPTER 5

IT'S ALL IN THE ENTRANCE!

The weekend passed by so quickly, they could hardly believe it when Monday arrived. Both Jack and Suzan were up early that day. They felt a strange mixture of excitement and fear. Both hoped that the school would be nice and that they would fit in well. Or at least Jack hoped he would fit in; Suzan hoped the school would fit in with her!

It was the beginning of term six and they were going to join almost at the end of the academic year, so even their father had his worries, but when he had phoned the school, to enquire about spaces, the friendly teacher had said that the sooner they attended, the sooner they'd settle in! There had been only a few spaces left.

Suddenly, their father's loud and spritely voice boomed upstairs: 'Rise and shine! You two, breakfast's ready, and we need to get going early this morning.'

Suzan and Jack ran downstairs, like a stampede of elephants, hustling each other for the seat with the cushion on it. Their father was already tucking into some toast and tea and was wearing his best and only suit, with a smart dark blue tie. 'I'll take you down to the school this morning, then I'm off to the main office for orientation meetings all day. I will still be working from home most days, but occasionally will need to travel up to the office.'

When they had all had their fill of toast and blackcurrant jam, Suzan and Jack went up to put on their school uniforms. Jack disappeared into the bathroom and spent ages checking his uniform was on straight and looked good. Suzan, on the other hand, had thrown on the trousers and white shirt, which she had already accessorised with a selection of her favourite pirate badges and had covered the whole lot up by her tatty black pirate jacket.

When they reached the front door, their dad glanced at Suzan, rolled his eyes, and pretended that she wasn't wearing *that jacket.* They enjoyed the walk, down towards the school, in the cool refreshing air.

Ten minutes later they arrived at an old gate that opened onto three steps and a path that lead around a large playground, to a beautiful old building build around 1900. The school had old sash windows and bright red tiles.

Their father marched them to the front reception desk, where a teacher was already waiting to greet them. Suzan was directed one way - towards the older year group and Jack followed the teacher, who turned out to be very talkative and friendly.

Suzan heard the hum of excited children all talking and shouting. She peered in through the slightly frosted glass and took a deep breath. *It's all in the entrance,* she thought to herself. She flung open the door, strolled in - as if she was the teacher - glanced around quickly for an empty desk and flopped down into the seat. The hum fell silent as a mixture of surprise and curiosity took over the class. They stared at her, like she was from another planet. She stared back at them and one by one they looked away.

'Ay, are you new?' said a boy, sitting close to the front.

'Yeah, freshly manufactured this morning!' Suzan replied, in fast wit. There was a chuckle from most of the class.

'Where did you come from?' said a tall girl, with ridiculously long hair.

Suzan looked around at the expectant faces and replied with a cheeky grin, 'My house, I think.' The class burst out laughing and the students decided to drop the questions and continue with their conversations about the holidays. Little by little some of them came and sat near Suzan, to chat to her.

Soon the door opened and in stepped a kind looking teacher, with fuzzy brown hair, wearing a smart jacket.

'Miss,' the boy from earlier said, 'There's a new girl over there.'

The teacher smiled softly at Suzan and said: 'Yes, but let's not make a fuss, her name's Suzan, and I am sure that you will all get a chance to get to welcome her later. But for now, George, could you give these books out.'

'Ooo… Ok miss,' he said, as he jumped to his feet and dashed around handing out the books.

Suzan gazed at the title: *Dry Cold History. Uuuuff, this will probably be boring,* she thought to herself. The teacher addressed the class and asked them several questions about kings, queens, and historical events. Each time a sea of hands shot up, but Suzan answered faster than anyone else could.

'That's great Suzan, have you already covered these topics in your last school?' asked the teacher.

'A few miss but mostly I like reading!'

The teacher thought for a moment and asked them to turn to page one hundred and eighty-five. Suzan reluctantly turned page after page. Then, when she found the right page, she was pleasantly excited!

'Pirates and Buccaneers will be our project for this term,' the teacher said.

Suzan sat up straight, in her chair, with a large grin on her face. The day seemed to pass really quickly and by the end of it, not only had Suzan made a few friends, the teacher had said that her jacket was great and *in theme* with the term project. Jack's day was way more subdued, but he was happy to have slipped under the radar and discreetly made a few new friends too.

Swiftly they settled into their new school, but times were hard for them. They just had enough money to pay the bills and buy food. They couldn't afford a TV or much furniture. They had to make do with what they had. Most of the time Suzan and Jack didn't mind, they were used to being poor. Things had been hard, as far back as they could remember. But they still had each other.

The time that they were really reminded of being poor though, the worst time, was at school when their friends remarked on their bags, or socks, or asked them to go to the cinema on the weekend. They had to politely refuse, making up excuses. But, as the weeks passed by, they settled more and more into their new school and bit by bit, they helped their dad fix up that old house.

On the weekends they spent their time planning and acting in pirate scenes together, just as they always had – scenes of pirates, treasure and adventure. They turned even the simplest things around the house into the props and scenes for their stories.

Their father seemed to be more relaxed each week with his new job. One day he even managed to find an old desk, that was outside one of the local houses, with a sign on it saying: *"Free to a good home"*. Suzan, Jack, and he carried it back, street by street and soon he set to work on it, sanding it down and cleaning it up. He set it up in the corner under the stairs and made it into his office space. Which was just as well, as he seemed busier than ever and worked, almost always, from home.

CHAPTER 6

IT'S A JUNGLE OUT THERE!

When they weren't at school – or planning and taking part in wild, exciting pirate scenes at home – they would lift the old family album from the window seat, and make up stories about some of the characters and places. Their dad recognised some people in the album, but others were before his time. Oddly, though, each time they crept towards the end, and the familiar sea smell began to overwhelm them, they would find it impossible to create any stories about Elgor's rock – it was as if it held its own mystery, beyond their imagination.

Every week they waited for a postcard from their mum, which they always took great joy in reading together - wondering what it was like, in each place she was working. They treasured each postcard.

Sometimes, just sometimes, Suzan would question *why* they were poor if their mother had a job that took her to so many exciting places. Surely, she must be paid well for such a job. Suzan once asked her dad and he simply replied, 'Well, things are not always easy, there are often many expenses, when you're working away from home.'

The term flew by and soon it was the last assembly and both Suzan and Jack were meeting their new teachers for September. Later, they strolled out of the school and said goodbye to all their friends, turned to glance at the old building that had welcomed them six weeks earlier and smiled at each other.

'That term went well!' said Jack.

Suzan's face lit up and she grinned in excitement.

'What? What is it?' asked Jack.

'Summer hols – *freedom*,' said Suzan in a voice that was probably heard across the channel in France!

They chatted about all the things they were going to do over the summer with each other, at the house. 'Let's camp out in the garden,' said Jack.

'Let's explore the attic and build a den there,' said Suzan.

'Let's tell pirate tales till we puke,' said Jack.

'Let's sneak into the shed and see what's in there,' said Suzan.

When they arrived home, Suzan and Jack made a list of hundreds of Summertime things to do!

The first week of the holidays, they decided to camp out in the garden, but soon realised that they had to first find it amongst the overgrowth!

'Remember I'm just here in my office, if you need my help, you two. Now be careful using the shears and tools and make sure you wear those gloves,' their father said, as he pointed towards an assortment of gloves that were all different sizes and none of which matched. Suzan and Jack worked their way through the assortment, to try to find a left and right each that they could fit their hands into.

Swiftly Suzan led Jack to the back door, that she had peered through all those weeks ago, when they first moved in. She unlocked it and gave it a nudge, but it didn't move.

'Let me have a go, I am way stronger than you sis,' said Jack.

'Keep dreaming baby bro,' said Suzan.

Jack's attempts were also of no use. Then they both barged it and bashed it, but it still didn't budge. However, the racket that they made, did manage to bring their dad out. He saw them trying to open the door and joined in with the team door bashing! After a few goes, with all three of them barging the door, it gave in. It was open, but only just, as there was a giant bush that had grown the other side of it.

'You go back to work, dad, we can take care of this,' said Jack.

'Yes, I've a million and one more emails to sort, but…' he paused, halfway to his office, 'remind me, one day soon, to make some little nesting boxes. Then you can fix them up, near the tall bushes, at the far end. And…' he paused again, 'don't get too carried away cutting back that huge buddleia bush, over there, or the lavender – they're both good for bees and butterflies.

Both children yelled, 'OK,' before squeezing their way out, into the garden, with a few tools and their gloves.

They set to work cutting back the bush, with the shears, and at lunchtime their dad lent a hand with the tougher stuff. They discovered all sorts of strange things that had been grown over by the undergrowth. An old wheelbarrow that had rotted through, some half-broken garden tools, an old fridge - that the bushes had grown around, a teacup and saucer, and a path that once led to what Suzan had suspected was once the shed but was now almost one giant bush.

Working really hard, each day they cleared and cut until, by the end of the week, the garden was … well, actually a garden. There was a clean path that led down to the old but uncovered shed, which leaned over to one side and looked ancient. A neat pile of cuttings sat in a corner.

Jack, Suzan and their father sat outside and drank a cup of sweet tea, that evening. 'What a difference! You two have done so well, cleaning this garden. Sorry I've been so busy with work this week,' said their father.

'No worries dad, we've had a fun week. And tomorrow we're going to spend the day out here, Suzan's going to be the unsuspecting rich merchant and I'm going to be the pirate captain who is going to relieve her of her gold!!' said Jack.

'Huh, dream on, you couldn't steal a teddy from a baby!' said Suzan.

'Well, I've seen tougher sponges than you!' replied Jack.

'Judging by your smell, you'd better use one!' replied Suzan, with her usual lightning-fast wit.

The sound of their affectionate banter became quieter as their father made a hasty retreat inside to get back to his emails. A while later Suzan and Jack came in laughing and giggling and decided to get cleaned up and go to bed. Soon they were all tucked up in their beds and fast asleep.

CHAPTER 7

DISCOVERY IN THE LOFT

Jack awoke the next morning to find his sister staring out of the window. 'What are you looking at sis?' he asked, as he sat up in bed.

She turned around with a disgruntled look and said: 'It's raining. Stupid weather! I'm going back to bed and not getting up till the weather is better!' And she did just that. She disappeared under her covers like a bear hibernating into a cave.

'But, but... What if it rains for days?' said Jack in surprise.

A muffled 'don't care,' came from somewhere under Suzan's covers.

'But what if we are in for rain every day for months, how will you eat?' replied Jack, with a hint of a smile.

'Don't care, I am not getting up for anything!' Suzan said, with another muffled defiant voice.

Jack's smile turned into a large grin as he stood up and began to loudly sniff the air. 'Oooo dad's cooking bacon and egg,' he said.

With that, Suzan's covers flew off, she jumped up and darted towards the door, running in the direction of the dining area.

Jack slowly and calmly walked after her downstairs. By the time he reached the bottom of the stairs he was being stared at by a rather unhappy Suzan, standing next to an empty table.

'You tricked me, you sea slug! You double-crossing, low-down barnacle,' she said.

Jack laughed and soon they were both laughing. They had breakfast together and made their father, who was already hard at work in his office, a cup of tea. They both gazed out of the back door, at the soggy wet garden and wondered what to do. They were disappointed after spending a week clearing the garden, ready to camp out, just for it to rain the very first day it was ready.

As they watched the large drops of rain plop onto the muddy ground, Jack smiled and said 'I've got an idea, why don't we explore the loft. I bet no one has been up there for years and it might be a fun place to create an indoor hide out!'

Suzan's face lit up, 'Jack that's a good idea, yeah let's do that. Let's gather a few things up, like torches and a few snacks and we can spend the day up there! We also better ask dad if it's okay.'

Their father said it was fine, but to remember that only part of the floor was boarded and to be careful not to go through the loft floor on the un-boarded areas.

On the landing they found the small loft hatch. It looked as if it had not been opened for decades, which didn't surprise them. Jack went down to the kitchen to get the steps and carried them up. He placed the steps below the hatch and slowly climbed, while Suzan steadied from below. He pushed at the hatch cover, but it didn't budge.

Eventually, after several attempts Jack managed to push the square wooden cover up and rest it on the loft floor, near the entrance. He turned on his torch and scanned around the entrance for a light switch. Finding an old Bakelite switch he flicked it on. There was a flicker and then a large and ancient looking bulb glimmered into a dull light. It was not as bright as the modern lights and struggled to light more than a few metres of the loft.

Jack flashed his torch around the partially lit loft. There were spider webs everywhere. And he saw quite a few large spiders glaring back at him.

'Come on Jack, let me get up there and have a look too,' said Suzan.

Jack climbed right into the shadowy wooden loft and stood looking down at his sister, as she climbed up. Soon both were standing peering around. Some of the areas were still very dark and many others were covered in cobwebs.

'Look at that beastie' Suzan said as she pointed, with a gawping mouth, at a gigantic spider.

'That's just a tiddler!' said Jack, as he pointed in the direction of behind Suzan. 'Now that is a spider.'

Suzan slowly turned around and saw that just about three centimetres away, from her head, was an even bigger spider. 'Let's see who can find the biggest spider Jack! Go and grab a ruler.'

'Well, I've already won! You won't find a bigger one than that!' Jack said, pointing at the one behind Suzan with a triumphant look on his face.

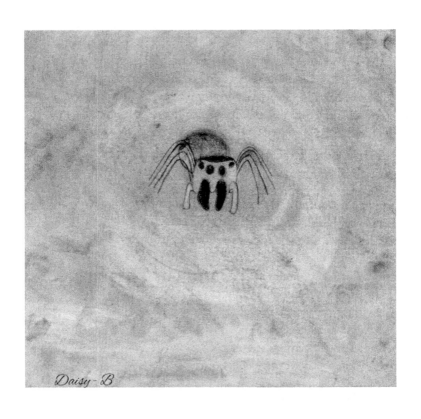

Daisy - B

'If I do, you do the washing up for a week and make us tea all day, today!' Suzan said.

'And if you lose, you do the same,' said Jack.

'Sure!' agreed Suzan.

They switched their torches on and began to explore the loft, while looking for the biggest spider they could find. The loft seemed for the most part empty, other than the large colony of spiders!

'Jack, look at this one! Looks like tea duty for you. I'll have two sugars in my teas today.'

'Not bad sis, but how about this bad boy!' called Jack, while pointing at an even bigger spider that was sitting on a rafter, watching them. And on it went, the spider hunt and banter. Soon the thick carpet of dust on the floor was covered in footprints leading to and fro.

Noticing that there were a few areas that they had not been to yet, Suzan decided to try to find a spider that would make all the others look like babies! 'Jack! Look at this! QUICK!'

'It won't be a bigger spider than that last one I found, but I will come and have a look.' Suzan had gone quiet, so Jack shone his torch in her direction. She was right in the corner, at the far end, of the loft and seemed to be staring at something transfixed. 'Coming sis, do I need to go and get the ruler for this one!' When he reached the edge of the boarding, he carefully stepped onto the rafters, balancing from rafter to rafter, like a tight rope walker. And slowly made his way over to her. He shined his torch around and found her still staring. 'There *is* something up here! I thought it was completely empty.'

'So did I,' said Suzan, 'but I found *this* tucked away, right at the back, in the corner.'

Both crouched down to take a closer look…

CHAPTER 8

WHO IS C.C?

From their rather uncomfortable crouched positions, balanced precariously across the dusty rafters, Suzan and Jack examined an extremely ancient looking wooden object.

'What do you suppose it is Jack?' asked Suzan.

'It's some kind of old chest, I think. Maybe the sort of thing people would use to keep their things in, when they travelled,' Jack said, as he reached out his hand to touch the top of it. It was very hard to make out more than that, because it was so thick with dust, because it had probably been up there for so long.

'Let's try to pull it out, to take a better look Jack,' said Suzan.

'Okay you take that side, and I'll take this side.' Jack said, as he reached down and felt around for something to grab. Between them they carried it over the rafters, to the edge of the flooring. Placing it down carefully, they began to wipe off the dust.

It was indeed an old chest, made from a rich dark red wood, which had an unusually large grain. It was about fifty centimetres long, thirty-five centimetres high and forty centimetres deep, with a curved lid.

On each corner it had ornate metal reinforcements and there were two decorative bands, that ran from bottom to top, to reinforce it. In the middle there was a large and beautifully cut metal plate with a keyhole in the centre. Although it looked like it was ancient, it had been preserved well in the loft.

Jack rushed downstairs to get some cloths to clean it up more. Swiftly he was back, gently wiping and cleaning it. Soon the natural sheen of the rich red wood was shining.

'Nice bit of cleaning Jack! But are we going to see what is inside!? Or just polish it all day?' Suzan said with her usual cheeky smile! Both looked at each other and knelt down in front of it.

'I bet it is locked' Jack said, as he pulled at the top. The lid reluctantly creaked open and the light from their expectant torches flooded in, for the first time in a long time. 'It's empty!' Jack said with a disappointed look on his face. He was about to close the lid when they both noticed that on the inside, of the lid, there were the initials *CC* carved.

'What do you suppose that means?' asked Suzan.

'I don't know, let's go and ask dad, maybe we can keep it too!'

Suzan and Jack climbed down the ladder and ran down to their father. Both arrived, one either side of him panting and bursting with excitement.

'Dad, dad, you never guess what we have found,' Jack yelled.

'Hang on Jack,' replied their dad, 'I'm just in the middle of an email. Now where was I? Yes, *I have attached the files that you have requested and I ... '* but he never finished, because he was abruptly interrupted by Suzan and Jack, one either side of him, like stereo speakers.

'Dad, really, you've got to come now, we've found a treasure box!' they said.

Their father was expecting many things, but not that. He turned to face them. 'What, you have found a what?' he asked, with a puzzled look on his face.

'*A treasure chest!*' both children bellowed out.

'But it's empty,' said Jack.

Their father creaked, as he stood up, after a whole morning behind the desk. He stretched and then gave them a gentle smile, 'Okay, come on let's take a look'. He followed them up upstairs and up the ladder. The three scrambled over to where Suzan and Jack had left the chest and knelt around it.

'Interesting,' said their father as he inspected it. 'It looks like an amazingly old sailor's, or captain's chest. They used them to keep their valuables and possessions in at sea.'

Suzan pointed to the carved initials that said *CC*, 'What do you think that that might mean?'

'Ah, that's probably the initials of the person that owned it. The strange thing is that I don't recognise the wood. It must be from a far-off land.' Said their father.

'Can we clean it up more and keep it dad?' asked Jack.

'Well, it looks like it hasn't been used for a long time and besides, your grandpa said we can make use and have anything here we like. So sure, it won't harm if you clean it up a bit more, and keep it in your room. As long as you look after it, in case he ever needs it.'

Suzan and Jack looked at each other.

'A real pirate chest for our room,' said Jack.

'Now I didn't say it was a pirate chest. It might have belonged to anyone at sea,' said their dad.

'Yeah, but it must be a pirate chest, it completely smells of adventure and treasure!' said Suzan.

Their father sniffed it, 'Oh yes, you're right, the delicate odour of pirate,' he said with a grin on his face. At that he closed the lid, lifted it up and carried it down to their bedroom.

Moments later, he brought them a selection of things to clean it. 'Polish for the wood, and the metal looks like brass, so here is some brass cleaner and a little machine oil for the hinges,' he said, as he placed each item on the floor, by the chest.

The two children got to work polishing and cleaning it. Soon they had it gleaming all over.

Sitting, with the lid open, they stared at the initials *CC*.

'I wonder what *CC* stands for…' Suzan pondered.

'Cabbage company?' replied Jack, laughing.'

'No, it's got to be captain…silly.'

'Captain Cutlass?' suggested Jack.

'Maybe… or perhaps Captain Cunning.'

'Yeah, I like that sis. I know, let's fill it with all our pirate things and loot.'

Swiftly they filled the chest with numerous treasured items.

'Wow, look at the time sis, it's almost dinner time already. We must have been up in the loft, almost all day!' Jack said in surprise.

Just then their father called upstairs, 'Are there a couple of no-good rascal pirates up there, who are hungry?' There was a rumble from above their father's head that sounded like a stampede. Soon they were all sitting around the table digging into shepherd's pie.

Jack smiled as he mopped up the last of the gravy with the last of the potato and then said: 'Suzan is going to do the washing up this week dad! And make us all the tea we want.'

Their father looked bemused and replied: 'Why ever is she going to do that?'

'Ah she lost the giant spider game,' Jack said with an aura of smugness.

'WHAT, but I found a pirate chest, which is far better than your stupid spider,' said Suzan.

'Now I really didn't say it was a pirate chest Suzan,' Their dad interjected.

'Yeah, but it isn't a spider is it sis?' Jack said as his smugness stepped up a notch.

'No, it's an ancient chest which I've decided you can't use, as I found it!' Suzan said with an aura of determination.

'Alright, alright let's share the washing up and the chest,' Jack said, realising his sister had a strong point.

'Hmmm, I don't know, I might let you look at the chest occasionally if you are polite to me!' Suzan said, knowing she was on a roll.

'Come on sis, sorry. Let's share,' Jack said.

'Alright but remember *who* found it!'

Their father was watching their dispute for a while. Suddenly he said 'Hmmmm, children I must speak to you both. I have some exciting news. Do you remember your two friends Annabel and Rachel who moved out to France last year?'

Both children nodded.

'Well, they're all settled into their new house, and they've invited the three of us out there, for a few days, to stay. As you know my new job is going really well and our money situation is stable now.

'You've both been so good, the last few months, in such difficult times – moving away from your friends and helping me with this place, that I really think you deserve a fun trip. Annabel's father has said that they have space to put us up and all we need to do is get over there.

'I've asked my company if I can have a few days off and I've found some really cheap coach tickets, from Dover to Paris via ferry. To get the cheapest tickets I had to book it for the day after tomorrow, so we need to pack and get ready now.'

Both children looked at each other as the excitement swept them away.

'Really dad?' Jack said in disbelief.

'Yes, it isn't going to be a luxurious holiday, but if you don't mind an adventure, on a bus for six hours, then we can go! Besides, they're really excited about seeing you both! We can pack sandwiches and cards and we will have some fun on the bus.'

Jack jumped up and ran upstairs without an explanation.

'What are you doing?' their father called after him.

There was a rumble, of objects being moved around upstairs, and then a pause. 'PACKING,' Jack yelled, before further rumbling.

'I'd better go up and help him,' Suzan said, in a calm voice, masking her excitement, for a brief moment, before dashing upstairs, and the rumbling sound doubled.

'I'll do the washing up!' their father muttered to himself.

CHAPTER 9

ON THE WRONG SIDE OF THE ROAD!

The next day went by like a whirlwind. There was a flurry of activity, in the house, with passports being found, clothing folded and by late that evening they had the suitcases all packed and ready by the front door. Their father had double checked the tickets, times and passports, several times.

Turning in for an early night, they set their alarms for five in the morning. Suzan and Jack lay in their beds, too excited to sleep, chatting about what they were going to say and do with their friends. They wondered what France was like too.

The alarm pierced the silence, early the next morning, and everyone scrabbled to turn it off. Moments later Suzan had on her favourite pirate jacket and a tatty old pair of jeans. Jack, also, was wearing his favourite jeans and shirt. Soon they were tucking into tea and toast. The three of them did the washing up and cleared away, brushed their teeth, and left. It was just light when they shut the front door and stepped out onto the empty street.

The three of them rolled their suitcases along behind them, blurry eyed and still half asleep. They strolled down past the little river, through the town and then down, towards the Eastern Docks in Dover, where the coach was due. They passed very few people, a few cleaners, and other early workers.

When they arrived at the dock, they saw the white coach, with red and blue writing, waiting at the bus stop. The driver greeted them in a Spanish accent, checked their tickets and helped them to load their large items of luggage into the luggage hold.

The three of them climbed onto the coach and looked around for seats. It was already almost full, but they spotted a double seat free, about halfway down the bus. Sitting opposite was an old lady who was squinting at a mobile phone screen, trying to make out the letters. She moved over to let Suzan sit close to the aisle and her brother on the opposite seat.

The driver stood looking around by the coach door, with his clipboard firmly in his hand. He peered down the list of names and gazed at his watch. Eventually he swivelled round, climbed the three steps onto the coach and sat in the driving seat. Pushing the button, which closed the door with a *swish,* he started the engine and soon they were following lines on the roads, directing them to the coach section of the ferry boarding.

Just before they reached the ferry, they were stopped at passport control, where everyone had their passports checked. Suzan and Jack stared out of the window as a huge ferry docked and lowered the loading bay door, like a hungry beast opening its mouth. The coach slowly edged its way towards the loading area, following a line of other coaches. And eventually it drove right up into the ship. Inside it looked like a giant car park.

Moments later there was a loud bang as the door closed, squeezing the last bit of the sunshine out, and with a judder the ship engines started. Everyone on the coach jumped up and scurried towards the coach door. Suzan, Jack, and their father followed. They climbed off the coach, stretched and followed the long converging lines that were heading for a set of doors.

Inside there were several flights of stairs which revealed seating and shops at the top. Suzan and Jack looked amazed to find shops and even a café on the ship.

'Hey pirates, come this way. Let's go and stand on the top deck,' said their dad. They hurried through a series of doors that led to the top deck. It was blustery and the shuddering growling of the engines was louder on the open top deck. They found a good place to stand and watched the ship crash its way through the waves towards France.

'I can't believe we're on a real ship and going to France,' said Jack, smiling from ear to ear. Suzan who was equally ecstatic said, 'Yeah, me too. Look at the waves. If I half close my eyes, I could imagine being on a pirate ship right now.'

Their father pointed behind them and a warm smile came over his face, 'Look we can see the white cliffs.'

The children turned to see the white cliffs and the three watched them slowly shrink and eventually drift into the horizon. The ship roared on, and soon the three were looking out for the first glimpse of France.

CAW-B

51

Suddenly Jack's view was obscured by Suzan.

'Ah yes, I can just make it out,' said Suzan, as she peered through her battered old telescope that she had picked up in a junk shop.

'What can you see sis? Tell me!' Jack said impatiently.

'Ah, well I can see a man sitting on a bench reading a newspaper, drinking coffee,' Suzan replied.

'Yes, yes, what else,' Jack asked, even more impatiently.

'Well, the newspaper says there is a special on in the supermarket and the weather will be sunny tomorrow,' Suzan said, with her usual cheeky smile.

'You must think I am Captain Gullible,' Jack said.

'Well Captain Gullible, I can see the dock!' Suzan said with a giggle.

'You will walk the plank for that,' Jack said.

'I'll have a word with the crew and ask if they can lend us their plank,' their dad said, joining in the banter.

The ship engines changed tone and then there was a great burst of sound, as the ship blew its horn and began to manoeuvre into port.

'Let's get back to the coach kids, just another three or four hours of driving and we'll be in Paris. Who is up for a game of cards?'

The three walked back down to the coach deck and onto the coach, which had just been opened by the driver. The other passengers arrived in dribs and drabs. Then the ship bumped something, the engine roar died down and the mechanical loading door ground into action, slowly lowering and eventually clunking onto the ground.

There was a cacophony of rumbles, as all the vehicles, on board the ship, started their engines at once and a small army of people directed the coaches and other transport, with a series of frantic hand and arm movements.

Soon it was their coach that was rolling off the ramp and driving off, onto the right side of the road. 'Dad we're on the wrong side of the road,' both Jack and Suzan said, as they covered their faces and ducked behind the coach seats in fear of crashing.

'Don't worry kids, they drive on the right in France.'

'Ahh, that's good,' said Suzan. Next, they were bumbling along highways with trees, small villages and fields flashing by. Suzan and Jack were glued to the window, watching it all go by, looking for differences compared to England. They passed the time chatting, playing cards, eating lunch, and polishing off the last of the snacks.

CHAPTER 10

PIRATE's REUNION

Eventually, the small villages became bigger and incrementally less spaced out, until they turned into a city and soon, they were in Paris. Steadily the coach pulled into a large curvy concrete building, with row after row of coach bays inside. The driver announced, in English, French and Spanish, that they were now arriving at the coach station and not to forget their luggage.

The coach pulled up with a satisfied *pshhh,* that was followed by a swish of the door as it opened smoothly. They were there, in a foreign land, across the sea. For the first time ever, and even better than that, they were going to see their best friends Annabel and Rachel!

Just then Jack spotted a familiar face, peering up at the coach. As soon as they climbed down, there was a deafening, 'Ahhhhha mi ship mates,' in Suzan's gravely pirate voice. People close by fell silent and looked around, wondering what was happening.

Suzan rushed over to hug Rachel and Annabel, closely followed by Jack. Their dad managed, by himself, to drag all three suitcases over to where they were. He shook hands with Rachel and Annabel's dad, George, a gentle man with a warm smile. Within moments the four children were deeply encapsulated in excited chatting, about pirates, the coach journey, and their new house in France. Meanwhile the two fathers were soon deeply engrossed in a conversation, about climate change, technology, and the world. The two groups, completely in their own worlds, stayed close to each other, as they manoeuvred through the corridors and eventually into a large metro station.

Annabel and Rachel's father stopped speaking for a moment and called for everyone's attention. He produced a wad of small rectangular tickets and gave one to each of the children and one to Suzan's father. 'Now there is a knack to this, especially if you have a suitcase,' he said pointing to a machine with two doors that seemed to slam shut, after people walked through them. He stepped forward to demonstrate. Inserting his ticket, he then rushed to get through, with one of the suitcases, before the barriers closed on him.

The children went next, scurrying through. Then their father. He almost made it through, but the suitcase was eaten by the barriers. He had to tug and pull until it slid through. Next, came a series of escalators and then they boarded a very lush overland train.

Fifteen minutes later they emerged into the bright sunshine, at a small train station. George led them all up a long busy street and then turned to a smaller pathway. They followed up a steep hill until, about midway up, they came to a high metal gate which George opened. He beckoned them in.

Annabel led the other three children straight through the front door and bellowed out, 'Mum, they're here!' in an excited uncontainable loud voice.

Soon the three adults were all sitting down, tucking into a delicious home cooked Italian dish that Ren had made, richly engrossed in conversations and catching up, while the four children sat around another table giggling and engrossed in their own conversations. After dinner, Jack, Suzan, Annabel and Rachel cleaned themselves up and were ready for bed.

They set up Annabel's floor with sleeping bags and decided to camp out together, just like old times – telling each other stories by torch light, late into the night. One by one they drifted off into a contented dreamland. The house, which had suddenly become brimming with laughter and chatter, fell silent and peaceful once more.

The sunshine snuck around the curtains the next morning and stirred the four sleepy heads. Suzan awoke first and immediately felt that everyone should also be awake. She shook Jack, Annabel and Rachel, until they were all rudely awoken from their epic dreams. The four stared at each other, processing the fact that they were all together again. Sweet smells drifted up, from the kitchen.

Annabel's nose twitched as she smelt the air. 'Crepes, last one to the kitchen stinks like a pirate's socks, after they've run a marathon,' she bellowed out, just as she made a rush for the door.

The four children jostled each other, not wanting to be the last. All arrived, in a heap in the kitchen doorway, after falling over one another – just to get to the crepes!

Soon the seven were sitting down, tucking into Ren's handmade crepes, sipping coffee. After more crepes than is humanly possible to eat, the four children snuck away to create a den, leaving the parents chatting away over more coffee.

'No, the den needs to be bigger,' said Suzan assuming place as captain of the operation, being the oldest. We need at least three more sheets and many more cushions.'

Jack and Annabel scurried off into various rooms in the house to plunder the things they needed. Soon the four were sitting inside an intricate den, made from most of the sheets, cushions, blankets and other linen from the house.

Suzan held her torch up and shone it around inside. They began to speak about their favourite topic, pirates.

After a few pirate tales, Jack looked at Suzan. 'Tell them THE story sis.'

'Which story?' asked Suzan.

'You know sis, the story of *The Mist*.

Suzan grinned, 'Aha THE story! Yes okay, but they may not want to hear it. I've told it to them before you know!'

'Yes, we do, we do,' yelled Annabel and Rachel in unison.

'Alright, come closer then, because this is the story of a real pirate,' said Suzan quietly.

The three children gathered close to her, and Jack smiled. It was his favourite. Suzan peered around at the three expectant faces, and she began to tell the tale in her best pirate voice. Pausing for tension in places.

The three were captivated with the story. Even Jack, who had heard it so many times before.

After Suzan had finished her tale, there was a flurry of discussion about whether the Mist had managed to escape and where his treasure was hidden and then Suzan stood up and held out her boffer-sword, whilst telling the story. 'Right, I'm the Mist.' Soon they were re-enacting some of their favourite tales. They took it in turns to be the Mist and made up wild and zany scenarios.

The day fluttered by, like a bird effortlessly sailing on the breeze. And before they knew it, they had been told to tidy up the chaotic quagmire of cushions, sheets, blankets, plus other random linen, strewn on the bedroom floor and get cleaned up for dinner.

Soon the four hungry children were sitting around the table, tucking into more of Ren's delicious food!

After eating everything on her plate, Annabel looked at her dad and said with curiosity, 'Dad, I was wondering whether you have heard of a place called *Argenteuil Hill*, somewhere around Paris?'

'Hmm I've heard of it. I think it is about an hour away. Why do you ask?' said their dad, between bites of salad.

'Oh, just that I heard it in a pirate story that Suzan told us and wondered if it was a real place in France.'

'Oh, yes, it's real alright. I seem to remember it has something to do with pirates actually. But the hill is a beautiful park now.' He tucked back into the rest of his dinner. And then moments later paused, looked up and said, 'Why, do you fancy going there? It's supposed to be a really nice park now.'

Four faces, with wide eyes, all stared back expectantly, '*Yes*, please,' they shouted excitedly.

'Ok, that settles it then, we'll take a bus out there tomorrow,' said Annabel's father.

CHAPTER 11

THE FALL

The early morning sun squeezed its way through the gaps in the curtains the next morning and fell on four sleepy children all camping out on the floor. Rachel awoke first and remembered that they were going to go to check out the hill park that was mentioned in the story. She pushed her fingers through her dark hair which was matted from sleeping in sleeping bags on the floor. She was the youngest of the four, and she was brimming with excitement.

Rachel smiled. She had an idea! Quietly she snuck across the room and took the boffer-swords that the other children were clutching as they slept and put them back in the wardrobe. Then she dressed in the most fearsome pirate clothing she could find and chose the longest sword she could get her hands on. Then she quietly zipped the other three sleeping bags up, stood above them and shouted 'AHH haaa, I'm the Mist and I've come to steal all your treasure you mollusc brained, sea slug faced scum!'

The three awoke, with an absolute fright, wide eyed with shock. They looked terrified, for a moment, as they wriggled in their zipped-up sleeping bags, then their terror turned slowly to grins and finally the four children fell around laughing.

'Well done, Rachel, you really had us there! Truly fearsome!' Suzan said with a smile and a hint of admiration.

Jumping up, the four children dressed quickly, so that they could do their *job* of waking the *rents* and generally making their mornings chaotic, noisy and full of energy! Soon, however, the house became tidy and ship shape, seven packed lunches were made, and they were ready to leave.

The mid-morning sun was already bright and sizzling. Their parents led the way down the hill, towards the bus stop, as the children ambled behind, engrossed in another conversation about the Mist. Moments after they arrived at the bus stop, the bus arrived. 'What perfect timing!' said George.

Ren spoke in French and asked for tickets for three adults and four children to *Argenteuil Hill*. And soon they were sitting down watching the roads, houses and people flit by.

The bus bumbled along small roads that twisted and turned. Jack and Suzan were especially glued to the windows, as they were still excited about how different everything looked to England. They watched as the bus stopped and people got on and off. And they listened to the French that the people spoke and tried to work out what they were speaking about. It was truly an adventure to realise that every small detail, they assumed to be *normal* in their country, was slightly different in another country.

After driving for about four minutes, the bus was brimming with people and there were almost no spare seats left, they felt like sardines crammed in a tin. A hum of people were chatting to each other, others speaking on their phones. Then little by little the people started to get off, until the bus was completely empty, other than Suzan and her motley crew.

Swiftly the bus pulled up at a small bus stop, in the middle of nowhere, and the driver turned to Ren and George and said something in French. He opened the door, which slid open with a clunk, and they all jumped off. He informed Ren that they needed to go down this road, and then turn left. And that it was about a three-minute walk.

The two families walked excitedly down the road. As they turned left, they saw the entrance to a huge park on a hill. It was marked by rusty old railings that allowed people to enter, but no cars. A well-kept gravelly path wound its way here and there up the hill and the seven started to climb up it. As they crunched their way over the gravel the warm breeze smelt of grass and woodland and they could hear bird song drifting in the wind.

The gravel path seemed to fade out towards the top, and an old mud path gradually took over. The mud was hard after having been baked in the long summer days. As they reached the brow and peaked over, they stood at the beginning of a vast plateau that was partly fields and partly trees.

'Ah now that is conveniently placed,' George said as his eyes caught sight of a bench, right next to the path. The *rents* looked at each other and without a word, as if in synchronisation, all sat down.

Ren took out a flask of coffee and some home-made snacks. 'Kids, you can go off exploring together, but just stay together as a group. And Suzan is in charge!'

No sooner Ren had finished her last sentence, all four children had sped off at top speed.

'Just remember I am in charge. And you have to call me Captain Boss,' Suzan said, with a smile.

'Ok Captain *Loss*,' Jack blared out.

'No, get it right Jack, it's *Captain Floss*, she's a tooth decay captain,' Annabel said, quick-wittedly.

Suzan stopped and glared at them. 'Well let's see if your running is as fast as your running away mouths! I'm going to catch you all in ten seconds.' She counted down as they scarpered in all different directions. Then without delaying for a single second, she ran after them, like a cheetah.

The top of the hill was like a warren with small dirt paths that crisscrossed all over and splayed off in all directions. Suzan chased them down, like a wolf and soon she had caught them all. 'Not so fast now!' she said.

Rachel stepped forward with a glint in her eye and said: 'Now I'm the Mist! I'm coming for you!'

The other three dissipated, shooting off down dirt paths as she counted, as fast as she could. Moments later Rachel was hot on their heels. She decided she would go directly for Suzan as she was the fastest. And while she chased Suzan across the top of the hill, determined not to show her year or two difference in age, the other two kept on running, in opposite directions.

Jack peered behind himself and kept going, ahead the path narrowed further and went into a rich green cool woodland. His feet were glad of the softer foliage ground.

The breeze, that meandered through the trees, brought soft smells of sweet flowers mixed with leaves. He looked round to see Rachel in the distance coming towards him, so he sprinted a little faster and decided to get off the beaten track. Jumping over a small, fallen tree he was soon sprinting through the undergrowth.

It was darker and quieter in the forest and there were no tracks. His eyes scanned the ground for obstacles and to pick out the best places to put his feet. Fully alert he went deeper into the forest, rich green moss covered the ground and parts of the trees in places where people had no reason to walk usually. Then the ground started to slope downwards, and he picked up more speed. His eyes and mind alert and sharp.

Suddenly the ground dropped right away, from a slope to a hill, Jack misplaced his foot, it caught on one of the roots and he tumbled. The sky flashed by several times as Jack went over and over, bumping and crashing into the ground every time.

He closed his eyes in fear. Fortunately, the ground was very soft and mostly made up of moss and old leaves, from previous years, so Jack was not badly injured. The last tumble took him head over heels and brought him to an eventual stop...

CHAPTER 12

A MESSAGE FROM THE PAST

Jack opened his eyes trying to work out what had happened and found himself gazing up at patches of blue sky glinting through the great branches of the trees. Slowly he looked around and clambered to his feet. Looking himself all over, checking for injury. He gazed back at the hill he had fallen down, and for a moment was surprised he had not broken any bones. He had escaped unscathed.

He peered at the old trees surrounding and then realised that he had fallen at the foot of a tree that seemed different than the rest. It was older, ancient in fact, but that was not the only difference. It was much taller than the rest too and was a deep red colour.

Botany was one of his favourite subjects at school and he prided himself on knowing most of the tree names. But he didn't recognise this tree at all. He remembered his teacher's advice that one of the best ways to identify a plant is by its leaves.

CA W-B

Jack jumped up and looked around the base of the giant tree for the most common leaves. He found a sample and made sure it matched the ones on the branches.

It was a very large leaf and he turned it over and over many times. Its shape was very distinctive, and was similar to an oak leaf, but it was much bigger. He went closer to the trunk to inspect the bark and noticed a strange large mark that had been carved into it.

Suddenly, startled by a noise behind him, Jack spun round quickly – to see Suzan, Rachel and Annabel bumbling their way down the hill towards him.

'Are you okay bro?' Rachel said she saw you completely tumble all the way down this hill?' said Suzan, with concern, looking him all over to make sure he wasn't injured.

'Yes, yes, I'm somehow fine. But look at this tree. Have you ever seen one of these trees before?' Jack said, in an excited voice.

The three other children gazed in wonder at the tall, ancient tree. They looked at the red bark and the leaves too.

'No, I have never seen one like this before. It must be really ancient. Look it's by far the tallest and biggest tree in the forest,' Annabel said, the others agreed.

'It's a kind of oak, I think. The leaves seem similar, but much bigger. Also, the bark seems very red. But there is something else too,' Jack paused and looked at the other three, then pointed to the large, deep carved mark.

The other three stared at the mark in curiosity. As they walked over, to take a closer look, they saw acorns around the base of the tree. Acorns, but giant ones.

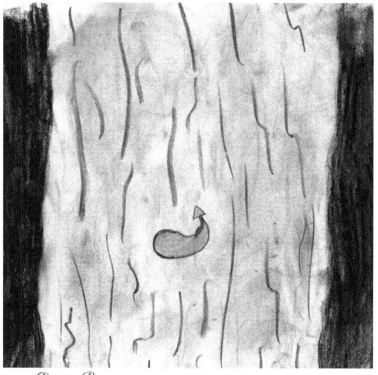

Daisy - B

'That's funny,' said Jack, 'I'm sure it's too early for acorns, especially giant ones like these! And… why is this tree the only one of its kind if it's producing acorns?'

The children studied the strange carved mark on the tree and noticed that it had been carved a long time ago but was so deep that it was still clear. It resembled a sort of round bulbous whale, but the line, which made the tail, went upwards and finished in an arrow.

'It's pointing up, there must be something up there,' said Rachel twitching with excitement. The four children's eyes slowly followed the arrow inch by inch up the trunk of the tree, up toward the top until they spotted a hole about halfway up.

'There's a hole up there, we need to check it out,' Rachel said.

'It's probably just a hole that birds nest in,' Jack said with a slightly sceptical tone.

'I can get up that tree before you can say "Hippopotomonstrosesquippedaliophobia!"' Suzan said with her usual cheeky smile.

'That isn't even a real word,' retorted Annabel.

Jack interjected, 'Sorry, but actually it is. It means to have a fear of long words.'

Suzan looked up, planning her route up the tree.

'You're going to need a torch sis,' Jack said, as he emptied out his pockets. He always liked to carry a few things he thought might come in handy, like string, a nail, a folding screwdriver, and a torch. He tested the torch and handed it to Suzan.

She winked at them, put the torch between her teeth like a pirate and shimmied up to the first branches. Suzan climbed like an agile monkey.

'She can out-climb anyone at school,' Jack said, as the three watched her scramble up the tree, in awe.

Moments later she was sitting on a branch far up in the tree and was shining the torch into the hole. Realizing that the hole went back quite far, she shone the torch in at different angles, then paused and froze in surprise.

The three watched intently as they saw her face fill with excitement. Then they saw her carefully reach into the hole, her hand disappearing almost to her elbow, as she reached to pull something out. 'It's an old leather pouch and there is something inside!' she called down. She put the torch and the coin pouch safely in her pocket and climbed back down.

The four children sat in a tight circle and the three watched silently and expectantly as Suzan carefully pulled out the leather coin pouch. The buzz of silence was only broken by the sound of their hearts thumping in excitement.

Three pairs of eyes were glued to Suzan as she placed the pouch in the centre of them. It was a dark brown and had a leather string that closed it. She delicately opened the leather pouch.

CAW-B

70

Reaching in, she pulled out a folded piece of paper. It was very yellow, but had been preserved by the pouch and the dry hole it had been in. Suzan gently unfolded the piece of paper. Three of the edges were straight and one was wavy, as if it had been torn from something. There was a short note written on the paper in swirly scrolly ink writing. And just below the words were two long numbers. It read:

"If you have found this, then you must have passed my first test. What is more, you must surely know my name and the name of my ship."

'It must be some kind of treasure map!' Rachel said with wide eyes.

Excitedly, the four children decided to go back to their *rents,* to show them the *treasure map* that Suzan had discovered and to tell them about the amazing tree.

CHAPTER 13

RETURN TO BASE

The hill was dusty and slippery to climb back up; they all helped each other, using tree branches to hold onto and the roots to climb on. Once they reached the top they walked, being sure to keep together in a straight line, but because they were fairly deep in the forest without paths, Jack suggested that they could use the sun, now peeping through the trees, as their point of reference and that this would allow them to walk in one direction.

Eventually they emerged onto a narrow dirt path. They followed the dirt path until they found their way back from the forest, to the open fields at the very top. Like emerging from a dark cave into the bright sunlight, they squinted as their eyes adjusted. And then they bounded over the open fields at the top.

They found their parents, exactly where they had left them. Everything looked the same, except the picnic and snack boxes – they looked considerably lighter. There was a hum of energetic, excited speaking that filled the air as they drew close, which tailed off – into an abrupt silence – when the four children barged in almost exploding with excitement!

'Look what we found in a hole in a tree! Suzan climbed right up the tree to get it,' Rachel exclaimed.

Their father's face twisted through a spectrum of expressions, firstly pride, then fear, before finally settling on shock, which he indicated by raising his eyebrows – almost to the clouds. 'I hope it wasn't a tall tree, Suzan, you know how I feel about you climbing trees,' he said.

Suzan, for once, looked regretful at her father's words. 'Sorry dad, I was very careful and look, this is what I found!' Suzan said as she pulled the leather pouch out of her pocket.

The three parents watched intently as she unfolded the piece of paper. And they listened, like detectives, as the four children retold how they had found it.

'Right, well let's take a look at this giant tree,' they said.

The four children led the three parents across the fields and into the dark coolness of the forest. But, after forty-five minutes of different paths and trying to retrace their steps, they could not find the tree, so they decided to head home, and towards one of Ren's home cooked meals!

'It must be pirate treasure,' Rachel said, as they headed back down the windy path towards the road.

'It's unlikely to be pirate treasure, it is just some kind of old note. It isn't even complete.' The parents all agreed.

'But it is a fun story, and you can pretend it is treasure if you like,' George said.

Back at Rachel and Annabel's house the children were soon cleaned up and enjoying another of Ren's home cooked meals. After dinner, Annabel and Suzan got the room ready for another one of their epic indoor camps, setting out the sleeping bags pillows and torches.

The four children decided to go to bed early and hang out reading stories to each other. But by the time they were all settled, and Suzan had opened the story book, she realised that the other three were already fast asleep. She too felt tired after so much fun and fresh air.

Laying the book down beside her sleeping bag, Suzan lay back and relaxed. She gazed around at her brother and two close friends and then wriggled into a comfortable position and drifted like a ship on a still sea, gently off to sleep.

The next few days flew by for the children, as they packed in as much play and adventure as they could. Finding the strange note in the park had fuelled even more excitement in pirates and long conversations about what it was and how it came to be in the hole in the tree.

It was soon the sad time to say goodbye to each other and for Suzan, Jack and their dad, to set off on the long coach journey, back to England. Suzan put on a brave face as they waved goodbye from their seats at the back of the coach, until Annabel, Rachel and their parents shrank into the distance and finally disappeared completely. Suzan and Jack sat in silence, after having had such a wonderful time with their best friends.

Back in Dover once more, they climbed wearily from the bus and trudged their way home. The sky was grey and drab and it looked like it was about to rain. Ducks on the river were already sheltering under the bushes along the bank, as if they knew the clouds were about to open and throw down their contents.

Just as they reached their front door, and their dad had done the special, wiggle jiggle, bash dance that it took to open it, the first few drops of rain plopped onto the pavement behind them. And by the time they had turned to close the door, spears of rain were falling everywhere.

The kitchen roof began its loud clattering cacophony of taps. Suzan looked around and felt strangely contented to be home. The place had really changed since she had moved in, and she had only just realized that it had now become *home*.

'I'll get the kettle on,' said Jack.

'Yes, please. I really wanted to buy us a tea on the ferry. But they had to close the café because the sea was so choppy. Strange how the weather can change at sea so quickly,' their dad said.

'Yeah, did you see the size of some of those waves?' Suzan asked, with a mixture of glee and fear.

'That was a long journey. I can't wait to get cleaned up and get into my own bed!' Jack said.

They ate, drank tea and all turned in for an early night.

CHAPTER 14

A HIDING PLACE

Jack awoke the next morning sleepy-eyed and gazed at the clock next to his bed. He rubbed his eyes and gazed over to Suzan's bed. It was empty and he could hear sounds coming from downstairs. Slowly he emerged from the covers, like a bear from its cave after hibernation. He trudged across the bedroom floor, stepping over several miscellaneous objects, and went downstairs to find his sis and dad already eating breakfast.

'Oh, nice of you to join us. There might be some crumbs left!' Suzan said with a grin.

Jack peered around and sat down. He served himself some egg and bacon from the pan in the middle and seemed to wake up a little more with every bite.

Just then the familiar sound of the letterbox, creaking and snapping back shut, took the children's attention. Suzan leapt up and grabbed the pile of mail, then she sifted through till she found what she was looking for and winked at Jack. 'It's here,' she said and at that, both she and Jack ran upstairs to read the latest postcard from their mum.

They sat in their usual place together and eyed it all over.

'Sydney! Look there's the opera house!' Jack said as he pointed to one of the pictures on the front. They read the card together and spoke about where their mum might be next.

Suddenly Suzan jumped to her feet and pulled out her boffer-sword, brandishing it at Jack. 'Let your guard down baby Jack!' she said, in a teasing voice.

Jack jumped to his feet, as quick as a cobra striking, and met her slashes with his sword.

'You won't be fast enough to get *my* treasure,' taunted Suzan, acting the part extremely well.

Suddenly Jack held up his hand. '*Stop*, no sorry, I refuse to fight you!'

Suzan looked bemused, 'What's wrong Jack, lost your tough streak?'

Jack laughed. 'No, I want to wear my eye patch for this, so I look more the part and give you the advantage!' he teased. He slid the old chest they'd found in the loft out from under the bed, opened the lid and rummaged through the various pirate items they had in there.

Jack rummaged and rummaged but still couldn't find his eye patch. Refusing to give up, he became frustrated and pulled things out, tossing them over his shoulder – one by one. 'Ouch,' he exclaimed suddenly, as he withdrew his hand and grasped it, as if he had been bitten by something.

After a moment, he uncurled his hand and inspected it. There was a large wooden splinter in his finger, which had just started to bleed. 'Grab me my Swiss army knife sis, please.'

She passed it to him, and he took out the tiny tweezers. Carefully he pulled the splinter from his finger.

Jack then threw the last of the items from the chest and shone his torch, deep inside, in curiosity. He inspected it, inch by inch, until he found an odd join in two pieces of wood, at the bottom. On the edge there was a tiny splinter sized piece missing.

As he inspected the join, he realised that the two pieces of wood had a different grain direction from each other. The rest of the chest was made from single lengths of wood, but the bottom inside was made from two. Jack knocked his knuckle on the two pieces of wood. The one on the right seemed a little loose. 'Look at this sis, this bottom panel seems loose,' he said, with a look of utter curiosity.

Suzan reached in and ran her finger around the edge of the panel. 'Look at this,' she said, as she pulled at a scrap of fabric, protruding from the wood.

All of a sudden, the fabric lifted up the right-hand piece of wood – revealing a secret compartment. As it lifted, a smell of old paper drifted up and the children peered in. Just below the surface was a dark brown leather-bound book. The leather was scuffed and damaged in places, but still held the book together.

Suzan reached in and very delicately lifted the book out. The cover was embossed with slightly faded patterns and the spine had ornate ridges that ran around it. The pages were yellow with age.

Jack and Suzan sat staring at the antique book, with their mouths open, astounded. After a few moments of two fish-like mouths opening and closing silently, Suzan regained control of her face! And slowly placed the book down on the carpet, in front of her, as Jack moved closer.

Suzan opened the book, very cautiously turning to the first page. In flowing writing, it said:

"The memoirs of CC."

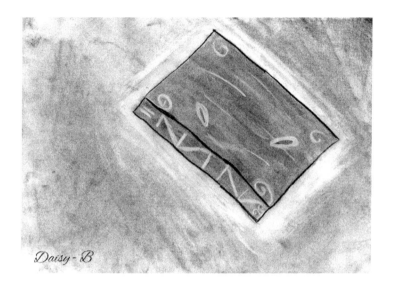

Daisy-B

'Who was *CC*? Was he a sailor? We need to find out sis,' Jack said bursting with excitement.

Suzan delicately turned the page and read chapter one to them both. Both children were transfixed by the story and accounts that were written. They followed the story of a young person and their journey becoming a sailor and then later a pirate.

'CC became a pirate!' Jack exclaimed, with a raised voice, as he gazed over to Suzan, looking for her reaction.

'What, we found the journal of a real pirate? Are you sure it's real Jack?'

'Well, judging by the way the book has been handbound, the colour of the glue pointing towards an animal fat-based glue and the way the paper has been made and cut, I would say it's real and it's certainly at least a hundred, or two hundred years old!'

'Er, a simple *yes* would have done!' Suzan said with a smile.

Before the conversation could continue, they both found themselves drawn back into the stories in the journal. They read page, by page, sometimes slowly rereading sections. It had been handwritten, in some kind of dip pen. As each chapter passed, the stories and adventures became grander, more daring and more flamboyant.

Suddenly their engrossed world was fractured, like a delicate egg, by the loud '*Dinner is ready!* Come on, it will get cold,' that echoed off the walls, as it bellowed up the stairs.

'Quick, put it back in the box, and put the chest away. We can't let dad see the journal. He might confiscate it or be sceptical about it.' Suzan said in an alarmed voice.

They fumbled around until the book was safely back in the chest and the items back in – then slid the whole thing under the bed.

Opening their bedroom door, Suzan said, in her softest voice, 'Sorry dad, were you calling us? We were engrossed in a book!'

'No worries, you two do like your reading,' he said, in a tone that showed that Suzan's soft reply had successfully derailed his anger.

Over the next few days, they read many of the stories from that book. By now, you will know just how much they loved pirates, and can imagine how truly excited they were to find the memoirs, of a real pirate, within a book in their attic! The stories filled their imaginations and became the topic of their discussion and curiosity.

CHAPTER 15

GIANTS?

Over a month or so, they forgot about the tree, France, and the old piece of paper they had found. They even forgot about the city, they once lived in and about missing their old life. Their attention was on the book.

Towards the end of the book, though, there was an odd story that reminded them about the tree. It seemed more like a story than all the rest. Like something from a fantasy, or even fairy-tale. It spoke of visiting a far-off and distant land that cannot be found, and is on no chart, map or record.

It spoke of finding strange giant oak trees, with acorns as big as your fist. Trees that towered above them like mountains. And, most weird of all, it described a strange civilisation. A civilisation of giants…

The children looked at each other in disbelief. Pirates were one thing, but *giants*, they were *something else*.

'There are no islands like that on the internet and no records of giants. They are just myths and legends,' Jack said in a sceptical voice.

The story went on to say that CC became friends with a giant and that they shared many a moment together. When CC and his crew set sail, they were given a single giant oak seedling, as a sign of their eternal friendship.

Everywhere they sailed they took the seedling with them on their ship.

That was the last story in the book. After that there was a note that said:

"And on the day that I disappeared and retired my cutlass, I planted that seedling in a foreign land, not far from my own, at the bottom of a steep hill. It is where my journey as a pirate ended, but not my adventures!

If you search, to journey in my footsteps and seek great treasures, you must eventually find this tree. For hidden within it is something that you will need to begin your journey. Without it you cannot find the ultimate treasure.

But be careful my friend, treasure is a strange thing. It can be many things, in many forms. Not just gold and gemstones. Sometimes we can search the farthest reaches, yet find the greatest treasures under our noses. Be careful, dreams and desires of treasure can cost. Morality, friendships, family, soul and even sanity! Whoever you are, and whenever you are, take care to not lose yourself.

Now, all great journeys begin with preparation. And yours is no different. Before you set off, you must find the magnifying glass that doesn't work, solve the riddle, know my other name and reveal the location of the tree!"

AWB

84

As they read those final words, Suzan jumped up unexpectedly and darted off, leaving Jack with a surprised look on his face.

'Siiisss,' his words trailed off, as he heard her thumping her way down the stairs. Just as he was about to stand up and make sure she was okay; he heard the same *Suzan commotion* ascending the stairs again.

She burst back through the door, with a gigantic grin on her face, and strutted across the room. 'Little bro, take notes, for I am the greatest clue solver ever!' she said as she pulled from behind her back an old tatty magnifying glass.

'That can't be it sis. This book was written a long time ago, that is just an old thing grandad left in the cutlery drawer with other odd items,' Jack said sceptically.

'It has to be, look it is a magnifying glass that doesn't work,' she said as she handed it to Jack.

Jack put it to his eye, and then pulled a face of puzzlement. 'It's just blurry. What use is that?' He was about to throw it back to Suzan, when upon closer inspection of the deep, dark oak handle, with its tarnished brass lens surround, he noticed that the edge had some kind of writing around it. 'Look, there's something written on it. Not very clear though.' He squinted and tried to read the writing around it. But though well preserved, it was tarnished and dirty.

'We need vinegar,' said Suzan, suddenly remembering a science lesson about acids and that vinegar is an acid that can clean some metals. Swiftly and carefully, they put the book back in the chest and then went down to kitchen, with the magnifying glass. Suzan took a bottle of vinegar and cleaned the brass.

AWB

Eagerly, Jack looked at the sentence and noted down each letter. 'It's a sentence in Latin. Then it has CC in tiny letters. I've studied a bit of Latin at school.' He stumbled slowly over each word, trying to remember the meaning. Eventually he translated it all. 'If the Latin, that we studied at school serves me correctly, it says:

"Vanity is a weakness look in the mirror."

'Jack, you should know about that! you spend ages in the bathroom every morning,' Suzan said, with her usual cheeky smile.

'Well, in that case, step into my office,' Jack said with a sarcastic tone.

They both ran to the bathroom, full of excitement, and almost crashed into each other when suddenly Jack came to an abrupt holt. 'This is just the cheap green plastic mirror, that dad got online,' he said. 'Looks like the search had gone cold.'

'Yeah, but dad put that mirror up because there was a tiny old mirror there before. So small, in fact that it was almost impossible to use as a bathroom mirror, unless you got really close to it. Don't you remember dad tried shaving in it and then decided to change it?' Suzan said with a glint in her eyes.

There was a moment of silence as they both paused and puzzled over it, and then, '*The shed*,' they both shouted together and ran downstairs.

They were as far as the back door, before their father boomed, 'Where do you think you two are going this time of night?'

'The shed…' Jack said in an innocent voice.

'Rhetorical question, dear boy! It is night-time and far too late to go to the shed now. You both have school tomorrow. Go on, get cleaned up and into bed, before you start smelling like the pirates you act like!'

Both children did an about turn and trumped upstairs as if they were four years old.

Suzan turned the light off as they settled into their beds for the night. 'I bet the mirror is there. We need to get hold of it tomorrow,' she whispered to Jack.

'Yeah, but we have school first thing, we'll have to wait till after school,' replied Jack, in a disappointed voice.

'Ok we'll go straight to the shed when we get back from school!

CHAPTER 16

THE MIRROR

The next day Suzan and Jack awoke blurry eyed. Reluctantly they trudged to school. It had been difficult to sleep after the events of the day. They had both been thinking about the magnifying glass and letting their vivid imaginations run away with themselves.

Things were no better at school. It was really hard to concentrate on each lesson and Jack's teacher was infuriated with him. '*Jack!* What is the answer to question number twelve: one thousand, one hundred and three plus one thousand, one hundred and twelve minus two thousand, two hundred and thirteen?' she screamed, as she tapped a long pointy stick at a cold hard math question on the board.

Jack glanced over the numbers, gave up and said the first thing that came into his head: 'Knee,' which coincidently is Japanese for *two* and was in fact the correct answer; however, as neither of them spoke Japanese, this eluded them both.

'Jack are you alright today, what has your knee got to do with my math question? You seem to be away with the giants!' his teacher said, as she peered over her bifocal glasses, which sat on the very end of her nose.

Jack heard her scolding trail off, into a mist of background noise, as he found himself thinking about the magnifying glass, the book and most of all wondering who *CC* was – for the one hundredth time that day. In fact, both he and Suzan were preoccupied all day.

Finally, the jagged ring of the school bell echoed through the school, followed by the unified dragging of chairs and cacophony of chatter. Kids flooded out of classrooms into the corridor and like water finding the nearest exit, gushed through the front doors, into freedom and fresh air.

Jack and Suzan were amidst the wave of kids all heading for the front gate. They both had one thing and one thing only in their minds: *get home and look for that mirror.* They ran all the way home, arrived at the front door panting, rushed upstairs, changed, and dashed downstairs to see their dad.

'How was your day dad?' Jack asked.

'It was pretty good thanks, how about you?'

'Good,' said both children, in unison.

'We're just going to play in the garden and the shed,' said Suzan.

'No worries, remember to help yourself to snacks, if you feel hungry.'

They stepped out into the garden and walked down the narrow path that led to the tumble down shed at the end. Jack wriggled the rusty bolt lock open and unwedged the door. It juddered and creaked open. Inside the shed was filled with old boxes, overflowing with random things. Some items belonged to them, and others must have been left by their grandad.

Suzan and Jack glanced into the boxes, until they came to a box of their dad's tools and house hardware. Jack pulled out the torch, which was permanently with him and shone it into the box.

Both children dug through the box, pulling out screwdrivers, pliers, door handles, clothes hooks and finally, right at the bottom, they spotted the tiny mirror. It was only about four centimetres in size and had a brass surround. Suzan chuckled as she remembered her father trying to shave in such a small mirror and becoming annoyed.

Jack slowly turned the mirror over in his hand and shone the torch on it. His eyes lit up when he noticed the writing on the back. They perched down on the shed floor and shone the torch over the words.

'Is it in Latin Jack?' Suzan said in an expectant voice.

'Yes, it is Suz. Let me see,' Jack said, as he squinted at the letters. 'Hmm this is a bit tricky for my Latin, but I have a book, on Latin, from the school library. Hang ten sis, I'll be back before you can say Sesquipedalian,' Jack said, with a giggle as he belted up the garden path and into the house, leaving Suzan, in a cloud of dust, wondering what *Sesquipedalian* meant and whether it was a real word.

Moments later a rather red in the face Jack reappeared with an old well-read tatty book called: *Latin a Beginners Guide and Dictionary*.

'That wasn't a real word was it, Jack?' asked Suzan, with a scowl.

'Actually, it is. It means to love using long words all the time!' Jack replied.

Suzan giggled.

'Right, let's translate this Latin sentence. Some of the words I recognise, but I want to check these ones in my book,' Jack said, as he fingered through his Latin book to find the same words. Then with a pen and paper, that he pulled from his well-stocked pocket of provisions, he began to write down the sentence in English. 'Ah!' he said as he wrote the last word down. 'It says:

"THE SUN SHINES THROUGH ME BUT WIND CANNOT" - it's another riddle. **It has CC engraved in tiny letters as well.'**

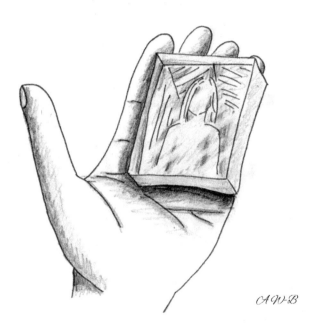

CA W-B

Both children sat, for over an hour, thinking of possible answers to the riddle but could not crack it.

'I know, let's ask dad,' suggested Jack.

'Sure…. Dad, we've found an ancient pirate's journal and are hunting for objects he's left us clues for, so we can then find a great treasure… That'll work - not!' Suzan said, in a deeply sarcastic voice.

'Or we could just say it was a riddle your teacher asked us!' Jack replied, in an even more sarcastic tone.

'Right, got your point. Let's go ask dad.'

Closing the shed up, they made sure the tiny mirror was safe in Jack's pocket and made their way back to the house.

'Dad, my teacher asked us a really, crazy, doubly tricksy riddle today,' Jack said.

Their father's curiosity was awakened. 'Really, what was the riddle?' He asked, eager to have a go.

'Well, it was: the sun can shine through this, but the wind cannot.'

Their father tapped his fingertips on his desk and pondered the riddle, for a few moments, and then said in a loud and enthusiastic voice: 'A window.'

'Wow, dad you're awesome, thanks,' Suzan said.

Both children wandered away and began to look at the windows in the house. They examined each one thoroughly, inside and out, but found it difficult as it was becoming dark.

'It's Saturday tomorrow, let's take a better look in the light, first thing, tomorrow morning!' Suzan said.

'Good plan sis, besides dinner is ready and it's shepherd's pie!' Jack said, licking his lips.

CHAPTER 17

GREEN LIGHT

The cool, early morning, air gave way to the warmth of the sun as it spread its arms over the sleepy seaside town. Jack and Suzan were already up to see the sunrise. They had woken up extra early, as they were so excited about following the next clue.

'Au u eddy?' Jack asked, while stuffing his mouth with his fifth round of toast and marmalade.

'Yes, *captain toast* I am!'

Both children left the table and started looking, once again, at the windows throughout the house, from top to bottom, one by one. But they all seemed to be very similar, traditional wooden sash windows that slid up and down. They ran their fingers along every inch of the frames, looking for marks, or anything that might be their next clue.

'We've been doing this all-morning Jack,' Suzan said, in a glum voice.

'Let's stop for a cuppa,' suggested Jack.

'And some biscuits,' Suzan added. They put the kettle on and made tea for themselves and their dad.

'I don't want to sit at the table. Let's sit at the sunniest end of the room,' suggested Suzan.

Although they had bought and made lots of furniture, there was still no sofa, so they drank their tea and munched their biscuits, perched on the floor. The low midmorning sun streamed through the front windows and danced on the floor.

'Ha Suzan, I always thought you were a green goblin!' Jack said, in a mischievous voice.

Suzan gave him a puzzled look and pondered whether her brother had finally lost his marbles!

'Your face Suz, is green from the light coming through the …' But he didn't finish the sentence because something dawned on them both.

They slowly turned their heads towards the source of the coloured light, a small but beautiful stained-glass window that sat proudly above the entrance. Jack grabbed one of the chairs from the dinner table. Standing on tiptoe, on the chair – hoping he wouldn't fall off – he inspected the window.

It showed waves and a tall sailing ship. In the sky there seemed to be seven moons, which were all green - each one a different shade. Jack inspected the window very closely and noticed that the lead that held the sections of glass all in, did not seem to go around the seven moons. And in fact, each of the moons seemed to be just loosely fitted into the window.

Jack opened the front door, and gently prised one of the circles out, while supporting it on the other side of the window, with his other hand. The glass circle was perfectly circular and had a fine brass surround, with a small hole in one side of the brass. He passed it to Suzan, and then tentatively prized out the other six.

Daisy - B

The two looked at each one, in turn, trying to find the next clue. Soon they realised there was a word written on the brass surround of each one, in Latin.

Jack laid them in different orders. 'What are we supposed to do? Jack asked, in a forlorn tone 'There could be hundreds of possible combinations of these seven words, each one with different meanings'.

'Let me have a look,' Suzan said, as she moved the circular green items around. 'Hmm, they were the moon in the window, and the clue that led us to them was about light,' she muttered to herself, as she pondered. 'I've got it! They need to be put in the order of a moon rise,' she said, in an excited voice. She ordered them from darkest to lightest and then looked at Jack expectantly.

'Hmmm,' said Jack, 'It says…

"cave trahere me cum cogitas te relinquere."

I'll look the words up in my Latin dictionary.' He noted the corresponding meaning, for each one, in his note pad. 'It roughly translates to:

"Be sure to pull me when you plan to leave"

hmm, that's a strange thing to say.'

'That's more than seven words,' retorted Suzan.

'Languages don't always translate into the same number of words you know,' replied Jack. He said the sentence aloud, over and over again. And looked at Suzan, in the hope that she might have an answer to the riddle.

They both puzzled over it for a while.

'I'm not sure what it is we are looking for, Jack, but let's leave it and look at the front door and the entrance. In case there's anything we've missed.'

Putting their tea and plates on the table, they slipped out of the front door. Suzan grabbed the high wooden handle and the ornate brass door handle and pulled the door shut behind them. Slowly both inspected the old wooden front door. They ran their fingers around the frame and looked closely at the letterbox and at the six panels.

Just then the door opened, to reveal a rather curious looking father. 'Whatever are you two doing out here?' He asked with one eyebrow raised high enough to almost touch his hairline.

'We are, er we are…' Jack stuttered, before Suzan swept in to save the moment with, 'We're looking for my hair clip,' she said.

'Oh, I see.' Satisfied with the answer, their father did an about turn and walked back into the house, leaving the door wide open.

Suzan reached up to the high wooden handle, between the top two panels of the door, and was just about to pull the door to, with the help of the old brass handle, when she froze and stared. Jack noticed and immediately took a closer look.

The handle back plate was ornate and a very unusual shape. They had never really looked closely at it before, but now they began to study its every detail. In fact, the back plate had a series of numbers at the bottom, in an arc. And the wooden handle looked strangely out of place, attached to such an elaborate backplate. There were four screws that fixed the plate to the door, and even the screws didn't seem to go with the brass plate.

'That *has* to be it!' Jack said in an excited high voice!

'O…. K, but we can't just unscrew bits of the front door! Suzan said, in her most sensible tone.

'Well, Suz it isn't the main door handle, it's just used to help pull it to,' Jack said, with a cheeky smile, as he rummaged in his pocket. He pulled out a very old pen knife and looked over the various tools that were part of it. Unfolding a screwdriver, he gave Suzan an extra cheeky, up to no good kind of smile and proceeded to unscrew the four screws.

Finally, he had to use his knife to prise off the brass plate, which looked as if it had been painted round many times, over the ages. Reluctantly it came away, leaving a mark where it had been and exposing a rich wooden section of the door below.

Jack inspected the brass handle, and on turning it over found some words engraved into it. 'Another message,' he whispered, in a discreet manor. 'We might need to clean it though.'

'Let's smuggle the handle up to our room and see if we can work out what's written on it. I'll smuggle some cloths and vinegar from the kitchen.'

They snuck swiftly up to their room.

CA·W·B

101

CHAPTER 18

WHAT IS MY NAME?

Jack set up the desk lamp, right nearby and they cleaned the back of the brass handle carefully.

Both squinted to try to read what was written on it and then Jack read the words aloud: 'It says..

"Now put us together and you will find your way. In a tree, beneath a hill in Argenteuil lays the final page of my memoirs and the first page of your journey! Good luck, may the seas be kind and riches be great!"'

Suzan peered at the bottom under the hand engraved writing. 'What's that?' she asked, as she pointed to a mark below.

Jack cleaned it with some vinegar and the rough side of a sponge. 'It says *CC*, but there's something else. It's a word or two, maybe … the writers name, it says…it, it says *"I am the Mist".'*

A thick cloud of silence washed over them, as they both stared at the two familiar words.

'WHAT?' Suzan exclaimed, 'Why is *the Mist* written on this? All the others have the CC mark.'

'Is that *the Mist*, as in the story mum told us?' Jack asked, in a puzzled state of shock.

'It is, but it can't be… but it is,' Suzan said.

'So, *CC* was the Mist?'

'But hang on, Argenteuil is where that park was. The one we visited and where we found…' Suzan's sentence tailed off into silence, then she explosively jumped up, and disappeared under her bed.

Jack raised an eyebrow as he heard her rummaging around the bed and saw her suddenly reappear on the other side, dragging a cardboard box out. She opened the worn lid and gently plucked out post cards from her mum, some family photos from years ago and finally the old leather pouch she had retrieved from halfway up that tree in France earlier that year.

Then she slid the wooden chest, they had found in the loft, out from under the end of her bed, opened it and took out the leather book of CC's memoirs. She sat back on the floor next to Jack.

'The book written by CC,' she said as she gestured to it. 'The letter we found in France, in that tree, which we thought was connected to the story of the Mist,' she said as she pointed to it. 'I wonder…'

Slowly and delicately, Suzan unfolded the letter from the tree. Then she opened the book of memoirs and turned to the very end. She pointed out that there was a ragged edge, next to the last page, where something had been torn out. Tentatively she placed the letter from the tree on top.

'*It fits*,' they both exclaimed.

'The tree in Argenteuil is the one planted by CC, or otherwise known as the Mist and these are his memoirs. One of the most infamous pirates ever! His ship didn't go

down that night and his treasure must still be out there!!!'
Jack said, hardly stopping for spaces to breathe between
words and sentences.

'In which case these strange brass items and this letter,
have something to do with him and might even lead to his
treasure,' Suzan exclaimed.

'Do you think it is still out there?' Jack said, with so
much excitement he almost exploded!

Suzan's eyes flitted, from box to book to brass items,
as she pondered it all. And after some time, she said: 'It
has to be. These things have been hidden for a very long
time. I think the Mist went to a lot of trouble to hide his
treasure. So, it must be still out there. In the vast world.
Thousand...' Suzan stopped, as she noticed Jack, staring
at the pile of post cards from their mum.

Tears were trickling down his face and he muttered,
'Yes, the world is vast. And that's why we never see mum!
Wish she didn't have to do that stupid job.'

Suzan put her arm around her brother and comforted
him, feeling his sadness, wishing she could help. Then her
eyes lit up, widening as she exclaimed: 'I have an idea!'
The sadness in her face was washed away by a bright
smile. 'CC, or rather the Mist, was a great pirate and he
had so much treasure. If we could find it, mum wouldn't
have to work away anymore, doing that stupid job, and
we could all be together again. We could have holidays
and money for things.'

Jack smeared his tears with his t-shirt and a smile crept
onto his face too. 'That's a great idea sis. Look we've
already solved the riddle and found the things. We must
be halfway there. If we could find it...' He gazed off into
oblivion for a moment, as a stream of ideas and images
filled his mind. 'Dad wouldn't need to work so hard

either, mum could come home. It has to be still out there. Even just a tiny bit of it would be enough!'

The two of them were carried off on a long, enchanting discussion of fantasy, imagining what they would do if they found it! Until Jack suddenly grabbed the items and looked at them in scepticism. 'But all we have is a bunch of odd brass items and a letter we found in a tree. What are we supposed to do with these? What are they all meant to mean?'

Suzan suddenly remembered that she had visited the local museum, with the school, earlier in the year and that the people there were very kind. It gave her an idea. 'Let's take the brass objects to the museum tomorrow morning and ask if they know what they are,' she suggested with excitement.

'Great idea sis,' said Jack!

'Then that settles it, we'll go first thing tomorrow morning. But we must *not* speak about the chest, book, or tree while we're there. Just say that you found the items in the house.'

'I agree, if they really *do* all lead to the Mist's long-lost treasure, we don't want anyone else beating us to it!'

After dinner, they prepared for bed. Then, carefully, they packed the items safely into a bag, ready to take to town.

CHAPTER 19

THE MUSEUM

The next morning Suzan and Jack told their dad that they might go to town. Just a little after breakfast they set out. Walking by the river, towards town, they saw the familiar lines of ducks and moorhens on the way. A single acorn was drifting down the river, ambling along, making its way round the twists and turns and they were reminded of the unbelievably large acorn discovered in the Argenteuil Park.

Daisy-B

The town museum was an old and mysterious looking building and looked as if it had its fair share of tales to tell too. Suzan and Jack walked up the worn curved steps and through a large wooden door and were met by a kind lady who greeted them with a soft and warm accent: 'How can I help you two?' she said.

'We've found some old items in our house, and we would like someone to tell us what they are, replied Suzan, taking control of the situation.

'Ah,' the lady said. 'You will want Jacob,' she purred softly, as she picked up the phone.

The children heard her say: 'Two children with something old they've found.' The lady put the phone down, 'Jacob can take a look at them now, if you like.'

The lady showed them to the back of the reception area, her finger jabbed an old dimly lit button, which summoned the lift. When the lift arrived, the lady pushed the *B1* button.

Suzan's eyes flicked around the inside. *We didn't visit B1, with the school,* she thought to herself. But she knew that, like all museums, there was likely to be a storage and cataloguing area, under the museum, to house eighty percent of the items that were not on display.

The lift doors opened, and the children stepped out to see a very old man with glasses, slowly walking down the corridor. The man had a long grey beard and kind warm eyes and as he drew close, he smiled. The children noticed that his face was full of wrinkles. Smile lines, not from frowning, but from smiling and laughing.

Introducing himself as Jacob, he spoke softly and gently: 'You have some things you would like to show me?'

The children replied, 'Yes,' in unison.

Jacob led them down the corridor, to a large room with tables in the middle. The walls were filled, from floor to ceiling, with shelves and boxes and two young assistants were working away, in the distance, cataloguing items.

The old man beckoned Suzan and Jack to sit down at the table. He sat opposite, smiled and said: 'So children, what have you found?'

Jack took the brass items out of his bag and placed them on the table. 'These. Do you know what they are?'

CA W-B

109

The old man gazed at the objects. They seemed to spark an excitement in him. He stroked his beard and nodded, as each item was placed on the table. His eyes sparkled and he appeared to drift off, into a sea of memories. After a few moments, he exclaimed: 'Ahhha! Do you know what you have here children?' Without waiting for them to reply he continued: 'These are very old pieces of a navigating instrument. It's called a sextant. Before computers and electric and GPS, sailors and pirates used these to navigate the seas, all around the world.'

He picked up the lens and held it up to the light. 'Beautiful,' he said. 'It's strange to see such a perfect lens, in such an old one.'

'But how does it go together?' asked Suzan.

The old man stood up, creaking as he did. He walked over to the wall, gazed up at the rows and rows of boxes and held his finger to his lip in contemplation. The uncountable rows of boxes were all simply identified by numbers and letters.

'Jacob,' shouted one of the young assistants, 'what are you looking for? why don't you use the computer catalogue system to find it?'

Jacob peered, over his glasses, at the young lady and laughed, 'I don't need that silly fandangle computer. I know the contents of every box here.' He returned to his gaze at the boxes and ran his finger along until he reached a box that was about ten centimetres tall and about thirty centimetres wide.

He lifted the box and blew the dust from the top - it had sat there for decades! He walked back to the table, placed the box down and opened it. Pulling back some protective tissue paper, he lifted out a brass object that consisted of a flat plate with a curve on the bottom, with many numbers on it. And attached to it were lenses, filters and a mirror.

Jacob smiled, gazed at it for a while and said softly, 'Hello my dear old friend.' He placed it next to the objects that the children had brought. 'This, children, is a sextant. It is in fact my sextant. When I left school a long, long time ago I joined the merchant navy and captained tankers around the world. I navigated almost entirely with this.'

'But why didn't you just use GPS?' asked Jack.

'Well, because… though it worked for many places, there were still many places where it didn't work, and I've never trusted it! I sailed till I was fifty, using this.' Jacob picked it up gently and the children noticed that the wooden handle had worn finger spots that fitted exactly to Jacob's fingers and hands.

'It is like an old friend to me,' said the old man. 'Two hundred countries, in thirty years. I could tell you a few tales! When I reached fifty, I decided to retire and become a historian. It was always my other great love! And I've worked here ever since.' He placed their brass pieces in the same order as his sextant.

The children let out an excited: 'Wow!'

'Though this is very old, there are some things that I don't understand about this, for example it has *seven* green lenses, not six and the numbers on the main arc are very different than usual. I've seen many of these in my time, but never one quite like this,' puzzled Jacob.

'But how can we put it together?' Jack asked.

'Ah,' said the old man, 'unfortunately it's missing the screws bolts and fixings. Without them, you cannot use it.'

The children looked a little down.

'The problem is that you will not be able to find the screws and fixings in any shop. They were handmade and only someone like a master watch maker would have the skills to make them.

'If you *can* find some though, and put it together, I can show you how to use it!' The old man walked over to his desk and came back with a card that read: "*Jennifer, master clock and watch maker.*" The card was amazingly old and had almost as many wrinkles as the old man's face.

'Children, give her a call and mention my name – Jacob –she might just be able to help you. That's if you're determined to put it together!'

The children walked back down the corridor and the kind old man showed them back to the lift.

'Thank you for explaining what the things we found are,' Suzan said, just as they were getting into the lift.

'My pleasure. Ask the lady upstairs if you can use the phone to call Jennifer, if you like,' he said, just before the lift doors closed and it began to climb with a reluctant squeal.

The kind lady on the front desk was more than happy to let them use the phone and they rang the number given on the card. An elderly lady picked up and asked who was calling.

The children explained that Jacob recommended her. And she agreed that they could come over. They took her workshop address and used most of their pocket money to catch two buses, along the coast, to a small town by the sea.

CHAPTER 20

THE CLOCKMAKER

On reaching the little town, they walked the rest of the way to the address and arrived at a very old wooden framed tumble-down house. The door and frame were crooked, as were most parts of the building and the thatch lay heavily on the roof, golden in the sun.

They knocked and a sweet cheerful elderly lady answered the door. She was short and a little bent over, with rosy round cheeks.

'Jennifer?' Asked Jack.

'Yes,' replied the elderly lady. 'You must be the children Jacob sent. Come in.'

The children stepped into what was once a lounge but had been a workshop for a long time. As they stepped in, they noticed that every wall was filled with clocks and wherever they looked they saw watches, clocks and more clocks. Great grandfather clocks and table clocks. All ticking together. In fact, the whole house seemed to tick!

'Sit down dearies,' said Jennifer.

They sat at a table in the middle of the room. Jack took the pieces of the sextant out of his bag and placed them on the table.

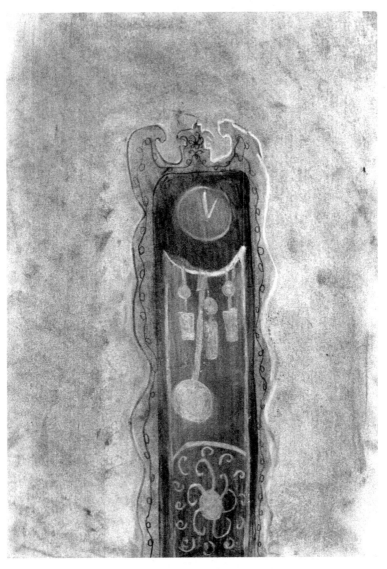

Daisy - B

'Oooh,' said the lady, 'I usually work on clocks. But I've worked on a few navigating instruments in my time. What seems to be the problem?'

'We don't have the fixings for it,' Jack piped up.

'Ah,' said the lady. She took out a small box with many different compartments. From several compartments she took screws and tiny bolts, and then gently tried them in the holes on the sextant.

'Just as I thought,' she said. 'This is exceptionally old and will need special handmade fixings.'

'Where from?' asked Suzan.

'Wait and see,' replied the elderly lady. Skillfully she took out two small vials of liquid, one blue and the other clear. She measured, a little from each, into a small bowl and mixed them up. Then she took a syringe and squirted some of the liquid into the screw and bolt holes, on the sextant. Standing, she asked: 'Cuppa tea?'

Both children said, 'YES PLEASE!' And the lady disappeared down a corridor.

The children heard the sound of china cups chinking and a whistling kettle. Soon she came back with an old tray with three china cups and saucers and a plate of biscuits arranged on it.

'Dig in my dears.'

The three of them all sipped their tea and dunked their biscuits. After ten or so minutes, when they had finished, the lady took the tray away and returned.

She explained that the blue liquid in the screw and bolt holes had gone hard now. She unscrewed each one, set up a large magnifying glass with a light on it, and studied each one, taking careful measurements and drawing corresponding designs in her notebook.

When she had finished, she told Suzan and Jack to follow her. They were led into what was once a dining room but had been used as another workshop area for a long time. There were parts of clocks everywhere and many watches and clocks, in the process of being repaired.

In the corner, the old lady went to work on a lathe making the fixings. The children watched intently, as she created each fixing. After a little while, she led them back through to the other room and assembled the sextant.

Soon it looked similar to the one that Jacob had showed them, except for a small telescope that was missing. The children were beaming with excitement and thanked the old lady several times.

Luckily Jennifer insisted that they didn't pay her: 'You are alright dears, don't worry. Say hello to Jacob for me. Goodbye dearies.'

'Thank you, Jennifer, you've been so kind,' Suzan said, with her warmest smile.

With the sextant carefully wrapped and in Jack's bag, they travelled back to their town.

'Let's go straight to the museum and ask Jacob to show us how to use this,' suggested Suzan.

But when they arrived, the museum was closed.

'Gosh, have we really been out all day?' said Jack

'I guess so, and now we'll have to wait another whole week, before we can come back and find out more about how to use this sea navigation object,' Suzan said, in a glum tone.

The same lady who saw them earlier, at reception, had just finished locking the front door and was turning to leave, when she saw them. 'Hi, sorry we closed early today, but we'll be open again tomorrow,' she said in a cheerful tone.

'We would love to come back tomorrow, but we've got school,' said Jack, in a disappointed tone.

The lady gave him a curious look, raised an eyebrow, and said: 'But tomorrow's a bank holiday, isn't your school closed?'

Jack turned to Suzan to see if she knew anything about the bank holiday. She gave him a look back that was equally as surprised as his. 'I didn't know it was a bank holiday tomorrow,' Jack said with an intrigued voice.

The lady came closer and showed Jack and Suzan a diary, that she kept in her bag, and sure enough it said: *"Bank holiday"*. 'We're open for most of the day, you're welcome to come back, and Jacob is around too!'

'Thank you, that's very kind. We'll come back tomorrow. Have a nice evening!' Jack said.

They walked briskly back home and carefully put the bag in their room.

Moments later their father called up: 'Dinner's ready. Don't be long.'

The two children ran downstairs as fast as they could. They sat down to a piping hot steak and gravy pie with chips and mushy peas.

'My favourite,' said Suzan.

Their dad sat down and smiled at them, as they dug into the food. 'What did you get up to today?'

'We went to the museum and…' Suzan began, but stopped, because she received a sharp nudge from Jack. She realized that she might have said too much, but she continued and said, 'We went to the beach, some shops and then popped into the museum to see an exhibition there.'

117

'Ah, I had heard that there was a new exhibition of paintings there,' their father answered knowledgably.

'Yes,' said Jack. 'They're interesting.'

After dinner both children went upstairs and looked at the sextant again.

'I wonder how it works,' said Jack.

'Tomorrow we'll go down to the museum first thing and ask Jacob to show us,' said Suzan.

They showered, jumped into their pjs and lay in bed, with the lights dimmed, speaking about the long-lost *ultimate treasure* and what they would do when they found it.

CHAPTER 21

EYE PATCHES

Next morning, they awoke to the smell of egg and bacon. Both children rushed downstairs, remembering it was a bank holiday and sat down.

'Thanks dad,' they said, in unison – in pirate voices – as they tucked into lashings of bacon.

'I'll be at home working hard all day. What do you think you'll both do today?' their father asked, with interest.

'We will go to the mu...' Suzan started but was given another sharp nudge by Jack. She shot him a glare as if to say: *You'll pay for that.*

'What Suzan is saying is that we want to have the day on the beach and maybe pop back into the museum, to finish looking at the new exhibition.' Jack said, trying to take control of the situation and avoid suspicion.

'I didn't know you like art so much!' said their father. 'But it's great that you do. You have a lovely day.'

The children washed up and were soon making their way along the river towards the town. They arrived just in time for the museum opening and asked to see Jacob.

The lady gestured to the lift and the two went down to B1. She phoned down and Jacob met them again.

'Did Jennifer manage to help you with the fixings?' Said Jacob.

'Yes,' the children replied, as Jacob led them back to the cataloguing room.

Jack pulled out the sextant.

Jacob looked it over. 'Yes, she's done a beautiful job,' said the old man. Then gave them a look of a little concern. 'But it's still missing one part. It needs a small telescope attached here to view from,' he continued, whilst pointing to a space on the device and stroking his grey beard. 'Hmmm.' He stood up slowly, creaking like an old tree in the wind, ran his fingers along a series of boxes, on one of the walls, and took out a fairly new, large looking box, wandered back over and sat down.

Placing the box in the middle of the table, he pulled off the lid. Inside he rummaged through an eclectic mixture of nautical instruments and took out a few broken sextants. 'No, too old... No, far too broken. Hmm, I wonder,' he said, as he sifted through the items. He picked up one and began to take a small telescope from it. 'The rest of the sextant is broken, but the telescope on this is still ok and should fit your device,' he said, as his fingers went to work fitting the telescope to the CC sextant.

Finally, squinting through the little telescope, he stroked his beard, thought for a moment and then brought over a box that was filled with an absolute assortment of tools. From brushes for cleaning, to screwdrivers.

Jacob selected a few very tiny screwdrivers and began to twist and turn different points on the device. After a while, he said: 'That will do ya. It should work now.'

AW-B

'Can you show us *how* it works, please?' asked Jack.

'Of course I will,' said Jacob, as he stood up and beckoned them to follow him.

They all walked back into the lift and Jacob selected an R button. The lift went all the way to the top of the museum. Climbing out of the lift, they went up a small set of steps and out onto a rooftop.

The roof of the museum was flat and had railings round the edge. In the middle was a small table and a chair. Jacob gazed out to sea and for a moment; his sparkling eyes were lost in a sea of memories and stories.

After a while he turned to the children and said, with a youthful glint in his eye, 'This is one of my favourite places, I often come here to look out to sea.' He lifted the sextant up and as the two children focused on it and listened, he explained: 'Sextants can use celestial bodies, like the sun, moon, and the stars to navigate with. During the day you could use the sun. But you would have to use lots of the green filter lenses. You should never look directly at the sun without the green filters,' he said with a serious face. 'Do you know why pirates had eye patches?' he asked, in a quiet whisper.

'Because they lost their eyes in fierce battles,' suggested Suzan.

'To make them look more fearsome,' said Jack with enthusiasm.

'Ha-ha,' said Jacob. 'No, the *pirates eye patch look* was due to their lifestyle, not fashion! The reason is that if you look at the sun, with a lens without the filters, it will burn your eye and make it blind. That's often why some wore eyepatches. They had damaged their eyes.'

He showed Suzan and Jack how they could see both the horizon and the celestial body, at the same time, because of the special mirror and lens. He showed them how to point it at the sun, using the strong filters, and how to slowly pivot the centre to take an angle reading.

Then he explained that you had to record the exact time and then cross reference the information in a navigation book, to get your latitude and longitude. He had brought an example, to show them, of a navigation book.

'Yes… but what *exactly* is latitude and longitude?' Jack asked.

'Ah,' replied Jacob, 'that's your horizontal and vertical position on the planet.'

They spent a few hours together, practicing how to take readings safely with the filters and how to use the navigation book. And Jacob regaled them with stories of his sailing days.

Though his face was rough and old, he seemed to take on a youthful spirit when he reminisced and shared his stories. When the conversation fizzled, Jacob explained that he had to catalogue some new items soon, so should be getting back.

'Thank you so much for a wonderful morning, Jacob. It must have been brilliant to spend so many years at sea, having adventures,' Suzan said, with a twinkle of excitement in her eye.

'Aye it was missy, but it was also a dangerous and risky life. It was no fairy tale!' Jacob said, with a glint of fear in his eye.

The children said their goodbyes and agreed to come back another day, to hear more stories.

CHAPTER 22

THE PAINTING

Back in the main part of the museum, Jack turned to Suzan. 'I think that we should have a look at the painting exhibition, in case father asks us about them.'

'You're right, he will probably ask!' Suzan agreed.

They both went into the gallery room. It had paintings from around the world, around the walls. As they slowly walked around, the two children spoke about the Mist, the treasures that he might have hidden and of course: *The ultimate treasure*. They discussed quietly what they thought it was. Both were excited after such a great morning.

In the corner, of the museum, there stood a thin wiry man, dressed in shabby black clothes. He had a crooked nose and short goatee. He gazed dreamily, from a little distance, at a painting that was behind very thick glass.

It was a famous painting on loan from a Paris Museum. The thin wiry man was making notes with a pencil in a notebook.

Not notes about the composition, or the delicate balance of colours, not even about the style or era, but notes about the thickness of the glass, the height, the position of the CCTV the alarms, the distance to the door and the habits of the security guard sitting in the hall of the museum. A small smile rose in the corner of his mouth as he whispered, 'Soon you'll be mine, my beauty.'

Just then the security guard stood up and walked in the direction of the toilet, very quickly. It seemed that the soup he ate for lunch had given him terrible stomach problems.

The man with the crooked nose slowly walked down the gallery space, closer to the picture. His eyes fixed on it. His gaze locked, like a leopard stalking its prey.

As he passed the two children, something broke his attention. Something made him stop and break his gaze. He turned his head and listened intently. His eyes widened. The words *ultimate treasure* seemed to evoke great excitement in him.

Listening keenly, the man heard everything that they were saying. He grinned from ear to ear. And without breaking concentration, he reached down into his pocket and took out an old folding mobile phone. Flipping it open, he jabbed some numbers, then put it to his ear.

'It's me,' he said, '*ultimate treasure,* museum. Quick! Two children, one girl, one boy.' Swiftly he flipped the phone closed, put it back in his pocket and strolled out towards the front door. Just before exiting, he turned his head, towards the painting. 'Next time,' he said, giving it one final look.

AW-B

A few minutes later a coach full to the brim with tourists, turned up outside. The tourists flooded into the gallery and museum. Soon the room became a chaotic, noisy hubbub of humans, all speaking in a foreign language.

No one could understand what they were saying and why they looked so disgruntled. But if you could speak their language, you would know that they had bought tickets to the great museum in London and that they were absolutely sure that this small museum was not it.

Some of the tourists were so disgruntled that they were shouting and looking for the tour guide, who had driven them there, and assured them that London really was just a short ride from the ferry crossing.

If you were standing in that room, you would have been confused at the strange languages and vast pandemonium from the noisy chaotic crowds. Everyone was too distracted to notice two rather burly unsavoury characters putting fabric sacks over Suzan and Jack and carrying them out.

The security guard and receptionist were too busy dealing with so many aggressive, disgruntled tourists – all shouting at them and asking questions in a variety of languages – that they did not notice the two children being bagged and put in the luggage compartment of that very same coach, or the coach leaving otherwise completely empty.

Suzan and Jack were terrified. They were not sure what had happened after the bags went on them. They were really uncomfortable being jolted around in the luggage compartment and they kicked and flailed out, until they were too exhausted to move any more; then they cried.

Suzan called out to Jack. He answered shakily. They were happy that they were still together, but frightened.

'Where are we?' asked Suzan.

'No idea,' said Jack.

After many hours, they eventually felt the coach stop and they were picked up and put down somewhere else. They overheard several people discussing payment and then the children felt the floor under them gently rocking. Several more hours went past.

Finally, the bags were opened and the sunlight streamed in. Both Jack and Suzan could not see, after being in the bags for so long. Two large men pulled the children out of the sacks.

One man had a long scar down his face from his hair to his chin, a roundish face, a crooked nose and cauliflower ears. The other man had a smaller scar, from above to below his left eye and wore an eye patch.

The man with the long scar spoke in a deep gravelly voice, 'My boss wants a word with you.'

Suzan and Jack were half walked and half dragged along the deck of a large metal tanker. As Jack looked up, he could see a great chimney, higher than a house, billowing out smoke. And the end of the ship seemed a long way off. It was a cargo tanker and was rather old, and dirty. They reached a door and the man with the eye patch knocked firmly on it.

'Enteeeer,' came a silky-smooth voice.

The two children were marched in and told to take their shoes off. They gazed around the great cabin in amazement. The cabin looked like the inside of an old mansion house. The walls had wooden boarding and the furniture was old and made of wood with gold and silver inlay.

At the far end of the room a smooth voice coldly, but calmly said, 'Sit down.'

A large leather chair swivelled round and a man wearing a red velvet jacket, gold rings on every finger and necklaces, stood up. The man was clean shaven except for a very well-kept moustache, which had been waxed into two points. His hair was neatly combed back, and he seemed to have a strong effect on the two men who had brought the children in.

The great men cowered back towards the door and went out, backwards, without turning around. Very softly the door closed with a tiny click and then they were alone with the strange man in the velvet jacket.

AW-B

130

'I trust that your journey was comfortable!' said the man with a hint of sarcasm. 'Now let me introduce myself, I am known as the Hound.'

Jack was feeling submissive and afraid after the whole ordeal, but Suzan had always been tough and not one to show her fear easily. She looked the man square in the eye. 'How dare you kidnap us. What do you think you're doing? My father will be looking for us now and he'll find us and then you will regret treating us like this!'

The Hound tried to laugh, but the best he could muster in return was a scoff. He walked a little closer to Suzan. 'I admire your attitude girl, but you are in *my* world now. You are on *my* tanker, surrounded by *my* crew, in the vast stretches of an ocean. No one is going to find you. My world! My rules! Not some fun fantasy fairy tale!'

Suzan looked away and said nothing more.

'Now tell me about the *ultimate treasure*, you silly children. Tell me everything and don't leave out any details. Tell me about *the Mist*,' demanded the Hound, in his silky-smooth voice.

'We don't know about any of that,' said Jack.

'*Don't* lie to me!' uttered the hound, with a slightly raised voice, but still as silky as ever. 'I am no fool, you were talking about it in the museum. Now tell me.'

Suzan bucked up. Again, she looked him in the eye, 'No, we won't tell you anything.'

The Hound smiled and said, 'Well, you two little children, maybe some time in the brig will loosen your tongues and teach you manners!' He gave a short sharp double clap and the two men, who had brought them to the Hound, appeared and picked up the children, hoisting them over their shoulders and carried them off.

Both children, especially Suzan, flailed out, kicking and punching, but the large burly men didn't seem in the slightest disturbed by being hit. They took them to a large space below deck.

CHAPTER 23

THE HOUND

The prison cells in the brig were cold, damp and dark. They were in a terrible place, a place that no adult should have to endure, let alone two scared children.

It was so dark and silent that the silence buzzed around their ears and the darkness played tricks on their mind. Although the children had experienced many aspects of poverty, they'd never experienced such a terrible place in their lives.

The old rusty cells had nothing in them except for an old dirty blanket, in each one. The children sat along each side of the dividing cell bars to try to be close to each other. They were scared. Even Suzan, the tougher of the two, was scared.

The only familiar thing, that told them where they were, was the rocking of the ship, the swaying as it charged and bulldozed its great metal self through the waves. Other than that, they could have been anywhere.

They sat next to each other - one in each cell, with bars between. For how long they didn't know, but for what seemed a long, long time indeed.

When evening came, although they were not sure if it was evening, because in the darkness they had no sense, or perception of time – but they were very, very happy to finally see the main door open. They were happy, although it seems strange, to see that slightly familiar

CA W-B

burly large round face of the rounder of the two scoundrels.

He stomped his way to the cages with a candle lamp, which he placed on the floor, and he slid one tray under each cell door. Each tray contained a plate with some pieces of bread and a cup with some water. Not exactly hotel food thought Jack, but he didn't dare say anything.

The burly no-good man was about to turn and leave when he looked closely at the children. 'Look children,' he said in his deep gravelly voice, 'I know you don't want to be here. I know you're scared. I don't even think that we should have kidnapped you at all, but as you know, the Hound is quite an important man round here. I can't really say too much, but he is a legendary treasure hunter and when he sets his eyes and sights on something, when he wants something, he gets it.

'I have never, in all my twenty years serving him, seen him fail to acquire something that he wanted. My advice to you children, is tell him what he wants to know, give him the information he wants, swiftly. It will be much more comfortable for you that way. I'll leave you the lamp children, it should burn for a few hours, so you can at least see your food and drink.'

He turned around and walked back down towards the door. The children heard the metal door slam shut behind him and they were alone again, but this time they had the lamp, thankfully. They could just make out a few other cells that seemed to be empty and the old rusty metal floors and walls.

Jack was hungry and so was Suzan, but they waited for a few moments in case anyone came back. When they realised that no one was coming back they grabbed the food and ate. After eating and drinking they sat looking at the shadows flickering in the distance, from the candle lamp.

A while later there were footsteps, not thumping, beating boots, but the delicate tap of beautifully handmade brown leather shoes, that slowly walked down towards them. The door opened again. It was the Hound, as he was referred to, but the children didn't know whether they should call him that or sir or please don't hurt me! For although he was smooth and sophisticated, he was clearly not a man to be reckoned with.

He took his time walking towards the cells and when eventually he arrived, he was wearing a red velvet jacket, his hair just as tidy as in the morning when they'd seen him last.

The Hound spoke in a cold, but smooth voice: 'Children, are you ready to tell me about the ultimate treasure? I know you know about it. I know you know a lot about it, or you wouldn't be here.

'It wouldn't have been worth my while bringing you here, if you didn't know so much. Let's cut to the chase, you've got two options children, you tell me, or you stay here longer, maybe forever!'

The children were quiet, they didn't know what to say. Eventually, Suzan plucked up a little courage. 'I'm not going to tell you, it's *our* secret. We found out about it.'

'Found out about what?' said the Hound.

'Found out about the ...' Suzan stopped completely, for she realised she was being lulled into telling him exactly what he wanted.

'Ah, so you don't deny it then,' said the Hound.

Suzan looked away.

'You're going to tell me everything,' said the Hound.

'NO! NO, I won't tell you about it. NEVER!' said Suzan.

'Very well then,' said the Hound. He paused to give the threatening tone, of his last sentence, time to percolate in their minds. 'I am going to be busy for a day or two, there's a wreck that has been found off the coast of South

America by some archaeologists. They have found some rather interesting treasure there and it's something that I need to complete one of my collections, so I will be going to… er, how can I put this… be looking after it for them, keeping it in a safe place!'

The Hound chuckled to himself, and the children heard two more rather uncouth chuckles, going on in the background. It was the two burly men. They hadn't realised the two men had also followed the Hound into the hold.

The Hound cleared his throat and the two burly men stopped laughing immediately. They became just as silent as before, as the Hound prepared to speak.

'So don't worry children we are going to be at sea for a while, I can wait… I can wait, don't you worry! Sooner or later these damp cells will break you and you will tell me *everything* that you know about the Mist and more importantly about the *ultimate treasure*.'

The children watched as the Hound turned and eloquently tapped his way back to the doorway, with his beautifully handmade leather shoes, followed by the thumping of his two sidekicks. The door shut behind them and the children were alone again.

The candle in the lamp was getting low and an hour later it fizzled away back into darkness. That night they slept, maybe it was the shock, maybe it was exhaustion, or maybe it was just the cold, but they slept all night, under the old blankets, despite being in such a horrendous place.

The next morning the same thing happened again: one of the burly men brought them some bread and water, left a candle lamp, and slammed the metal door shut. This was repeated at lunchtime and that evening too. And the same again on the day that followed.

Time passed so very, very slowly for the children. The only reference they had were the meal visits and falling asleep. The only way they could keep themselves happy and take their mind off their kidnapping, was to remember their mother and father. To speak about the fun times as a family and the hope that they would be rescued soon.

CHAPTER 24

FAR REACHING HAND OF THE HOUND

Two days later, in the evening, the Hound returned. He was wearing a blue velvet jacket and his moustache looked just as well kept as ever, twisted, and waxed at the ends into little points. He seemed to look happier than the evening two days before.

'How are we this evening, enjoying your roomy accommodation?' asked the Hound as he laughed to himself, a sinister and horrible laugh.

Jack had plucked up a little courage now, after sitting brooding and thinking for two days, so he looked directly at the Hound and said, 'Happy with yourself today aren't you ... Hound?'

The Hound looked at Jack with a piercing sinister look. 'Who told you, you could call me the Hound?' he said. 'And yes, now you mention it, I am rather pleased with myself today. That treasure I spoke about two days ago, is safely locked away in my collection and those archaeologists... well... I do hope they can swim, because it's a long way to the nearest land and their boat seems to have sprung a leak.' As he finished the sentence, he gave a great sinister laugh. 'I do like it when I complete a collection! Now are you ready to tell me about the ultimate treasure? Have you two children had enough of damp dark cells?' said the Hound.

The children had had enough of sleeping and sitting on horrible blankets and eating nothing but bread and water.

'Yes, Yes, I'll tell you everything,' Suzan blurted out.

Suzan and Jack told the Hound about the trunk, and they told the hound about the sextant.

'Really?' said the Hound, as his eyes lit up with great glee. 'Where is the sextant now?'

Suzan's eyes looked towards Jack's bag. 'We left it at the house,' she said.

'You're lying, it's in the bag, your eyes deceive you girl. Pass me that bag now,' demanded the Hound.

'Yeah alright,' said Jack, as he reluctantly passed him the bag, knowing that there was nothing left they could do. The children had spent three days and two nights in the damp, dark horrible prison cell and it had truly made them feel powerless against a mighty villain like the Hound.

The villain unzipped the bag and pulled out the beautifully shiny special sextant. His eyes widened and he seemed transfixed by the object and the inscriptions on it, as it shone in the candlelight. 'The legend is true!' he said. 'Now carry on telling me the story,' he continued.

Suzan told him about how they'd found the different parts of the sextant and how the letter from the tree had some strange numbers on it and that they didn't really understand what the final clue was. And she told him about the book as well. Jack was hoping that she wouldn't talk about the book - they could at least keep that to themselves - but she blurted it all out.

'Where's the book? I want that book! I need that book!' said the Hound.

'It really is at home in the trunk. We didn't bring it with us, we don't like taking it out of the house, because it seems so very old and precious,' replied Suzan.

The Hound double clapped his hands and in came running the two burly henchmen. He walked over to them and whispered something about the book and the children's address into their ear. Then they disappeared back out of the metal door.

'Don't worry children we will have your book tomorrow morning and then you are going to help me find the ultimate treasure. I want it! In my thirty-five years as a treasure hunter, I have found many rare treasures. I have hunted and stolen my way around the seven seas! My collection spans the globe and it spans the history of humanity.

'I love treasure, I was born to find treasure and born to collect it. Gold is the only constant in humanity. Civilizations come and go, people, friends, family come and go, but gold never tarnishes, it is always a constant. That's why I've dedicated my life to finding treasure. But there's one treasure that's always evaded me, one thing that I've spent so many nights dreaming of.

'A treasure that whispers in the winds. *Yes*! that legendary treasure of the *Mist, the ultimate treasure*.' The Hound paused for breath, then continued his rant: 'No one even knows what it is, although some fools think they

141

do, and others say it is just a fanciful dream, cooked up by drunks.

'Now we can see plain as anything that the tale of the ultimate treasure is true! Needless to say, it's made of gold! That beautiful, yellow, dreamy material we all lust after.' His eyes glazed as he said this.

He turned to look at the children again and said: 'You know that's what makes the world go round children, gold! Not love, not friendship, not science, but gold! And the ultimate treasure will be the best gold. I want it! It's the jewel to finish the crown of my collection, I need to prove it exists and I must have it and you children … you children … you're going to help me find it. So don't worry, your book will be with us tomorrow.'

The children were shocked and scared to see their captor in such a greedy ranting state.

'But how are you going to get the book? asked Jack, puzzled and scared. It's back in our house.'

'Don't you worry, boy, I have accomplices and an underground network of criminals who run right around this world. If I need a simple book from your house, it will be with me by tomorrow morning. And when it is, I would like you to show me everything about the sextant and the book and I would like you to tell me the story again in *great* detail. Then we'll find that last clue together,' he said, as he gazed in the lamplight at the strange numbers they had written down, from the message found in the tree. 'Do you know what these are, children?'

The children shook their heads.

'I don't know,' said Suzan. 'We spoke about those numbers for many days, trying to work out what they meant.'

'It's very simple, they're coordinates, latitude and longitude.'

'I'm not going to tell you our address, so you *won't* be able to get that book,' shouted Suzan, in one last act of defiance.

The Hound laughed. 'Don't you worry girl, I don't *need* you to tell me your address. I'm the Hound, I've sailed the seas and collected treasure for many a decade. I've friends all over the world, dark underground networks.

'It will be a couple of clicks of a mouse, for someone who knows what they're doing. They'll be only too glad to find out where you live and someone will be only too glad to break in and they will be only too glad to deliver the book – no questions asked – to a port, where someone will be only too glad to sail it, double time, to me on a fast stealth motorboat.

'As I said, gold makes the world go round... girl. People are *only too glad* to do *anything* if you can pay them enough gold. Thank you for telling me what I wanted to know children.

'You will be shown to some proper quarters. I'm afraid it won't be a hotel for you, but it will be better than these damp cold cells, naturally.'

The children were freed and shown to a small room, with a bunk bed for them to sleep on, a small wardrobe with some extra blankets, a chair, and a desk to sit at. There was also a porthole, to see the sky. They were really glad to not be in the darkness any more, despite the fact that they were still kept under lock and key.

CHAPTER 25

THE EMPTY SEA

In the morning Suzan and Jack were freed for breakfast, which was toast and butter with bacon, eggs and a cup of tea. Just after breakfast they heard the very low pitched sound, in the distance, of a powerful motorboat, although they did not see it until the sound was extremely close and a gleaming silver, very sharp angular boat pulled alongside the tanker, way down in the water. The metal was polished so highly, that the reflections all around it meant you could barely make out the shape.

The Hound informed the children that the sound they had heard was the stealth boat. Stealth, because not only was it almost impossible to see with the human eye, but it also could not be seen on any radar.

A brown parcel was brought in and unwrapped in front of the children. A wad of cash was exchanged. Soon they heard the stealth boat buzz back into life and zoom off, glinting in the sunlight. Sure enough, the parcel contained the book, the book that they had hidden safely inside the chest.

'Now let's go to my office and let's work out where that treasure is,' demanded the Hound.

The children followed him submissively, broken. They went through the story again, but in greater detail, speaking about where each piece of the sextant was found. And they showed him the clues that were written on the sextant.

The Hound read some of the book, but some words were in Latin, which only Jack could read. He sneered at the last story, about the giant. 'There's no such thing as giants,' he scoffed.

They set sail using the ship's navigation for the coordinates, which were written on the last page that they had found in the tree. When they arrived, after a long time at sea, there was nothing there, just empty sea. The Hound clicked his fingers and pointed to the sea. Two of his crew quickly suited up, in diving gear, and dropped into the ocean.

The two crew members dived for about thirty minutes and took quite a quantity of equipment with them. At the same time, other crew members seemed to be looking at some screens, inside the cabin of the ship, which showed information from equipment sweeping the seabed below them. Time and time again the divers returned with nothing. Each time the Hound demanded they try again, after only a short break. After many hours with divers, they realised that there was nothing on the seabed.

The Hound was furious. 'We must be missing something. I'd like you to go away and think about where this treasure is and I'm going to do the same. We need to work it out. If you ever want to see your family again, you'd better help me with this and do your best.'

He left them locked in their room. The two children discussed what had gone wrong with the coordinates, desperate to help him as quickly as possible and get back to their father. After some time thinking about it, Jack worked it out.

'It must be the sextant that we need to navigate to those coordinates with, not the boats GPS. It must be slightly different than the GPS. In fact, Jacob said that the numbers on it were slightly different than even a normal sextant.'

Suzan nodded but then her eyebrows crinkled up and she said in anger, 'But don't tell The Hound that.'

That evening at dinner the Hound asked them about their parents. When he saw their reactions, he delved deeper with his questions, until they caved in and told him about their mother always working away and that they really wanted her to stop her horrible business job and come home and to not be so poor. They explained that they had hoped to find the treasure, so that they could change all of this.

The Hound looked strangely compassionate for a moment and a smile crept over his face.

'Well, if you help me find it, I will give you a small share. Enough for that. Work with me, the sooner we find the stash, the sooner you can see your folks and help your poor, poor mum. He whispered enticingly.'

Suzan smiled, for the first time since she had been kidnapped. 'Do you really mean that?'

'Yes,' said the Hound. 'I might be a treasure hunter, but if there's anything I have learnt, it's to stick to your word. And I will.'

The children believed him and were suddenly motivated to help. They could only think of being reunited with their parents and their mum coming home for good.

Jack explained that the sextant must be integral to finding the treasure, or why else would CC have gone to the trouble of hiding all its parts all over the place? He explained that Jacob, the man in the museum, had said that the sextant was a little different than other sextants and that the numbers and layout were unique.

The Hound began to smile and said, 'Nothing like gold to loosen the tongue, aye Jack?' He took out a gold coin and rolled it around his fingers, as he pondered what Jack had said. 'Yes, Jack you're right, clever boy. Very clever, you don't miss a trick do you? And nor did CC. Clearly even now he's living up to his name, making us guess and weave together clues. Making us work hard to find his treasure.'

The Hound opened the memoirs of CC, and he took an old, yellowed almanac from his desk drawer. 'Do you know what this is children?' he said, in a soft and purring voice. He didn't wait for them to answer and continued:

'This is a navigation almanac. Sailors and pirates used them to navigate with sextants and similar instruments to cross-reference the readings taken. It is the final part of the tools we need!'

He told the crew to turn off their GPS and they sailed, charging through the waves. Jack navigated using the sextant, just as Jacob had shown him. He took it in turns with Suzan and used the stars by night and the sun by day, making sure to cover the telescope with the protective lenses.

They navigated to the very spot, to the very latitude and longitude that was written on the note from the tree and in the distance, as they approached the very spot, they saw a small and beautiful island with golden sandy beaches that glistened in the sunshine.

Jack peered up at The Hound and said, 'You did promise, didn't you? You did promise that you'll give us enough treasure to help our mum to stop working in her job and come home and that we won't have to be poor anymore.'

'Of course, I will, of course!' said the Hound, with a subtle, cunning smile. The children, unfortunately, didn't see the smile of that master villain; they trusted him.

CHAPTER 26

DEADLY BEAUTY

A little way off in the distance they saw that beautiful shining island, like a gem set against the ocean. It shone with golden sandy beaches and beautiful blue turquoise corals around the outside, beautiful but deadly. They could see that many ships had fallen victim to that beautiful, but deadly coral.

The coral ring that surrounded the island stretched deceptively far out into the sea, so that ships could not get close to the island, without crashing onto the coral jaws and bursting their bows. Only a small boat could navigate its way through safely.

The Hound stopped his ship. As an experienced sailor and treasure hunter, he knew that it was perilous to get too close. They dropped anchor a little way out from the island and the whole crew closely followed his every move, because they had caught wind of the fact that this might be the island that contained the *ultimate treasure*, the legendary treasure found by the Mist.

The whole crew climbed into smaller dinghies, with the hound at the lead. And inside one dinghy, with the Hound, sat Jack and Suzan, both submissively aligned

CA·W·B

with the Hound – on a mission to find the ultimate treasure and get back their mother.

They didn't want to think too much about the fact they had been kidnapped by the Hound and his crew, just days earlier. For this was the moment that they might solve the strange mystery. A mystery of not only the book found in their house, or the pieces of the sextant, but also a story that – for some strange reason – their mother used to tell them when they were small children. The story of that cunning captain, the Mist as he was often called. The same person. A pirate, so surrounded by mystery and legend that he might as well be Mist!

The dinghies moved closer across the outer stretches of the reef and slowly those teeth, those jagged, sword tearing edges, drew closer to the surface of the water, until they became so close that they had to move very, very slowly indeed – for one wrong move, or a wave in the wrong direction and they would be ground to a halt, on to the coral teeth. They navigated through. It was like a maze of waterways.

Eventually, after a long time of painstaking sailing, the Hound and the two children landed on the beach. Armed with modern day, semi-automatic pistols and good, old-fashioned cutlasses, the Hound's entourage, a thirty-man strong group of no good, nasty, terrible, cutthroat, blood thirsty, pirates, followed close behind.

The motley crew were modern day pirates, not the kind of pirates you get in the stories, or fairy tales from old. But ruthless treasure hunters, criminals, cold hearted and part of a connected network of underground crime that spanned the globe. The kind of people who could receive anything they needed, they only had to ask.

With so much gold behind him, the Hound was above the law, and anyone who sailed, with him, was too. As soon as someone discovered treasure in the world, as soon as someone struck something of any value at all, the first person to know was the Hound. He was the first person to decide whether he wanted it and if he did: watch out, for he would get it - by hook or by crook.

The Hound led his entourage of no-good scoundrels across the beach, with the two children closely by his side. They decided to walk around the beach to look for a way inland, for there was nothing but a sheer cliff face.

There was something odd about this island, maybe it was the coral or maybe it was the sheer, sharp, rocky, jagged edge of the cliff, but it seemed extremely beautiful yet extremely deadly. It looked as if no person had set foot, on this island for many hundreds of years. The surrounding reef had many a wreck.

It looked like a timeline of ships, some of them extremely old; just outer shells, like skeletons resting there – permanently beached in a great coral mouth; their outer boards torn off by the weather and rot, exposing their skeletons, the rib cage of each ship, with water lapping inside. The owners, the captains, the crew, long gone – perhaps taken by the sea, perhaps taken by the island, or perhaps rescued. But…the Hound didn't stop to query this, he had only one thing in his mind now: gold.

You could see it in his eyes, the stories in the book had fuelled him and no sooner had he seen the island, he imagined finding and owning that treasure, the greatest stash ever known, the *ultimate treasure*.

The golden sand of the beach reflected every ounce of the sunshine, it reflected every beam. The sea glistened away as they walked around the island, the cliffs on their left and the sea and reef on their right; their dinghies tied up the best they could - around the protruding, jagged coral – far off in the distance now.

It looked as though there was no way in. The Hound stopped for a moment and gazed up at the high, jagged, teeth of the mountain to his left. You could see he was pondering whether a gold-crazed man, with enough motivation, would be able to scale those rocks.

They looked so sharp though, they looked as if they were made of blades and swords. One wrong move and you would cut yourself to pieces, you would cut yourself to shreds, but nevertheless the Hound decided to order one of his men to give it a go.

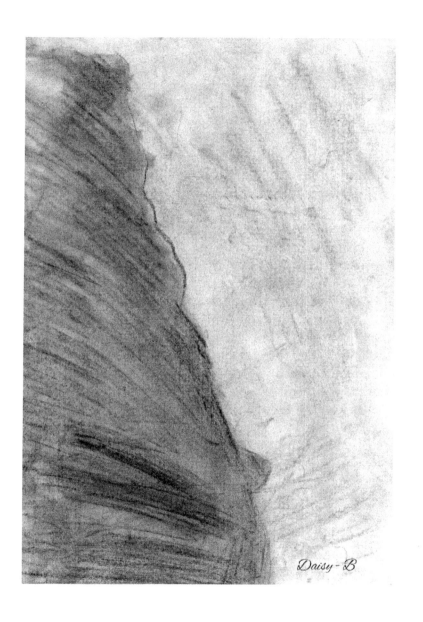

Daisy - B

He held up a gold coin, signalled to one of his men, and a short wiry kind of fellow, with a rope around his waist, threw the grappling hook attached to the rope. It wedged firmly within one of the rocks, high up on the cliff face. He started climbing, but he had only managed a few metres, when already his hands and legs were cut to pieces.

No one was sure what the rock was, but they thought it must be some kind of volcanic rock. It seemed to be sharp, sharp like glass and just brushing against it, just holding onto it, seemed to irritate and cut the skin. The man slipped back down the rope, covered in lacerations and blood.

'No, no, I don't think it can be done, look at me. Certainly not without some kind of protective suit. These rocks, they don't take prisoners,' the man said sheepishly.

The Hound withdrew the gold coin, slipped it back into his jacket pocket, gazed around, looking for solutions. 'OK,' he grumbled to himself, then glanced at the bloodied man, 'fall back in and get cleaned up. Let's continue walking round this horrible island. Yeah, I know it's here, it has got to be here.

'Only the *Mist* would choose a place so inhospitable, so tooth-like, so shard-like and utterly nasty, to protect his treasure. Only *he* would choose an island that is surrounded, like a fortress, by a sharp cliff face.'

They continued walking and were almost back to where they started from, when Suzan remembered a story from the book. It had mentioned some unusual rock colouring, near the entrance to an important island. Suzan carefully surveyed the area, and finally she noticed a slight difference of coloration in the rocks, to one side of the cliff.

They decided to walk towards it and realised that, by optical illusion, what looked like the same cliff face, which stretched all the way around the island, actually had an opening. The cliff face stepped back a little and from the side, revealed a hand cut shaft.

'Well done,' said the Hound, 'I knew there was a reason to keep you two around.'

'You promised, you'll…' Jack started, in a scared voice.

'Of course, of course boy, don't worry, I did promise you, of course I'll give you some treasure. Now follow me,' said the Hound, in a silky-smooth voice.

The three of them walked, followed by the entourage, through the narrow gap in the rock. From the sea you wouldn't have spotted it, from the beach you could barely spot it, unless you knew it was there. It was slightly cooler behind the rocks, as they followed the shaft that curved around and then ran inland.

Eventually, they came out into a beautiful green landscape. It was the strangest island that the Hound had ever seen in his life and the strangest place his crew had ever been to. They had followed him through thick and thin over the years and despite them all being thieves and bloodthirsty pirates, they had an ultimate respect for him, but more importantly for his gold, enough respect to stick around anyway.

The beautiful green landscape was surrounded by that very same cliff face, imprisoning them inside a large bowl. And in the middle of the fertile land there was a lake and in the middle of the lake there stood a very, very small island, almost entirely taken up by a beautiful white palace.

It was a bizarre sight to see, a lake in the middle of an island, with an island in the middle of it, with a palace on it. The palace, just like the walls of the cliffs, had no entrances. There seemed to be no windows and no doors…

CHAPTER 27

TIME TO SHARE!

The men were not sure how to get across the lake, as there was only one small boat tied up and ready to use. The only way to do it was to split up. The Hound and the two children went first. The boat could only carry two or three people safely and despite it being a lake, it would take more than one person to row across.

If you were shipwrecked here alone, if you came seeking treasure alone, you would never get across that Lake. It was too far to swim, and it was too difficult to row alone, due to the strange currents in the lake.

Perhaps the lake was connected to the sea under the ground in some way or another. They couldn't really work out why there seemed to be such strong currents, on an otherwise quite still and beautiful lake. The currents tried to take hold of the boat and two of them had to row hard to keep the boat moving towards the edge of that palace.

As they drew closer, they could see that the palace was built out of the most beautiful white marble. Marble that must have been quarried and cut thousands of miles away. Its tall elegant pointy towers reached up to the sky, yet no windows could be seen, no doors, just a beautiful white silky-smooth face.

If you know anything about marble, you will know that it takes a long time to wear, so despite the surrounding cliff rocks having been worn away by wind and rain, in the centre, protected away from all of that, was the silky smooth beautiful white marble. Between the marble of the walls of the palace and the lapping water of the lake, there was little space to stand.

As they stepped out of the boat, it started to drift back towards the shore. The Hound, Jack, and Suzan walked around the outside of the palace, just as they had on the island, looking for a way in. As they came around, almost to the front again, they saw something written in Latin. The Hound asked Jack to translate it for them.

Jack took a look. 'It's very simple. It says: no one person can enter alone.'

There were two steps on the floor below the Latin sign, one either side. On closer inspection, Suzan realised that, in fact, there was a faint line, or groove within the blocks, that ran around like a doorway in shape.

The three of them were confused about how they could open a door that had no sides, no handle, and no keyhole. The Hound stepped onto one of the steps. Suddenly he heard something moving behind the wall.

'Quick, get on the other step there,' he called to Jack.

Jack stepped on it, but nothing else happened.

'Suzan as well, come on, between you both, you must weigh about as much as I do,' said the Hound.

Suzan climbed on and suddenly many sounds came from behind the palace. Inside, it sounded like chains running, levers turning, and cogs winding and eventually the crack Suzan had noticed before became wider. And a whole marble section, the height of a door, slowly hinged open – on great iron hinges that must have been forged by a strong person, for only someone very strong, or very large could forge such huge, gigantic hinges.

The door swung open into a tiny chamber or porch, just big enough for the door to open and close and a little bit more. At the back of the small porch room, clear of where the door swung, there were two more steps.

As the Hound stepped off one of the platforms and stepped towards the open porch, he realised that the only way to go further into the palace, was by closing the door, because the open door was blocking the only entrance that led further in.

Glee came across his face. *Yes,* he thought, *I can close that door and shut them out, maybe I can even barricade it and I can claim this treasure for myself.* He stepped in, up onto one of the platforms, a gleam in his eye. There was some clunking, but not enough. The door didn't move.

Reluctantly, the Hound gestured to the children, 'Get off that step and stand on the step next to me.'

That worked, the clonking of all the cogs and mechanism moving happened again and the door, that had opened slowly, swung shut again. Clearly *only two people could get in and only two people could get out* at the same time.

They were now in a dark, dark room. It was made just for the size of the door plus a bit, but where the door had been standing, when it was open, there was now an open archway that led down into a corridor. The Hound turned his torch on and shone it around. Next, he found some very old oil lanterns. They were basically not much more than sticks wrapped in oiled rags.

Taking out his golden lighter, the Hound flipped it open and lit the rags. The cloth had probably been there for a couple of hundred years, so it was dry and perfectly flammable. The torch burst into life and the Hound lit some other torches that were also on the walls. Both children took one each and the three of them slowly moved down the corridor cautiously, for they knew that they were in CC's domain now and they knew that CC was just the kind of person who might boobytrap a place like this.

The Hound went first because deep down he knew that the treasure was his. He wasn't going to share it. He smelt the gold. If anyone could smell and recognise the smell of gold, it was the Hound. There was a yellowy light that flickered at the end of the corridor. As they walked it grew brighter and brighter.

As they turned the corner, the corridor opened into a huge central treasure room. Never in his life had the Hound seen so much treasure. He had dedicated thirty-five years of his life to stealing and gathering other people's treasure. He was one of the richest people in the world, but this treasure collection made his lifetime's work look like mere small change.

His fingers twitched with excitement; his eyes glistened as the beautiful brightness of the golden yellow flickered around the walls of the room. A trickling water fountain in the middle of the floor reflected golden shapes onto the ceiling. The shapes seemed to dance around and flicker, transfixing him like fireflies.

CHAPTER 28

IRRESISTIBLE

The Hound couldn't resist it any longer, he was so excited to have found so much treasure, that he ran towards the piles and piles of gold and dived onto it. He cried from excitement and from sheer joy.

He screamed, 'It's mine, it's all mine - my gold! I've so much now. Look at this, this is from the fifteenth century and this, look at this sword,' he said, as he pulled out a sword that looked as if it belonged to a great king. It had diamonds and emeralds set into the hilt. The stock between the blade and the handle was also inlaid with huge rubies and the beautiful blade curved elegantly back and glistened in the light, as if it had been made only yesterday.

There were shields encrusted with jewels, there were trunks filled with trinkets, golden cups, chalices, plates. There were coins, jewellery, suits of armour and artefacts. Artefacts from all manner of histories and times.

It looked as if CC – the Mist – had stolen from everyone. He had taken the very best of the treasure and the Hound knew it. The Hound felt a great affinity between himself and the Mist. But… the more he touched the gold, the more his face became twisted. 'It's mine,' he kept repeating.

Suddenly noises came from the corridor. They looked round quickly, and he saw the rest of his crew, the thirty odd men, had all made it across the lake and somehow worked out how to get in. They too saw the gold flickering, in that beautiful amber room. They jumped and dived amidst the treasure, and a great greed came over them...

Their eyes turned wide and glistened, their fingers twitched, they let the gold run through their fingers like a liquid. The Hound started to twitch, they all started to twitch. They looked around and become agitated, eyeing each other up, sizing each other up, to see who might make it out with the most gold.

You see... people who have spent all their lives looking for gold, wish for only gold. And here was truly their dream come true, a room filled from floor to ceiling with so much treasure, so many gemstones, so many artefacts, it was as if someone had gathered all the most prized possessions, from all the kings of all times and put them in one room.

The crew started stuffing the treasure into their pockets, filling every single gap they had in their clothing, every single space they had in their bags, each one glancing suspiciously at the other, to see how much each was taking. The Hound stood there in the middle, on top of the pile of gold, looking around at his crew. Although he was a nasty man, he'd been a good leader over the years. He was feared and respected by his crew and had led them on many a treasure stealing hunt. It had made them rich and that's why they followed him, the gold.

The gold was whispering to the Hound, it was like the room was alive with voices. The flickering lights on the ceiling, and the sound of the chinking treasure on

165

treasure, seemed to get inside his head. That whispering inside his head that said: *why should I share it with anyone? It's mine I deserve it more than anybody else.* And it wasn't just the Hound, they were all hearing the voice…

Like the voice of the poor souls who had owned this treasure, over the years. The voice whisked around the room, like a wind bouncing from the walls, getting inside their heads. That same story, that same whisper: *Why should I share, why should I have to give any of this away? I deserve it more than you.*

Then the most terrible thing happened, something that no children or indeed no person should have to see. The greedy whisper became a shout, it became a roar, a heart pumping roar.

The first to give way to it moved his hands towards his cutlass. Slowly his eyes widened and whitened, it looked as if the last of humanity had been washed out of him. He drew his sword, the sound of the sword on the sheath grazed as it drew, and then finished with a 'shing.'

Then the others realised that they were all drawing their swords too, even though they didn't quite know why. They were bewitched by the treasure, but more importantly by their own greed.

The Hound stood looking around at his forces, his men drawing their swords. He too slowly drew his double cutlasses. Jack and Suzan knew the way this was going to end, so they backed away. They backed into the corridor, they backed away from what they knew wouldn't end nicely.

That bewitched gold even got inside the heads of those poor children too. Jack was thinking that he should be the one to take all the treasure home not Suzan because he was better than her. And Suzan was thinking that she was better, and she wanted to be the one who saved her mum from her terrible job, and she wanted to be the one who owned the gold.

They gazed at each other with cold stares, their fists clenched. They heard sword on sword, pistol shots, screams, not screams of pain, but screams of pure madness, screams of bewitched people attacking like animals. And then blood curdling screams of pain of as they cut, shot, and ran each other through.

Jack grabbed hold of Suzan. Suzan grabbed hold of Jack. They hit the floor and they rolled and scrabbled around grappling at each other. Luckily, they were not carrying weapons and all they did was scratch and bite and hurt each other.

As siblings, the two children had had to make it through most of their life without their mother and with only their father. This had made them close. They were probably closer than many other brothers and sisters in the world. Having moved away from their friends and family in the city, being isolated in a place that they had never been to before, had also made them close. The love for each other was very, very deep and although they were overtaken, for a moment, by that terrible greed for gold, their love for each other was far, far greater.

Tears trickled down their faces when they realised that they were hurting each other. Quickly they came to their senses. The sound of the whisper stopped in their heads, they cried, they wept, as they realised that even all the gold in the world was not worth destroying their friendship and family for.

Both children turned and walked back to the entrance. As they came towards the end of the corridor and drew closer to the door, the screams, shouts, gun shots and crashes of steel on steel drew further away.

They didn't look back; they didn't want to look back. Those were crazy, crazy people, beasts, vicious animals.

Suzan and Jack reached the marble door. Above the door, fitted into the wall, there was a dull and dusty sign carved right into the marble itself, written – again – in Latin.

Jack translated it: 'The writing says…

"Only a person with empty pockets, but a full heart would have time to gaze upon this sentence. Look down."

I think it's telling us to search for something.'

'Quick then,' said Suzan, 'let's take a look, but we need to hurry.'

After a while, the children discovered that one of the marble floor tiles had a very small *CC* inscribed on it. The tile seemed quite loose, so they prized it up.

Inside was a scroll of paper, with a large, but very light, wooden ring around it. Jack slid it into his jacket pocket and the two children stepped onto the panels, one on each one.

It seemed that it wasn't a lot of weight that was needed to open the door, but it was important that it was roughly equal. Their weight operated the door. They stepped out and closed the door behind them.

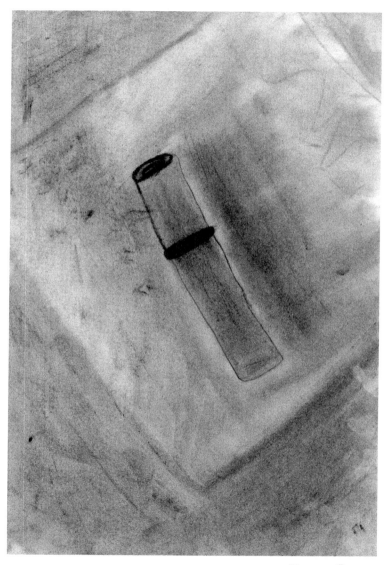

Daisy - B

That was probably the last that anyone heard of the Hound and his crazy crew. What became of them, nobody knows, and how many made it out of there alive? Well, that is another story. But for now, we must follow Jack and Suzan on their daring escape from this island and from their kidnappers.

CHAPTER 29

SHIPWRECKS

Both children struggled to row back across the lake, using the boat the crew had moored, with its fierce currents. It was far more difficult with just the two of them, but they managed it, determined to get away from that terrible place. That place where even the sanest person would be lost to the whisper of gold.

When Suzan and Jack reached the beach, they ran towards the dinghies, instinctively feeling they should escape from the island as quickly as possible. Neither of them knew what had come over them inside that palace. They didn't know why they had attacked each other; they were scared, they were frightened – they just wanted to run.

Quickly they climbed into the dinghy and started up the engine, trying to decide what to do. Both were about to sail cautiously through the maze of waterways, when Jack realised that they did not have the sextant, they didn't have the book and they didn't have the almanac.

Suzan and Jack would have to go back to the Hound's ship – hoping it was empty – hoping that there were none of his terrible bloodthirsty crew still on it. Those vital items could not be left behind.

They motored their way through the maze of water ways, missing the coral but only by millimetres. And

171

eventually they got back to the large ship that the Hound had moored just past the coral.

Climbing very quietly and cautiously up onto the deck of the ship, they looked around to see if there was anyone there. They didn't see anyone, so crept around the edge of the deck, towards the Hound's cabin.

As they drew close to the cabin, they looked carefully through the window, to see if anyone was there. Slowly, deftly, they snuck in and went directly to his desk, where he had left the sextant, book and almanac. Carefully they gathered the items, not daring to spend a moment longer in his cabin, or on his ship.

They came out of the cabin, just as cautiously as they had entered and crept around the side of the ship. It was deserted; probably because all the crew had wanted a piece of that pie, a piece of the *ultimate treasure*! Suzan and Jack now needed to get away from that place, as quickly as they could, in case the crew returned.

They climbed their way back down to the dinghy that was bobbing next to the Hound's ship at sea level. As they climbed, Suzan suddenly had the brilliant idea that there were so many shipwrecks on the island that there must be one that was still seaworthy. She suggested that it would be a clever idea to motor around the outside of the island, a little way from the coral, but still close to the island. In search of a wreck that might be salvageable.

Jack thought it would be a great idea too. There were hundreds and hundreds of ships here. Surely one of them must be of use to them.

They motored around the island and saw many a wreck. The first they came to, was a great wooden galleon. It looked as if it had first set sail in the 1800s. Its sails were all but nothing, the hull had great deep scars along the side. It looked as if it had been beached too many times. There was a great groove behind it where the giant galleon had hit the coral. They thought that maybe it would be seaworthy, but when they sailed around the other side of it, they saw a great gaping hole in the side of it. They weren't going anywhere, except downwards in that ship.

Next they found an old fishing trawler, which was also empty. The hull looked ok, but unfortunately the engine wouldn't start. On closer inspection, they realised that the propeller attached to the engine had been smashed to bits. And the engine had taken such a blow when it had hit the coral, it had lost its oil.

They sailed a little further around and caught sight of a white sailing ship that looked as if it was bobbing in the sea, away from the coral.

'That one looks like it's anchored and not caught on any coral,' said Suzan, 'and if it's still bobbing, it must be sea tight. We might have a chance,'

'You might be right sis,' agreed Jack, as he motored the dinghy towards it.

When they reached the white ship, Suzan and Jack tied the dinghy to one of the loops on the side of the bobbing sailing ship. Then they climbed up onto the deck.

'Is there anyone there? Please is there anyone?' called Suzan politely.

They looked around the deck and they could see that although it was a nice ship, it had been through a big storm. There was some damage, but it was still usable. They could see that the sail was slightly ripped.

'Hang on Suzan, there is blood over here,' said Jack, noticing a small pool of blood on the deck. 'It's not a lot, but a bit. I wonder if the person who owns this ship is injured. Maybe they were attacked by pirates. We should be careful.' He shouted out loudly, 'Hello, is there anyone there?'

There was a faint, but audible: 'Help,' that came from below deck.

'There's someone down there. We really must be careful; we don't know if they're friendly. Let me go first,' said Jack.

'NO,' said Suzan, 'I'll go first. I'm bigger and you know that I'm stronger.'

'No, you're not!'

'What? Do you want to sort this out right now?' said Suzan.

Jack backed down as he knew Suzan had a bit of a temper on her and had seen her get angry with boys and girls at the school and wrestle them to the ground in one fell swoop. She was strong and she had a strong mind to match it!

'I'm also the older one and responsible for both of us,' said Suzan, firmly.

'But …' Jack uttered. He tailed off into a silence, because he knew she was right – deep down. Swiftly he followed her…

CHAPTER 30

AN UNLIKELY ALLY!

Suzan led the way down the narrow staircase. 'Hello,' she called.

They walked down the corridor, towards the small sleeping compartment with two beds. In one bed they saw a rather unhappy lady, her hair matted with blood from a big gash on her head, that was still trickling and staining the sheets and bed clothing around her. But that wasn't the worst of it, she also displayed the beginning of hypothermia. She was weak, very, very weak. Suzan approached and pulled back the covers to see more of her face. The lady had pulled them, almost totally, over herself because she had been so cold.

If you have ever had a fever, you will know that you feel very cold and shivery, so cold that you go underneath the bedclothes, leaving just a small hole for your nose to breath, to try to feel as warm as possible. And that is what the lady had done, just her nose and forehead were visible. She was as white as the crashing waves. Suzan looked into her eyes and could see that she could die if they didn't do anything.

Luckily both Suzan and Jack had some first aid knowledge and Suzan had learned about hypothermia symptoms and what to do, at school. So, with their combined knowledge and experience, the children were able to help the lady. They helped her to take off her wet outer clothes so that she was drier and they wrapped her in as many covers as they could find. They stayed with her and gave her hot drinks with sugar.

Jack found some butterfly closures in the first aid box. These sticky strips would help to hold the wound together. He bathed the cut on her head, sterilised it with iodine, fixed it together with the sticky butterfly closures and dressed it.

After a day or two, Suzan and Jack had managed to bring the lady back from the brink of death. And as she stabilized, she became more coherent in her speech and a little more aware of her mysterious rescuers. They stayed by her side, nursing her.

The children were relieved, towards the end of the second day, when she was able to sit up and the clarity had returned to her eyes. A small smile crept across her face, as she looked at the children. A warm smile of gratitude.

Brushing her mousy brown hair out of her eyes, she tried to pull it into a ponytail, but soon gave up when her hand felt the dressed gash. She let out a wince. She squinted at the children, as if she could not make them out properly. Suzan and Jack returned the smile.

'Who are you?' the lady asked, in a slightly weak voice.

'I'm Suzan, and this is my baby brother Jack!' Suzan said, with a cheeky smile – followed by a sharp jab on the arm, from her not so baby brother.

The lady seemed a little perplexed by the comment and squinted hard at Jack. He looked back, with inquisitive eyes. The lady was wearing a dishevelled shirt, with a little notebook and pen that poked out of the top pocket. The notebook looked well worn, as if it was very well used.

'Who are you? And how did you get injured?' Jack asked, compelled by details, about the lady, that made him curious to the core.

The lady rubbed her eyes and her head, as she seemed to be casting her mind back to a torrent of memories, which were washing over her. 'It's a long story,' she replied simply.

'Well, we just saved your life, you could at least tell us who you are, and what happened!'

The lady considered the request, her face awash with emotions and memories once more. And when she eventually spoke, there was a tone of sadness in her voice. 'I'm Cecile, and I'm a *mystery* reporter!'

'A *mystery* reporter?' Suzan repeated, swilling the title around in her mind.

'Yes, that is right. I've spent my whole life travelling around the world, exploring, and often solving mysteries. As I solve them, I write articles for papers, and the internet, so that people can read about them…'

'Wow, what a cool job. What kind of mysteries have you solved?' Jack exclaimed, in awe.

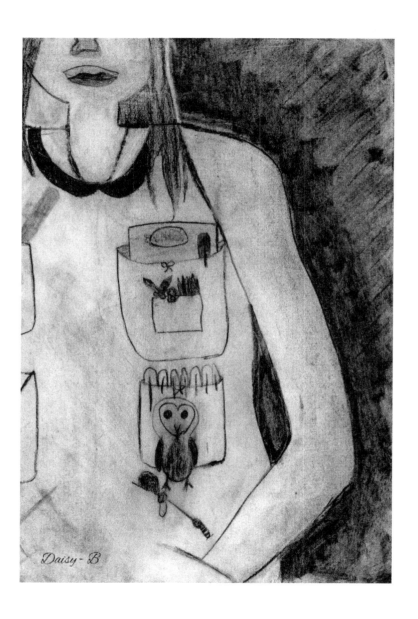

179

Cecile's eyes glistened, as a waterfall of exciting adventure memories cascaded in her mind. And trying to pluck one or two, she said: 'Oh, so many, but to name a few: missing towns and lost treasures. Strange creatures. Oh, all sorts of wonderful adventures.'

Suzan and Jack looked at each other in bubbling, brimming excitement.

'What's the oldest mystery you have solved?' Suzan asked.

'Ah, that would be the mystery of a missing town, which disappeared five hundred years ago and was thought to be unsolvable.'

'What, you solved a five-hundred-year-old mystery? What happened to the town?' Jack asked, in a flash.

'Oh, it wasn't that exciting, to be honest. It was a town that a rather crafty, famous cartographer, had added to his maps, to ensure they were not copied, but sadly they were copied by everyone, until most ancient maps included the town.

'When eventually people began to travel around more, many years later, they travelled there expecting to find a town, but found nothing. The people were baffled as to where it had disappeared to. Soon rumours became stories and it became a mystery.'

'And how did you find out the truth?' Suzan asked, her eyes wide.

'Well, sometimes mystery solving is all adventure and field work, and sometimes it's just sifting through information online – or, even more often, through old library documents and records. I managed to trace the original map back to the cartographer and stumbled upon his journal. And after a long paper trail, I managed to solve the mystery…'

A look of slight disappointment fell across the children's faces.

'Ok, what is the strangest mystery you have ever solved!?' Suzan asked, as she leant in closer to Cecile.

'Ah, now that is a good question! I have solved quite a few, but I guess it has to be the mystery of a talking owl!'

Suzan scooted back a little away from Cecile. Jack gave Suzan a tiny glance as if to say: *be careful, this lady is bonkers!* Suzan, was very sceptical, but decided to prod a little and asked: 'A talking owl, you can't be serious?'

Cecile shifted herself, to get more comfortable, squinted and then pointed to a bag that was stowed in an open locker. 'Up there, grab that bag and take out the folder,' she said.

Jack did so and soon was staring wide eyed, with Suzan – a gnat's whisker away from him –also stooped over the folder. There were clippings showing a collection of mysteries Cecile had solved and written about. And the children soon realized that Cecile was both very seasoned and also quite famous. They flicked through, glancing at each headline, till their eyes rested upon several that read: *talking owl.*

The two children gasped, as they realized there was an element of truth in what Cecile had said. Suzan and Jack listened to several more exciting tales from Cecile, including the mystery of the talking owl.

Finally, Suzan asked, 'So how did you end up here, injured?'

When Cecile answered, her voice was filled with sadness. 'Well, there's one mystery I've sought to solve, for the best part of my career. The great mystery, which has always evaded me. The problem is, every mystery I aim to solve, or investigate, must be passed by my boss, in order for the company to fund the great expenses, needed to explore them.

'I spent the last few years listening to legend, researching, and trying to persuade my boss that I should go after this legend! But every time I asked, she's laughed at me. Then, one day, my reports and story about the talking owl took my career to another level and I finally managed to persuade her.

'It had taken me years to get that *yes* but finally I was able to set off – on the mystery of my career! I arrived at a sleepy port in the middle of nowhere and set about trying to charter a boat.

'All the captains laughed at me, when I told them what I was looking for, but finally, in a smoky bar in a dead-end street, I found a captain sitting in the corner, drowning his sorrows. He agreed to sail wherever I wanted, even the impossible, as long as the price was right. I think he took my mystery with a pinch of salt, but I gave him the coordinates of an island and we set sail.

'He said it would take about two weeks, and as we weighed anchor and motored out and as the sails went up in the fair wind, we were off! I was finally chasing that career long mystery and my dream to solve it, my trusty notebook in my pocket and my pen poised!

'I was – however – hoping to charter something a little faster, as I didn't want to waste a moment longer to find that island, but a boat was a boat.' Cecile's eyes were twinkling, at the thought of the moment when she was finally inching towards the unknown.

'So, what happened?' Jack asked.

CHAPTER 31

CECILE's TALE

Cecile's face turned pale, and her eyes began to well up as she remembered the accounts of the following days after leaving the dock. 'Well, I'm no captain, but I'm no stranger to sailing and between us, the captain and I soon established a routine as I assisted him. The fair wind filled our sails and he soon trusted me to muck in with all the sailing tasks.

'We were making good time, and on course too. But suddenly, a day into our journey, we spotted a storm in the distance. The clouds bubbled and boiled, black and angry. We were both experienced sailors though, so we didn't worry too much about it. But by the time it was upon us, we realized that it was no ordinary storm, it was the tail end of a typhoon, which is like a hurricane, but given a different name because it's born in the Northwest Pacific.

'When it hit, it battered the ship and the captain told me to go below. But I protested and demanded to stay on deck to help him. He reluctantly agreed, but on the agreement that he would take charge.

'We fought our way through the great crashing mountainous waves. We fought through the spray that crashed down on the deck. It stung our faces… the wind blew us. As the small ship crooned and rocked in the waves, I took a wrong footing and slipped. I bashed my head when I fell. Luckily, I didn't lose consciousness.

'As I lay on the deck with a large gash on my head bleeding, I saw a turn of unfortunate events. The captain was trying to change direction, to try to keep the boat aimed for the bow of the giant waves, so the ship would not capsize. He had to keep the wind on the sails, at the right place. As he tacked, the boom swung from one side to the other side of the ship, and it caught him square on the head. He went over the ship, into the chasm of the sea below.

'I was unable to get to my feet, so I crawled to the edge to look over, but he was gone. Lost to the sea…'

Cecile dropped her head and wept, as she remembered staring down at the inky black sea, in search of the captain. After a moment or two, she wiped her eyes and pushed herself to finish the story: 'With the sails down and no one in control of her, the ship was at the mercy of the sea. I had a headache and blurry vision, but I was alive. My glasses had broken when I had fallen too. So, I grabbed on and held on the best I could.

'The ship crooned and rocked violently, like a giant untamed horse. The immense sound of the waves crashing into the ship hammered my head and the cold bitter rain stung my face.

'How long it went on for, I can't remember as I drifted in and out of focus. But then as the storm started to subside a little, I saw the glint of a small island in the distance.

'The ship was being swept towards it. As I drew closer, I was scared that the ship would crash into the island. I crawled over to the anchor and using the railings and other support, I pulled myself to my feet and dropped the anchor.

'As the anchor hit the seabed below the shallows of the island, there was a great tug on the ship. It was like slamming the brakes on in a car. The chain attached to the anchor suddenly became taut and the whole ship creaked and screamed and rang out in agony.

'Luckily, the ship held together and came to a stop, bobbing around in one place. I dropped back to the deck and lay there. Losing blood from the deep cut on my head.

'Eventually, after I realised that the ship was anchored safely, and the adrenalin wore off, I felt tired and exhausted. I crawled down to the lower deck. I found something to wrap my head in, to attempt to stop the bleeding. And I lay here, with the worst headache I had ever had in my life, peering through my broken glasses. Exhausted and broken, I was cold, wet and shivering. And to be honest I thought I wouldn't make it.'

The children looked a little white, at the ordeal Cecile had just experienced. Then Jack felt the need to ask a question, that he had wanted to ask at the beginning of her account but hadn't wanted to interrupt. 'So, what was the mystery and the island you were searching for?'

Cecile, squinted at the children, trying to make out the intricate details of their faces. 'Well, I had set out to try to find an island, that according to my research, might have evidence of ... giants, having lived on it. If I could find it, it would prove that they really had existed, and they were not just stories from legends and fairy tales.'

Suzan and Jack were silent...

185

CHAPTER 32

THE MIST DISAPPEARS

Cecile looked at the children expecting them to laugh at her giant story. She felt bemused by their response. They looked intrigued, but they were not surprised, they were not sceptical.

Suddenly the silence was broken. Excitedly the two children told Cecile of the book and showed her the story, of C.C. on the island of giants and his friendship with them, in the book.

They were about to tell her the rest of the story, as the three of them sat down in that bunk room of the bobbing ship, when suddenly an expression of fear swept over Jack. He realised that they were still on the outskirts of that terrible island. In all the panic and worry of saving Cecile's life, they had forgotten about the Hound, and that terrible palace and the terrible, but beautiful treasure.

Quickly they told Cecile about the island. She looked shocked, filled with terror and fear.

'I'm going to get onto the top deck. I don't have the strength to sail myself, but I will have to talk you through it,' she said as she foraged through draws for her spare pair of glasses. 'Are you ready?'

The children nodded in agreement. And Cecile talked them through how to raise the sails and set off. They didn't worry about directions, they just needed to flee as far away from the island as possible. They sailed for many hours until the island was but a speck on the horizon.

Every moment, they kept looking back, expecting the nightmare to begin again, sure they would be followed by that great ship and the Hound. But the Hound's ship stayed static, like another souvenir belonging to the teeth of that island, another medal hung on its wall.

Eventually the island completely disappeared altogether. They could not even see it with a telescope. They relaxed for a moment and took time to decide what to do next.

Jack explained more of the story and Cecile listened, taking notes. For she was feeling better and more like her old self. Her mind and her hand were fast at work on the stories of how the children had found that trunk, that tree in France and the book and the pieces of sextant. And how Jacob had helped them.

Their faces went white with fear as they remembered and told Cecile the part about them being kidnapped and sold to the Hound and kept inside a horrible brig. They told her about the alliance they had made with the Hound, in exchange for some of the treasure, so that their mother could come home and not work abroad anymore.

Cecile's pen was moving so fast, there was almost smoke coming off it. Frantically she worked hard to get the details down.

AW-B

188

For Cecile there were so many mysteries in the children's story. There was the mystery of giants, the mystery of the ultimate treasure, and then of course there was the mystery of CC.

'I thought his ship went down, how can it be?' asked Cecile, as they continued their tale.

Then suddenly, she realised something that even the children hadn't realized… CC's ship, the *Beluga,* had indeed *not* gone down that night. Cecile knew the old smuggling lanes and the geography of France. She suspected that on that fateful stormy night, the night that CC was said to have gone to the bottom of Davy Jones locker, he had actually sailed his ship around the coast of France, with a decoy ship that had gone down instead.

Then he probably sailed, up the estuary river that begins in Le Havre in France. He had sailed that river as it twisted and turned all the way to the outskirts of Paris. She asked Jack and Suzan where their friends lived and where the park was.

Suddenly it all fell in place, like the pieces of a jigsaw puzzle brought together. Yes, that was an old smuggling spot, that route was used by many a scoundrel. It was also said to be, according to her research, a famous spot for the alleged sightings of the *Beluga*, the ship belonging to the *Mist.*

It all made sense to the three of them now. CC – the Mist – had pulled off the most daring and cunning thing of all! Pulled the wool over the eyes of the whole armada! And escaped scot-free on land. But, more importantly, with his treasure.

The three of them were deeply excited, now that Cecile had put together all the pieces. The children continued with their story, in high spirits, until they came to the worst part. The part that they didn't really want to speak about, but knew they had to. Something they would rather erase from their memory. But unfortunately, some things can't be unseen. And some things can't be unheard. Tears trickled down their faces as they spoke about how they had found the treasure, and the gold and artefacts in that palace.

'Why are you crying? And why are you leaving it now and sailing away from it?' interrupted Cecile, in a gentle voice.

'Wait,' said Jack, 'there's more, we need to tell you the rest.'

Then the trickling tears turned into streams of tears, as they told her of how that strange bewitching ambience overtook them with greed and how the Hound was still there and that they didn't know how many survived.

Despite being a woman of the world and having seen many a thing, Cecile's face went white as they told her about how those pirates had turned on each other. People who were loyal and had been a crew together for more than twenty years had turned, overtaken by greed.

'Let's never go back there. Maybe some treasures are better unfound,' Cecile said.

Suddenly, Jack remembered the scroll in his pocket. He told Cecile of the Latin on the wall and how they had discovered the scroll under a marble floor tile. 'We haven't looked at it yet, we've been so busy running, looking for a safe ship and then helping you,' he finished. He reached in his pocket and pulled out the scroll.

It was written on a yellowy coloured parchment. Not like the bright bleached paper we have nowadays. Around it there was a large, but light wooden ring, the size of a napkin ring. It was a deep and rich red, similar to the chest, found in their loft.

Protecting it from the breeze, Jack very carefully and gently slid the ring off the parchment. The three leaned forward, towards each other, as they sat on the deck in a circle. It was written in calligraphy ink, that though faded, was still readable. In beautiful swirly letters, it said...

"You have found this note because your heart is larger than greed. It also means that you deserve to go on! You have passed my first trial! My friends, there are many kinds of treasure in this world and what you have just seen and experienced was indeed not my greatest treasure by far. I have had and found far, far greater treasures than that. That is nothing! Just gold. If you would like to continue in the footsteps of an old pirate, you will need that love that you found today, but you will need many other things too! For treasure does not come easily. Good luck and may you find the wind fair and the currents gentle."

After those words were a series of coordinates, just like those found on the note in the tree.

CHAPTER 33

SITTING DUCKS!

Cecile's face lit up with excitement as they read the small scroll together. However, after a few moments, her excitement turned to concern as she looked at the children and started to fully process the story and all its entirety.

She realised that she had become caught up by their adventures and by the mystery they were beginning to piece together, but she had forgotten about the fact that the children had been kidnapped and that their father and their mother were surely really, really worried about where they were.

As concern filled Cecile's face she looked down at both children and she smiled at them and said, that they needed to contact their father to tell him that they were okay.

'I agree,' said Suzan. 'But... I really, really want to see this adventure through. We've come so far - we really must find this treasure. We want to free our mother from her terrible business job. We've been in so much danger to not give up now. But yes, you're right, our father must be so worried about us. We do really miss him too. We need to get a message to him as soon as we can.'

Cecile said nothing, as she walked in the direction of the lower deck. A few moments later she returned, with a mobile phone. As she flicked her finger across the screen to unlock it, she suddenly looked very worried.

She tapped the phone screen and the side of it, as if it would make a difference. 'It got really wet that night, when the storm hit us. I thought if I left it below deck, it might dry out and I guess I kind of hoped it might work again. But it doesn't even go on,' she said to the children. 'We've no way of contacting the outside world. And what's more I've noticed that the GPS navigation system on this boat is also down. The boat took quite a battering in that storm, to be honest. We're quite lucky that she still floats at all! But somehow, we must find civilization. The problem is we've no way of navigating.'

'*Yes, we do… yes… we do!*' Jack said, excitedly. 'We've got the *sextant*. Look,' he smiled, as he pulled it out of his bag and the glistening brass shone in the sunlight. The old sextant that had once belonged to that mischievous pirate captain.

Cecile's eyes lit up and they widened in great excitement. She beckoned for him to pass it to her. 'Yes, but do you know how to use this?'

'Yes, I do. Jacob, the curator in our local museum showed us how to use it. And we used it on the Hound's ship.'

'But does it really work? I mean it's something from many, many years ago,' said Cecile.

'Yes, of course it still works, Cecile. That's how we found that last island. We sailed by this sextant,' Jack explained.

Cecile smiled and said excitedly, 'Then we have the tools we need to navigate, that's fantastic… but we only have one coordinate. Surely if we had a better coordinate… Somewhere where there's civilisation that we could sail to and then send a message to the police and your father, then you could go home safely.'

'I'm *not going home*,' said Suzan, raising her voice. 'Jack agrees. We both agree that we are going to the next island,' she continued, in a stern voice.

'Okay! Okay! I can see that you are strong minded about this,' said Cecile. 'But surely, we must let your parents know?'

'Yes, we must!' said Suzan, 'but I'm not going to go anywhere else, except those coordinates.'

After a long and lengthy discussion together, they came to a compromise. The two children agreed that they would follow the coordinates, the only coordinates that they had, to wherever it led them. And if there was any kind of civilisation, or communication equipment there, they would use it immediately, to send a message out to tell their father that they were safe, so he wouldn't be worried. And if there wasn't any way to contact their father, on the next island, then they would work out a way to reach somewhere that did. To signal their agreement, they shook hands.

Cecile felt a weight lifted from her shoulders. Being the only adult, she felt she had to take responsibility for their wellbeing and care. Now at least they had some form of plan.

Together they looked at the charts, that once belonged to CC and at the almanac that the Hound had found on his journeys – the one they had taken from his cabin. They looked at the sextant and they took celestial body readings – to work out where they were. And then they plotted and set a course.

Just then Jack's and Suzan's stomachs rumbled. They had not eaten since the morning. It was time for them to rustle up some food. Cecile was still a little weak, so Jack offered to cook because he was an excellent cook. There didn't seem to be much equipment or fresh food – it was mostly tinned, but he managed to rustle them up some scrummy soup and they sat on the top deck in the sunshine, dipping their bread in.

They spent the next few days sailing, taking it in turns to keep course. They had to take readings many times, throughout each day and night, because without regular modern-day navigation equipment, they had to do it *old school*, using the same old method that C.C. had used, all those years ago, sailing by the sun and the stars. Soon the three of them became almost expert at navigating.

Luckily, they had Cecile's tins of food and fresh water on the boat because Cecile had originally planned to be at sea for a while. However, after some days of sailing they realised that the boat's sail had been damaged in the storm. There was a tear in it. And with the fierce winds that blew them along on that Pacific Ocean, the tear wasn't getting any better.

After ten days the sail eventually gave up completely. The last shreds tore and became unable to catch even the slightest breeze at all. When that happened, the ship slowed down to a halt and was then simply at the mercy of the waves and the currents.

'What are we going to do? With no working phone, with no electrical communication equipment on the ship, and with no way of sailing, we're just sitting ducks,' exclaimed Jack, in dismay.

'Maybe… *hopefully*… the currents will eventually take us to *somewhere*,' suggested Suzan.

'Yes,' replied Jack, 'but we've no idea *where* we could end up or *how long* that could take.'

And... thought Cecile, *It's only a matter of time before we all start to grow weak, without food and drink. We've probably enough food, perhaps for another week or so and then that's it.*

Trying to sound calm, she spoke quietly to the children, 'Listen children, I think we need to ration our food, just in case the currents don't take us anywhere within a week or so.'

'I agree,' said Suzan.

'Yes, so do I,' nodded Jack. 'Our survival depends on how long we can last with our food and our water and on the currents of the sea taking us to people who may help us.'

Cecile knew, that at that moment, the nearest people may be those on the space station, above their heads! She felt that huge responsibility again, coming down hard on her shoulders. She had agreed to take these children to their next destination... the next set of coordinates. But she had got them lost on a boat, that now would not go any further.

She started to think of the unthinkable... she started to worry about what would happen if they ran out of food, or even worse, ran out of water or were caught in a storm. If they were caught in a storm, they would have no way of directing the boat.

Being a reporter and a researcher, she had heard many stories of the Pacific Ocean and how vast it is. And she knew how storms could turn it from the most beautiful silvery mirror to a great mountainous terrible place. Both beautiful and deadly.

CHAPTER 34

S.O.S

Suzan, Jack and Cecile agreed that they should try to flag down a ship and get help. It was their only chance. The Pacific Ocean is a busy ocean, however it's a very big ocean indeed – although many a ship sails it, some of them are so large, just to stop would take them about three quarters of an hour, just to turn around and find a small sailing ship – a speck on the horizon.

First, they would have to be seen. Next, they would also have to be lucky, for a large tanker, sailing around the world, delivering goods, was unlikely to stop for a sailing ship - unless the crew realised there was a problem.

Suddenly Jack came up with a very cunning idea: 'Let's remove the mirror from the sink and take it to the top deck. We can use it to try and flash sunlight signals towards any ships, in the hope that we can get their attention.'

'Good idea,' agreed Suzan.

Jack also searched the ship to see if he could find a telescope, so that they could look for ships on the horizon and could also see whether they had gained their attention.

'But what about night-time… it's not going to work at night-time unless the moon is full and bright,' said Suzan.

Jack agreed and so did Cecile. It was a daytime solution only. They thought a fire might be a good idea too, but they couldn't risk lighting a fire on the deck of a ship. Suzan was right, it had to be mainly daytime. They also pulled from the cupboard some of the white bed sheets, so that they could hold them up.

Jack had the clever idea of searching for a large black marker pen, so that he could write SOS in large writing. For any of you, who don't know what that means, it means: *Save Our Souls*, also: *Save our Ship* and that's what they needed...

They needed help desperately and they knew it. None of them mentioned it, after that moment, but they all knew that they could die on that boat, perhaps from a lack of food, but more likely from a lack of water.

'Apparently you can last a week or two without food, although it would probably make you very weak, but you can't go much more than three days without water,' said Jack.

They had to conserve as much as possible, which meant using hardly any water for cooking and avoiding having a shower. They had to save every single drop; it was finite... they couldn't go to a supermarket... they couldn't go to that tap in the kitchen, because they were in the middle of nowhere. What they had was what they had!

Yet they were surrounded by the ocean... water, everywhere, but as you probably know, the sea is salty, it is saline. If you drink a cup of sea water, it has so much salt in it that it would make you far, far more dehydrated than you were before you drank it. It would also make you very, very sick.

'Water, water everywhere, but not a drop to drink,' said Cecile, trying to uplift them, but Suzan and Jack were not uplifted. They missed their parents, their home, and their school. They sat bobbing… Bobbing along aimlessly, with the currents pulling them this way and that. They could steer with a rudder of the ship only, but that was it.

Jack carefully wrote "*SOS*" on the sheets, in the largest letters possible. With the mirror now in a safe place on deck and the telescope to hand, they took turns to scan the horizon for ships to see if they could find something… anything!

They sat there drifting aimlessly. They sat by day, and they sat by night. The children were tired, they wanted to sleep, but they could not sleep. They refused to give up. Using the telescope, the three took it in turns, no sooner the light came up, to scan the horizon constantly for ships.

Finally, they saw their first ship. Frantically they shone the mirror at it and held up the sheet with "*SOS*" – the ship was too big. It was a huge oil tanker, bringing oil from the middle of the world to Europe, so that people could fill up their cars. The captain of the oil tanker, was looking out across the sea and didn't even notice them. For the oil tanker, their little sailing ship was like an ant, compared to an elephant… How many times does an elephant notice an ant?

Time after time, almost on an hourly basis… tanker after tanker… passed them by in the distance. None of them even looked at the sailing boat, let alone noticed the mirror, or SOS sign, until - after several days - they were noticed by a smaller ship. And not a moment too soon, for they were down to their very last drops of water and their very last few crumbs of food.

The ship was much, much larger than theirs, but smaller than the tankers. Dark black smoke was billowing out of its chimneys. They couldn't make out the faces of the people who were looking out, but they could see through the telescope that there were people looking their way.

When they saw that the ship had suddenly changed course and started to move towards them, they couldn't believe their eyes. They couldn't believe their eyes when they saw it was gaining and gaining and gaining.

Finally, they had managed to flag down a ship on the Pacific Ocean and they were saved. They could eat and drink properly again. They would survive.

Daisy - B

CHAPTER 35

RESCUE

As the ship grew nearer, its size – compared to their little sailing ship – was colossal. As it drew close enough, they could see, peering over the edge of it, a grimy looking man who seemed to be in charge on deck. He was all covered in oil and grease and wearing a flat cap to one side of his head – his nose seemed to go in the opposite direction. In fact, his nose looked as if it had been hit by a train.

The man peered down at the small sailing boat 'Are in trouble, are ya?' he shouted down. When he saw the two children, he looked surprised. 'You're just wee children.'

Cecile popped her head into view, 'Yes, they're with me, under my care. We need help, our sails are torn, we have no way of sailing anymore and what is more: our navigation system is down. We need to get to somewhere with civilisation.'

'Really?' The man turned around and went away, calling out: 'I'll be back in five minutes.' It looked as if he was going to check with someone.

Five minutes might sound like a short time, but for those children and for Cecile it felt like an eternity, because their safety rested on whether or not he would come back… Whether or not he would agree to help them.

AWB

The man reappeared though, sure enough, five minutes later, with a big smile on his face.

'Yeah, we'll help ya, don't you worry.' He tied a rope to his ship, dropped the end down and then clambered down. Once down, he tied the piece of rope to the front of their sailing ship. Then he pursed his lips and whistled, in a kind of signal, to his crew.

The great ship chugged away, under power of its great smoky diesel engines and as they came very slowly around to the back of the ship, the man with the flat cap threw the end of the rope to a waiting guy, who was balanced on a small rusty platform on the back of the ship. The man tied the rope round a large metal loop near the platform and then slowly, slowly they stopped the great ship.

The crooked nosed man gave another signal whistle, and the other person single-handedly tugged the rope to pull the sailing ship as close to the back platform as possible. Then they dropped a rope ladder, directly above the ship, as the ship bobbed along.

'Come on aboard then!' called one of the crew. 'Watch your footing.'

Jack, Suzan, and Cecile climbed cautiously, one by one, up to the metal railings of the rusty old platform. They were helped over the rusty railings by the sailor and his mate, onto the small platform and then through an old brown rusty door that creaked open reluctantly.

They found themselves inside the engine room, about halfway down the ship. The engine filled quite a large space of the ship and it was obviously used to haul something heavy, guessed Jack.

'Your ship will be alright out there bobbing along behind us and as soon as we get to port, they will help you,' said the burly captain … Although, as you will realise very soon, that man was *not* actually *the captain,* he was simply a sailor.

They were about to meet the true master, the true captain of the ship. He was not there, covered in grime, in the engine room. *That* … was not his style!

The children and Cecile followed the man with the crooked nose, past great thumping engines. They could not hear anything except the engines chugging away.

There were some people working around the engine, like bees buzzing around a flower. They were all dressed in dungarees, dripping with sweat, and covered from head to toe in grease. Running around, they were busy keeping the engine happy, checking gauges and dials.

As they passed the engines and went up a staircase, the sound of the thumping engines began to quieten a little. And as they grew closer to the top of the stairs, they heard some other strange sounds. They heard a different kind of thumping and bashing. Strange cries. They didn't know what they were.

When they arrived on the deck, they were led to a cabin. But not your average grimy cabin. A very large room, indeed, that had a chandelier fixed to the ceiling and an amazingly long table, spread with all manner of food.

There was someone sitting at the very end of the table, in a beautiful large wooden chair, made of a deep rich aged wood, upholstered with red and gold fabric. The chair size was much larger than normal though and must have been custom made to take the size of the man sitting on it – a tall, yet extremely round man who wore a natural fibre tweed suit, with a rabbit's foot hanging around his neck.

Hanging over the back of the man's chair, for it was hot in the room, was a fur coat made from mink. And if you know anything about mink fur coats, you will know it takes quite a few of these cute animals to make one.

This was a man who liked his comfort. On the walls there were heads of animals mounted. And on the floor there were furs spread out like rugs, made from what looked like bears, wolves, and other endangered animals. The children couldn't help feeling sorry for all the poor animals used to decorate the cabin.

CHAPTER 36

The Boar

The large, round man sat in his oversized chair with a pile of empty plates, to the right, on the table. And with a large napkin hanging over and around him. His belly was so large that even his shirt, that was extra, extra, extra, extra, extra, double extra-large, struggled to hold in his waist. His shirt buttons were straining in the holes and looked like champagne corks about to pop. Great stretch holes, between the buttons, showed his t-shirt which was also struggling.

Rolls of fat hung around his chin and as he sat upright, in his ornate chair, he didn't look up from the plate he was gorging on. It was duck à l'orange.

Just then a small stout man wearing white charged in through the door with more plates.

'Eere is your order sir,' said the small stout man, with a deep French accent. 'Just as you like it.' He stumbled and half ran to the large round man in the chair and placed the dishes down, in a queue, with dishes previously ordered.

The large round man still didn't look up from his food, he was absolutely in a trance, engrossed in eating. He looked rosy cheeked from having had so much and his eyes sparkled from sheer joy. Some people eat to live, but this man lived to eat! The joy across his face as he reached out to take the next plate. A delicate dove, or pigeon marinated in a sauce.

Suzan and Jack gazed across the table. They forgot where they were for a moment and their mouths began to water. The table was filled with succulent dishes from all around the world and the children were so, so hungry – after eating half meals for the last few weeks, to try to conserve their food. Cecile started to salivate too. She stared at the food with eyes ablaze.

Eventually when Cecile and the children had been standing there, dripping with salivation, watching him eat for quite a while… Eventually… he paused… Eventually… he finished eating.

He moved the dish away from himself and dropped the spoon onto the white silk tablecloth. Brown sauce dripped off the spoon and pooled on the cloth. He peered up and smiled. 'Welcome,' he said, in an accent that the children found difficult to pin down.

Clearly, he was not the sailing captain on the ship. Clearly, he didn't do a single ounce of work on the ship, but clearly, he was the boss of the ship!

The chef stood poised, ready in case there was another order. The man looked Cecile and the children up and down and then the crooked nosed sailor, they originally thought was captain, very delicately cleared his throat: 'Uuuhum,' he said, with a fearful stutter, 'sir, these... these are the people, we found, who need help.'

'Yes, yes, yes,' the round man replied, in a deep strong voice. 'Give them some food, they look hungry... look how thin they are.'

The round man beckoned the children and Cecile to sit down. Then he clicked his fingers and the chef stood to attention and excitedly asked them what they would

209

like to eat. The children asked what the chef could make and what they were allowed.

The burly round man at the head of the table smiled and said in a deep voice: 'This is my chef. He is one of the greatest chefs in the world, trained under the chef master Pierre G. H. Francoeur in Paris. Under the great three-star restaurant and when he was too good for that, he rose to the greatest restaurant in New York where he became a sensation, with a ten-year waiting list. And only then was he good enough to serve me.

'He can prepare any dish from around the world. And trust me, I have put him to the test with that! Children, lady, it is lovely to meet you. Welcome aboard my ship, *The Piglet*! My humble ship. Now, ask my chef for anything you want, my guests!'

Jack giggled, thinking he might really try to put the chef to the test, as he said, 'I would like lobster in a crème sauce.' He had never tried lobster and had always dreamed of tasting it, having come from a background where money was scarce.

'Is that a garlic crème, or a sweet crème?' asked the chef.

Jack hesitated for a moment, realizing that the chef actually would make it for him. 'Both please,' he said, not wanting to miss out on an opportunity and feeling terrible pangs of hunger.

'No problem, one of each, coming right up,' said the chef, in his French accent.

There was a small chuckle from the round man, at the end of the table.

Suzan was a little more conservative and said politely: 'Are you sure we can ask him for anything, is it really okay?'

The man smiled, '*Yes*, be my guests. Eating is one of life's wonderful joys my friends. And if I cannot extend my arm of hospitality, to a few weary sailors now and again, what is the point of everything?' He seemed like a kind-hearted man, on their initial meeting, as he offered them such generosity.

'Really?'

'Yes… please ask him for anything. He is the greatest chef that has ever lived and will be a legend one day. There is nothing that this man cannot cook!' replied their burly host.

'Could I have beans on toast?' asked Suzan.

'*Huh*, you are asking him to cook you beans on toast?' said the round man. 'What is your name girl?'

'Suzan.'

'*Come on*! Please ask him for anything you would really like to eat.'

Suzan plucked up the courage and in a timid voice said: 'Well, there is something I would like. I've heard my friends at school, talking about their trip to Japan. They spoke about this thing called sushi, which sounds delicious and ever since they've spoken about it, I have wanted to try it. But I've never had the chance. Can your chef make sushi?'

'Ah Suzan, no problem, before studying in Paris, he spent five years as an apprentice under a great sushi master in Japan. He knows everything there is to know about sushi! Let me recommend the ebi and the maguro,' said the round man, warmly.

'What are they?' asked Suzan.

'Ah for you, they are prawn and tuna,' said the round man, at the end of the table. He turned his head towards his legendary chef. 'Bring her some salmon, ebi, magural

211

and a selection of others too. A tray of fifty pieces and make it good, my man!' Then he turned his head to Cecile, 'And for you madam?'

Cecile smiled and thought for a moment. 'Well, from all my travels, the most delicious dish I've ever tasted is when I solved a mystery, in a tiny village, deep in the heart of India. The people there made me a curry with a base of lentils and a delicate blend of spices with goat meat.'

The man grinned, 'Ah that one, I know. No problem. Would you like naan with that too?'

'Yes please. That's really kind of you ...um ... sir,' Cecile replied, searching for the correct way to address the man.

The round man clicked his fingers and the chef hurried away. Then his hands moved to the arm rests of his chair, and he began to sweat. A few moments later the three guests realized that he was getting up. But getting up took a while for a man of such stature.

Eventually his body creaked into a standing position. 'I don't think I've introduced myself... I'm the Boar. My real name is of no significance. I am always referred to as the Boar.' Very slowly and courteously he took a tiny bow and then slowly sat back down in his big chair.

CHAPTER 37

DELICIOUS

As they waited for their food, Suzan, Jack and Cecile breathed a sigh of relief. The Boar seemed friendly, *and* they were about to have some wonderful food…

'It's very kind, offering to help us after we were stranded, and thank you for offering to feed us too,' said Cecile.

'Oh, it's nothing, really nothing. My pleasure. Don't worry,' said the Boar, in his deep bellowing voice – like an echo from the depths of a great tanker ship.

'Thank you so much,' both children said. They were really taken back by his kindness.

'And don't worry we will be having dessert in a minute too!' The Boar gave an enthusiastic smile.

Just then the small stout chef came back in, rolling along an ornate trolley. It was polished to a bright shimmer. He stopped just behind Jack. He then turned gracefully and served Jack with his two plates of lobster. One cooked in a delicate cream sauce, from which – as he lifted the silver bell shaped cloche – a rich buttery steam bellowed out. As he lifted the other silver cloche a gorgeous garlic fragrance, that carried in the steam, swirled around Jack. Like a taunting gremlin!

'Enjoy your lobsters sir,' the chef said, as he kissed his thumb and fore finger and separated them in mid-air, in a huge *chef's kiss*, as if to gesture the meal would be impeccably exquisite in taste. Then he wheeled the trolley over to Cecile and took a beautiful authentic half circle copper pot, which looked as if it had come all the way from India itself and placed it in front of her.

He paused for a moment and put out his hand in a cautioning gesture. 'Do take care madam, it does pack a little punch this curry!'

Cecile's eyes closed, for a moment, as the smells reached into the depths of her mind and sparked memories of that mysterious adventure, when she had first tried that very curry. 'Ah yes,' she said, as she remembered. 'Yes, it's a spicy one.'

The chef smiled and then gently rolled the trolley towards Suzan and served her a large slate platter that was a rich bluey grey. It was filled with the most beautiful and colourful ornately delicate pieces of sushi. Each one had been lovingly crafted. The fish looked so fresh that it slightly glistened in the light.

Pointing to the top left of the platter, the chef said: 'This is salmon from the Hokkaido region of the North of Japan. And over here we have the *Ika,* which is squid. And down here we have prawns, five different kinds of prawns, from around Japan.'

As he pointed to each piece of sushi and spoke about the names and origin, Suzan found it difficult to remember and was barely listening. Ever since her friend at school had told her about sushi, she had dreamt of eating it, but had known that they could never afford to try it.

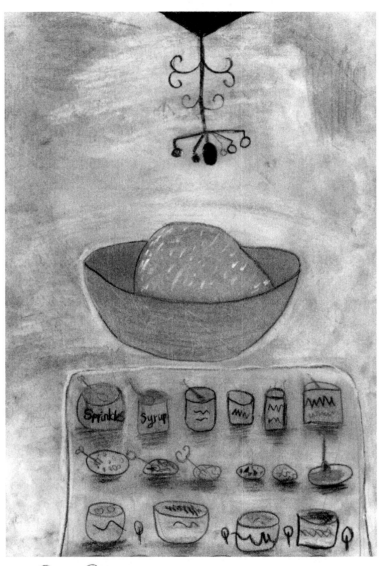

Daisy - B

Yet here she was sitting in front of some, freshly prepared just for her! She asked the chef how she should eat it and he explained that she could use chopsticks, but it was no problem to use her fingers too.

Suzan could not hold back any longer, she picked up a piece and took a bite. A range of great expressions washed over her face as she took that bite, and the flavours oozed out. Then she took another, and another.

Jack began to work at the lobster, cracking the shell and pulling at the meat. And Cecile began digging into her curry.

Soon there was a great silence in the room as the four of them ate. The chef stood in the corner, poised in case anyone needed anything else. His eyes flicked from face to face, to ensure the four enjoyed his great creations. He took his cooking deeply seriously and there was nothing better to him than the smiles and satisfaction of people enjoying his food.

After a long while, when they had finished all their food, the children and Cecile sat back, deeply contented. And finally, the Boar sat back, his plates all empty.

'Now,' the Boar said happily, 'I think it is time for dessert, don't you? Now children what would you like?'

Jack asked if it was possible to have Battenberg cake.

'Easy for my chef, he will make you one from scratch,' replied the Boar.

Suzan's face lit up, with a smile. 'You know what I'd love right now... rice pudding!'

'No problem,' the Boar smiled as he turned towards Cecile. 'And for you Cecile? What would you like?'

Cecile paused for a while, before replying: 'Well, a while ago I was in Paris helping a boy, who was cursed to be an owl, before he could find the true meaning of his name. Over there I tried this thing, it's absolutely delicious. It's small and round and made from egg. It's called a mac… a macr…'

'You mean a macaroon?' The chef asked, in his strong French accent, that seemed to come from nowhere.

'Yes, that's it!' said Cecile. 'Is it possible for you to make macaroons?'

The Boar laughed, 'My chef is French… of course he can make a macaroon. Macaroons will be a *walk in the park* for him.'

The chef scurried away again and came back a little while later with a trolley packed full of their desserts. How he had made them so quickly, no one knows, but he was indeed the greatest chef who had ever lived.

In front of Suzan, he placed the most delicious rice pudding you could ever imagine, creamy with a crispy caramelised top. Then he placed on the table a tray full of possible toppings. There were hundreds and thousands, there were chocolate flakes, there were syrups of every different variety.

It seemed to the children that the chef had a kitchen the size of Buckingham Palace and an ingredient store the size of twenty supermarkets. How did he do it?

Then he placed a large silver platter, full of macaroons, in front of Cecile – more macaroons than any one person could ever eat and not be sick. The chef ran through the flavours for Cecile in a strong and silky French accent. They included green tea, chestnut, coconut, apple, pear, strawberry and far too many more to mention here.

Cecile's head was swimming with the smells and the names of them. Each one was delicately smooth on the outside and light and slightly chewy on the inside and each bite released a spectrum of delicate flavours. Cecile took her time tasting them like a great connoisseur.

The chef wheeled the trolley around to the Boar and began to serve his multitude of desserts. He lined and queued up: a giant apple pie and custard, a whole chocolate gateau, a whole crème brûlée, a pear and syrup tart, an Indian yoghurt dish, cookies and cream doughnuts and Japanese Manju sweets.

Finally, he rolled the trolley back round to Jack and placed in front of him a beautiful handmade Battenberg cake. As the chef cut a slice, Jack noticed the slightly sticky soft yellow outer with a soft fine sugar coating that covered the delicate yellow and pink sponge.

The chef then went back to the corner where he liked to stand, poised and ready. He watched eagerly as all four people tucked in, to ensure that their expressions were of joy.

Although he was fast at making dishes, he was a true artisan and for him it wasn't about the money he was paid, it was about the look of joy and satisfaction he saw when someone tucked into one of his dishes. He was a perfectionist!

When everyone had eaten, the Boar asked the crooked nosed man to show them to some quarters. He told them that they would be dining with him every day, until they reached the port.

220

CHAPTER 38

A KIND OFFER

As the days passed by, they headed ever closer towards the port where they knew that they could contact their family and get that sailing ship fixed. The ship cut through the water, sure and proud, and the weather was fair and calm as the sun shone, and the rich blue sky stretched out in every direction as far as the eye could see.

Every day they ate like kings and queens with the Boar and every day his charm, charisma and his hospitality made them feel increasingly at ease. The terror and ordeal that they had experienced with the Hound seemed like a distant dream now – yet one that they would never quite forget.

They had comfortable, but humble cabins. One for the two children to share and one for Cecile on her own. There were small but soft bunk beds, a desk, and a port hole window. They could use the shower and the facilities on the ship, when ever they wanted to. Soon they settled into what the Boar had said was about a ten-day journey to the nearest port.

As they relaxed day by day, they put that chef to the test. Almost like a game, every day they would wonder

221

what they should ask that legendary chef to cook for them.

'Today, I bet he can't make this,' Suzan would say, and describe something really unusual.

Jack would then say, 'No I bet he can't make… '

Even Cecile would join in and say, 'I remember a mystery I solved once in such and such, where they cooked…'

They put that chef to the test… And every day he rose to the challenge and made the most beautiful perfect and scrumptious food, that exceeded all their expectations and imagination.

As the long sunny days rolled by, they grew to know a little more about the Boar and his ship. Although there was one thing that they never quite understood, and that was exactly what it was that he did.

Every time they brought up the subject with questions like: *What is it you do by the way?* – he would just give them a very general answer and say that he transported *luxury goods*. He said he transported them all around the world to clients who would pay extravagantly for the most magnificent things. He would then change the subject and offer them more food.

The strange thing about food is, and you may have noticed this if you've been to France, food creates social bonds, it creates relationships and it's one of the things that creates trust. It's the thing that helps to make us feel comfortable, at ease and relaxed. And meal by meal they all became increasingly relaxed with their host.

Soon they began to speak about their lives and Cecile spoke about many of her adventures. The Boar sat listening intently at dinner time and asked many questions. As a great host, he was genuinely intrigued by their lives and their stories.

One day, Cecile decided that it would be a great opportunity to interview the chef and write an article on him as it was very rare that she met such a master chef indeed. His story was interesting.

The chef agreed to have lunch with her on one of the days. While Cecile went off to have lunch and to interview him, the children were meant to have lunch with the Boar, but Jack was feeling a little tired that day and felt he wanted to be alone. He found a peaceful spot on the ship and sat gazing out over the sea. It had been a difficult few weeks for all of them, but especially for Jack because he was the youngest.

Suzan decided to go alone, to eat lunch with the Boar. There she sat, completely at ease with her host, and there they were chatting about some of her adventures, whilst drinking fine tea and eating cakes.

Maybe it was the warm relaxing atmosphere of the room and the good food, maybe it was just that Suzan had always had a weakness for letting secrets slip, but the conversation naturally led towards where they were going and as each story and explanation connected, like avenues, eventually Suzan mentioned the legend of the Mist.

The Boar was intrigued, he wanted to hear this famous pirate tale. He hadn't heard of the Mist, and he was genuinely interested in the story. So, he sat back in his chair, comforted by his food and listened intently to Suzan tell her tale of the Mist.

The Boar wasn't a pirate, and he wasn't a treasure hunter, he was simply a transporter of luxury goods, but he was curious and asked many, many, questions.

Unfortunately, though, the questions led to more questions and before Suzan knew it, she was spilling the beans! She was telling him about the sextant and explaining about their hopes and dreams of finding the treasure and solving the mystery, so they would be able to use the money to stop their mother from needing to work, as a businesswoman, travelling around the world. And so that they could perhaps live together as a family again and have enough money for food and bills.

When she spoke about these things, the Boar looked concerned and in a moment of kindness, offered to help them work out where the next location was. 'After all,' he said, 'I could take you there, if it's not too far.'

'Well, Jack and I need to contact our parents first,' explained Suzan.

'So, let's plot the coordinates with the sextant now. I'll still take you to the port on route. Then, as soon as the repairs and phone calls have been completed, I can take you all the way to the next island.

'Your little ship can tow behind, so you know it's safe and ready for you. This might save you time and I will be there in case you need any further help.'

After they had plotted the coordinates, they realised that the next island was on route to the next port.

'So why not stop there on the way?' suggested the Boar.

Suzan was excited, 'I wonder… I hope… there might even be a phone on the island too.'

'Well, if there's no way of fixing your boat and contacting your parents, on the island, then I'll simply take you on to the port – as originally planned, so you'll all be safe either way,' replied the Boar.

Later, that day Suzan told Jack about the Boar's idea. Jack was furious. He knew that they didn't really know this person well enough, and it was supposed to be *their secret*.

Cecile was quite concerned too, but after a lengthy discussion, they came to the conclusion that, if the Boar had actually wanted to hurt them, or to try to take their treasure, he would have done it by now. He was a gentleman and a great host, and it seemed like a genuine offer to help them. It *was* on the way after all! So, after much discussion, they agreed to his offer of help.

The Boar's only proviso was that he wanted to come on shore with them and have a look around. He said that, as a hobby, he was very interested in plants and animals, particularly animals and that he liked to collect them.

Jack, Suzan and Cecile used the sextant, to navigate to the coordinates on the letter. The destination was very close to where Suzan and the Boar had calculated it would be. But with the sextant and the almanac, they were all able to find the exact pinpoint location.

CHAPTER 39

FOR THE COLLECTION

After a few days of sailing by the sextant, a small but beautiful island appeared on the horizon. As they sailed closer, the details of the island came into focus.

Just as the sun rose and the beautiful warm glow washed over the horizon, they found themselves within a deep coastline that surrounded the tiny island. Golden sandy beaches surrounded a thick, rich deep green jungle that appeared to cover the whole island.

The beach very quickly dropped from shallow bright turquoise water to a dark bottomless blue, where they were able to drop anchor and row to the beach. It was such a small place, probably seldom visited by anyone. Too small to really build habitation on.

The children and Cecile were disappointed about the size because it meant that they were not able to contact the children's parents, but they were also filled with excitement because they were at another island. Another island that CC had been to. Another island that was part of CC's wild goose chase. His crazy treasure hunt!

They decided to go on an expedition to explore the island and the Boar insisted he'd like to go with them. He stepped from his rowing boat, followed by some crew and the crooked-nosed captain, who carried a large box, with jars, pipettes, magnifying glasses, and a few other bags of things that he said would be useful, if he found any interesting specimens of – as he put it – *fauna and flora* for his collection.

As they slowly entered the woodland, the gentle lapping of the waves on the shore faded and so did the bright sunshine that lit the beach like a great torch. They found themselves in a dimly lit lush jungle. Beams of beautiful green light streamed through the gaps in the overlapping canopy leaves, like a giant stained-glass window.

In the otherwise uncharted jungle there were faint, half overgrown paths, which were used by animals rather than people. They seemed to run all over the island, throughout the jungle.

Worried about getting a little lost, they decided to explore the paths methodically. After walking for about fifteen minutes, they saw the strangest and cutest little animal, sitting up on a branch, above them. It was furry and pure white almost all over and looked a little like a large mouse lemur.

Perching on its branch with its fine fingers and toes, it had large gooey, puppy eyes and a tiny round, dark brown nose. It looked around gently and slowly and seemed the most peaceful relaxed little animal, you could ever meet. Its beautiful soft, thick white fur gently moved in the breeze.

Daisy - B

The Boar with his small crew of five people, including his chef, walked on slowly. Two of his crew carried a huge wooden chair with ornate carrying handles, ready to transport him whenever he became a little tired. His chef pulled a large four wheeled trolley that contained a portable kitchen and some food, just in case the Boar became hungry, for he knew that the Boar was a gentle and kind man, but could become angry and beastly, if he was ever allowed to get hungry. It was his duty to serve him the finest gourmet food at any moment, at any time and in any place – even on an uninhabited island. He had the equipment he needed to make a few meals for all of them, but most importantly for the Boar.

The party of explorers thumped and slashed their way through the jungle while the little white creature turned its head to observe them in intrigue. It didn't flinch, or even blink despite the noises that were suddenly being made below. And as they moved further, they saw more and more of these animals.

The paths wound and frolicked their way through the jungle. In places they were bold, and in others no more than a subtle line in the undergrowth. Eventually the pathway led them to a series of tiny clearings.

They set up a temporary camp at the first clearing they reached, and the chef got to work. He put on his hat and unfolded a temporary yet extremely high-quality kitchen, complete with kitchen sink. He set up the cooking facilities and started dicing and chopping meat and other ingredients. Very quickly, almost like a magician, he had already made them a great stew. A rich gourmet beef bourguignon, made from the finest cuts of beef.

The Boar sat back in a chair that had been unfolded and set up for him as soon as they arrived. Buckets of sweat trickled down his brow and his whole top was drenched. It had been a hard walk for him, despite being carried part of the way in his wooden chair.

While the chef created his art, a foldable table was set up and laid by his crew. They had not brought sleeping equipment, as they planned to only be there for the day. The chef hurried over to the Boar with a gigantic bowl of the stew, with three whole loaves of his finest bread, made late the night before. He then placed a bowl of stew in front of each of them and finally sat down himself.

As they sat and dined, they became very aware that they were surrounded by lots of those beautiful, inquisitive little white creatures, sitting up on the treetops. And the creatures were all gazing at them with intrigue and curiosity.

When the Boar noticed them, he looked at his crew member, the one with the crooked nose. The man instantly knew what the Boar wanted. Out from a box he unfolded a tranquiliser rifle, took aim, and shot one of the little white creatures. Then another of the crew unfolded a large metal animal cage.

'For the collection,' said the Boar.

The children were surprised and horrified.

'How many are you going to take? How many do you need?' asked Jack.

The Boar grinned, 'Oh just a few samples for my collection. I've never seen this kind of animal before. It seems to be… let me see…' he said, as he waddled over, picked up a limp, tranquilised creature, from the ground and studied it. He took a magnifying glass from his pocket and carefully observed the little creature. Not more than twenty centimetres tall, it was round and beautifully fluffy.

'Hmmm, mammal, maybe a primate,' said the Boar, as he placed the creature down, took out a notebook and started to sketch the poor creature, as it laid there tranquilised. He poked and prodded it. 'Ah yes, judging by the teeth... a herbivore, interesting... judging by its large cranial area it must be highly intelligent... um yes remarkably interesting.'

The Boar took many notes, like a scientist. The children had relaxed a little, by then, as they had realised that the animals had not been killed, just tranquilised. They assumed the Boar was interested, in what seemed to be a completely new species of animal, until - unfortunately - the Boar looked over to his chef and said: 'What do they taste like?'

The children had eaten chicken, beef, pork, and a few other meats, in their lives, but the idea, of eating such a small and cute creature, horrified them.

'You're not going to eat one, are you?' asked Suzan.

'Yes, of course I'm going to eat it! It's all part of my study, my dear. We must see if it has any... palatable characteristics,' replied the Boar. He turned to the chef. 'I think we will begin by grilling one, shall we?'

The chef grinned in excitement. 'Oh, very good choice sir, excellent choice.' He hurried off to get charcoal. Speedily he dug a small pit in the ground, about half a foot down and a foot or two across. He then put in the charcoal, took out a long lighter and lit it.

The paper, that he had carefully added around and below the charcoal, burst into flames and soon the coal was alight as well. He waited a while, letting it burn down to bright even glowing coals, then he took one of the creatures and as he began to prepare it, the children and Cecile looked away in disgust.

When the chef had finished, he placed a plate in front of the Boar, with the cooked animal drizzled in soy sauce. As the Boar tucked in, great expressions came over his face. expressions of ecstasy, joy and euphoria were displayed. His eyes became wide and bright, with sheer delight.

Only when he had finished cleaning and mopping up the plate, only then did he turn and address the chef, who was still standing in front of him, poised, waiting to find out whether he was pleased with the taste. Waiting to know whether his cooking was good and whether indeed the meat from the animal was palatable.

'That was the most delicious thing I've ever tasted in all my life,' said the Boar.

The chef took a step back, in surprise because in his career he had made the Boar some of the most delicate and amazing food known to humankind, from all parts of the world. Yet suddenly a simple grilled animal was being described as the best thing that he had ever had!

Suzan, Jack and Cecile were nearby, trying to ignore the whole scene. They felt sad and confused. It all seemed so cruel.

The Boar signalled to the man with the crooked nose and the man tranquilised more of the cute animals. Soon the chef had cooked them all and was serving *seconds* for the Boar and some for the crew.

As everyone tucked in, their faces lit up with sheer joy. It was exquisite, a vast range of flavours and tastes absolutely filled them with joy and happiness. It was addictive too, they ate more and more, until after a long while they all fell back in their chairs contented and rosy faced.

The children and Cecile refused to eat even one tiny bite of it.

'It's very, very good,' said the Boar, persuasively. 'You really must at least try one bite. Then you'll know how good it is.'

'No, thank you, we're going to go for a walk now,' replied Cecile, firmly.

As they walked away, the Boar and his crew drifted off to sleep with pure relaxation and contentment after such rich food.

CHAPTER 40

THE MIST'S ROOM

The children and Cecile started walking further into the jungle, keeping a careful record of which paths they had taken, so that they knew the way back. And, after a long time, they came to a much, larger clearing. Around the outside of the clearing there seemed to be many of the beautiful cute white animals.

In the centre of the clearing, taking up a large proportion of the canopy, was a beautiful very, very ancient tree. The tree was about six or seven metres wide, and it looked as if it was about two thousand years old, although it can be difficult to gauge the age of a tree, because some trees grow very, very slowly and some very, very quickly. But it was certainly, incredibly ancient indeed.

Some of its branches almost touched the ground, hanging low by their weight and under the weight of its fruit; for it was a fruit bearing tree, but one that the children had never ever seen before. It was a bizarre fruit, a drab grey-green colour, nothing like the bright colours that we usually associate with fruit.

Daisy - B

The three picked some, and because they were quite hungry after a long walk, they wondered if it was possible to eat it. They could see that the animals around them had been eating them, for some of them had the fruit in their hands, so they imagined that it couldn't have been too poisonous. Unless the animals had built up some kind of immunity to any toxins.

Cecile, being so hungry, decided to take out her pocketknife and cut one open, to see if she could taste the tiniest amount. All three of them knew it is always a very, very bad idea to try and taste any kind of wild fruit, for there are berries out there that can kill you after eating just one. There are fruit and mushrooms in the world that would make you very, very ill indeed or possibly kill you, even if you only touched them and licked your fingers.

The three of them knew that it was taking a huge chance, but they were really hungry, and there was no way they would eat the little white creatures. Cecile decided to go first. She warned the children that they must not try it yet. She would taste a minute amount and then if she was okay, they could eat some. She tasted a tiny amount and said that it didn't taste bad. it wasn't bitter or sour, but it wasn't really very sweet either.

It was very, very bland, like cucumber and it seemed to be mostly liquid, with the tiniest sweetness. The strangest thing though, was that the tiny centimetre cube she had eaten, made her feel so very, very full indeed. It felt as though she'd eaten a whole meal.

Cecile felt no bad effects from eating the food, in fact although the taste was immensely bland, she felt not only full, but also rested and surprisingly energised. 'It's strange… how can such a tiny amount of fruit make me feel so full and rejuvenated?'

'Let's pick some, to eat later,' suggested Suzan.

'Good idea sis,' replied Jack. He cut one of them open, to take a second look inside. 'It's really dull in colour, the same as yours,' he stared at Cecile in disbelief. 'Very strange and look at the large stone in the centre. That stone is quite a beautiful colour, compared with the actual fruit. It's a really interesting shape. I'm going to keep a few of those.'

'The tree itself looks really ancient,' remarked Cecile.

They gazed up at the branches, in wonder and then they decided to walk right around the tree, because it was a great ancient majestic tree that stretched up to the very top of the canopy. As they reached the back of the tree, they noticed that like some other ancient trees, the tree had become hollow in the middle. Suzan explained that, when trees become really old, sometimes the centre of them rots, but they continue to grow and stay alive on the outside.

The hollow opening seemed to be about the size of a crouching person. Although it was daytime, it was extremely dark inside. Jack always had a torch on him, in fact his pockets were always full of random items that he deemed would be useful one day! He turned his torch on and gave out a great gasp of surprise: 'Look inside it's completely hollow it's like a room inside here.'

The other two peered in and gasped in disbelief. Inside the enormous trunk of the tree, was a room. The shadows flickered as he shone his torch around and could just make out furniture. Cecile had a torch, which she turned on. It illuminated the room. The three of them ducked their heads right down, to fit through the small entrance hole.

They found themselves in a great round room with undulating walls, that made up the inside of the tree. The room was obviously at least a few centuries old, and no one seemed to have lived there for a long time. It looked as if it was once home to a legendary explorer, or someone equally exciting. There was a dark wooden desk with a simple leather top, which was once a rich emerald green and had faded gold patterning around the edge.

At the back of the leather writing surface was a dipping pen and next to it was a delicate glass, open topped bottle, which showed the lines and residue of what had once been dipping ink. In the centre of the leather surface was a pile of crispy parchment charts.

In front of the desk there was a simple looking chair that had been made from thick branches and sections of wood. The four legs were all different thicknesses and still showed notches. It sat still sturdy, at a slight angle and had a natural charm about it.

The walls of the tree room were not quite flat and had charming nooks and crannies, used - by whoever had lived there - to create shelves. Suzan noticed a few books perching on one shelf and as she reached up to pick them up, they disintegrated into dust.

Daisy - B

Gently Jack pulled the wooden panel away. Behind it there was a nice dry cubby-hole. Inside was a scrolled piece of paper, held within a single large napkin-ring-sized, wooden ring.

The three companions sat in a little circle, shining their torches down on the scroll. It was very old, and it looked similar to the one that they had found in the palace.

Of course, they knew *who* had written it. They knew it was going to contain something interesting and probably another wild goose chase.

Carefully and gently, they slid the ring from the scroll of paper. Very gently and delicately Jack unrolled it, so that they could read it together.

They leaned in, eagerly and enthusiastically, to see what was written. And this is what it said:

"To my dear friends,
If you're reading this, it means that maybe many years have passed since my treasure hunting pirating days. It means that you have been to the Palace of greed and survived! It means that you found my clue and you've sailed here, and it also means that, despite such a long journey and a hungry stomach, you have not eaten my dear animal friends. This island is a dear place to me. A place where I spent many a time alone reflecting over the years: the uncountable treasures that I've taken and the deeds that I've done and on the life that I have led as a pirate. And, more importantly, how - one day in the future - the world might be different and perhaps people might have gentler hearts.

I trust by now you may have also tasted the fruit of this tree. Don't worry it is completely safe! It is a very, very special fruit indeed, for it will fill you as if you've eaten a whole meal in just one mouthful, and it will rejuvenate you, as if you've slept for many days. I have never in all my travels around the world, in all my adventures, found this fruit anywhere else.

And I trust you have met my dear companions of this island. the dear little beautiful white creatures who live here. I always used to call them Cujies. You will find that the longer you spend here the more relaxed they become around you.

After knowing me well, like companions, they used to come in my tree home, share meals with me and nestle up to me. They are in fact extremely intelligent creatures, but unfortunately, I never found a way to communicate with them, beyond gestures. But you'll know, by looking in their eyes, that there is great peace, kindness tranquillity and wisdom in their hearts. I have never found these creatures on any other islands, and I have been very careful to never document them, for the fear that maybe they would soon become extinct, if people started coming to see them or made them pets. Treat them with kindness. And my friends, I'll give you a word of warning... never ever eat these animals. If you're hungry on this island, you'll find that this tree will give you everything you ever need.

Treat my little retreat home with kindness and care and stay for as long as you wish. Do you know that out of all the most majestic, beautiful places, I've travelled to in this world, this is probably my favourite place? This is where I wrote my memoirs, after I retired. I came here to sit at my desk and be alone and I spent many years in solitude, here, reflecting on my life. Well, it's time for me to give you your next destination. But take care though, for only the purest and the kindest hearts will make it."

This time it was signed, unlike the other letters:

"Yours faithfully, your friend."

After the message was a set of longitude and latitude coordinates.

243

Their excitement mounted as they read the words.

'CC wrote his memoirs here,' exclaimed Suzan. 'He wrote his book in this very tree.'

'*And,* we now have coordinates for our *next* destination,' Jack said, excitedly.

Sitting on the floor of CC's tree-room, they chatted together – happy and elated. Eventually they grew tired. It had been a long day. They had been walking around the island most of the day and it was really nice to relax – especially after their exciting discovery.

There was a kind of peace inside the tree. A kind of wisdom too, a little like the cute little animals – the cujies – who seemed so calm and so wise.

Cecile had some spare blankets she had brought with her in case they were needed. They put the blankets round them and lay down for a while. Maybe it was excitement, or maybe it was all the walking, but the three of them drifted off into a great peaceful sleep. They slept all evening and all night.

CHAPTER 41

GLUTONY AND EXTINCTION

As the first light of the early morning crept into the hollow of the tree, and the spectacular dawn chorus began, the children and Cecile awoke to find themselves covered in tiny little cujies. They had all come in, to warm up for the night and to keep them company. They really were the sweetest, cutest, loveliest little animals you could ever imagine. Suzan, Jack, and Cecile were careful not to hurt any, as they got up.

They ate some of the fruit and they picked quite a lot of it, so that they could take some back. They wondered what had happened to the Boar and his men and where they had spent the night.

The three decided to take a walk back and tell the Boar about the exciting tree and everything else. But to their horror, when they arrived back to the camp in the small clearing where they'd left them the day before, they were in exactly the same place. But they looked duller and slower, and they looked like they had been sitting eating all night.

The children began to tell them about the tree, but the Boar and his crew really didn't seem interested at all. Their only interest was in eating more and more of the cujies. it was as if they were addicted to them. Sitting, the dribble slid down the sides of their mouths, as they started to talk and salivate about more and more dishes with cuji. The chef scurried around cooking more and more.

The children were in shock and horror for there was a great gluttony that had come over the crew members and the Boar. All they did was to eat.

After hearing the story of CC, with these creatures as his companions. And having stared deeply into their eyes, the three of them knew that it was very wrong to eat the creatures.

They tried to persuade the Boar to stop, but he wouldn't. He filled his cage with many of them and said he was going to take them back to the mainland, where he was going to breed them and sell them, but in the meantime, he must eat more and more of them. He refused to leave the island until he had had his fill.

The children didn't know what to do. Eventually, deciding they could not stand it any longer, they went back, and they spent time in the tree. They were not hungry because they could eat the tree's fruit, and they had water. Luckily, Jack had brought the sextant and the book, so they read some of the stories of CC and were amused by the thought that, maybe two or three hundred years ago or more, he had sat in that very tree and written that book.

It was almost poetic that, as they were stepping in his footsteps, they were also entwined in his story and he in theirs. In fact, it was more than just a coincidence. There was a strong thread that ran deeply through their lives and inexplicably intertwined them.

Many days went by and every day or two they went back to the Boar and every day he and his crew looked duller and lazier and more and more gluttonous than the day before. Day by day there were less and less cujies as well, until one day they woke up and there were none. They walked around the island, from path to path, and there was not a single cuji left in sight.

Feeling angry and sad, they returned to the Boar. To their dismay the only cujies were the ones left in the Boar's cage, the ones he was going to take back. He didn't seem to care about taking any for his collection, to breed and to sell anymore. All he cared about was eating them. And he didn't even seem to care about the treasure anymore.

'Please, stop eating them,' pleaded Suzan.

'The ones in your cage are probably the last left in the world. You've almost eaten your way through the whole population of cujis on the island. You've eaten them almost to extinction. Please stop now, *before it's too late*,' begged Cecile.

'There might be plants that taste *even* better,' suggested Jack.

The Boar was relentless, he and his crew were totally overcome with gluttony. Each day Cecile and the children had debated, each day they had pleaded, each day they had shouted - only to be quietened by the Boar's crew, who were so caught up in their gluttony that they would not stop, until the creatures were all gone... eaten to extinction.

The children and Cecile hung their heads and walked away, as tears trickled down from their eyes. Even Cecile who was a grown woman and had seen and experienced so many things, walked away, and cried. Silently they sat – alone in the empty, quiet hollow tree – crying.

The next day the children came back to find the Boar shouting and screaming and the cage of cujies completely empty. More tears trickled down the children's faces. That man… that great round gluttonous man had eaten his way through the entire population on the island. In frustration he and his men searched every corner of that island, for more cujies. They would do anything at that moment, anything at all, just to eat one more. Sadly, there were no more. All gone. Extinct. Extinct in just over a week.

Finally, certain that there were no more cujies left, no more food left… the Boar and his men left. The children and Cecile followed, with their heads hung low, tears still streaming from their eyes.

CHAPTER 42

THE LAST OF THEIR KIND

When they arrived back at the ship, they went straight to their cabins and cried, for it was a tragedy. Such a horrible experience, to have found a new and beautiful kind of animal, just to see someone make it extinct in just over a week.

Suzan and Jack lay back in their beds. Cecile couldn't sleep, she just stared at the wall. They could hear the Boar shouting and screaming. He was not his usual self: calm, hospitable and kind. He had turned into an angry beast, craving the taste of Cuji; nothing else quenched his appetite. He was angry… terribly… terribly angry.

Cecile listened to the bangs and screams and shouting; she stared at the corner of her room with the lights down low. Something strange there caught the corner of her eye, her peripheral vision. It was her bag. She had placed it on the desk, because it contained her notebook and some other important things.

Somehow it did not look quite right… somehow…it was moving! Or rather, *something* inside it was moving.
She gazed upon it with confusion and curiosity and to her great surprise she saw it flex, move and reshape itself. Something inside it was moving!

249

Help… she thought, *maybe a snake's crawled into it. I've heard about this; they crawl up into warm places, when it gets cold. I should run.* But… being a brave woman of the world, she decided that she must discover what it was.

Stepping boldly towards the bag, keeping her head and her body away, she stretched and reached out her arm, very slowly and carefully, and opened the buckle that held down the flap, at the top of the bag. Then, very carefully and cautiously, still keeping a distance, she peered in…

Suddenly, something jumped out at her. Something leapt out and grabbed on to her. It made her jump. She was scared that it might be a snake, a spider or a rat. After a moment of panic, she came to, and peered down to see what it was.

To her great thrill and excitement, it was a terrified, yet alive and well cuji! Cecile stroked it and cuddled it and after a few moments it became calm. Just then she noticed that her bag was still moving. She took a closer look. Huddled together inside her bag were four more cujies.

She placed the cuji, in her arms, back in the bag and spoke softly to them all. They felt the gentleness of her voice and relaxed, snuggling together inside her bag.

'What do I do? I cannot let the Boar know that you five exist,' Cecile said, as she loosely pulled the flap back over the top of the bag. 'Now, little ones, stay very still, just for a few moments.'

Cautiously Cecile crept out of her room, looking left and right. Swiftly she went next door, into the children's room. Quickly and quietly closing their door, she sat with her back against it, just in case someone decided to come in and ask them to come to supper or something. She didn't want them to be discovered at any cost!

The children looked at her rather odd behaviour, in utter bemusement, with gaping mouths.

'Come closer, both of you,' Cecile said, as she pointed down to her bag.

Suspiciously Jack and Suzan approached and crouched in front of her. Cecile put her finger, to her lips, gesturing for them to be quiet. Carefully she opened the bag and out jumped two of the cujis. They clasped onto the children, one on Jack, one on Suzan. Amazed and ecstatic, that there were still a few cujis alive, Suzan and Jack just about managed to stop themselves from screaming with joy and surprise.

Cecile, Jack and Suzan whispered to each other and discussed plans to make sure that the Boar would not find out that some cujis were still alive, on his ship, under his greedy nose.

Somehow they had to keep them quiet, and somehow they had to get them back to a similar habitat or, even better, the same habitat.

Eventually, they came up with a plan. They would say that one of them was not feeling very well and needed to stay in his or her room.

Cecile suggested that it would be better if it was her, as she could be more convincing and more cunning, at keeping the creatures out of sight and earshot. She also had plenty of the fruit left, so she could feed them. She could guard the cujies and in a few days they would smuggle them onto their boat and part company, politely, with the Boar.

That evening as the ship cut its way proudly through the rough waves of the open sea and the chugging engines pushed the ship ever closer to the port, the sun disappeared over the watery horizon in a spectre of fiery glory. And both Jack and Suzan dried their eyes and emerged from their cabins like creatures from a cocoon.

They had seen a very horrid side of the Boar now and really didn't want to spend any more time with him. But they put on smiles and pretended to be happy, so that they could keep the cujies secret and not arouse suspicion.

Arriving at dinner, Suzan explained that Cecile was feeling a little seasick and wanted to sit dinner out. The Boar bought the excuse, along with his crew. He didn't for a minute suppose that there were any cujies left – why would he?

The children enjoyed the chef's meal that evening, despite the company. After they had had their fill, they went back to their cabins to settle down for the night. In their bunks, they chatted together about CC and that humble house in the tree, wondering more and more about his adventures. They listened to the sea crashing on the bow of the ship and were rocked gently to sleep by the rhythmic sway.

Eventually, they were awoken by the early morning light streaming in through the window. After washing and dressing, both children spent the day maintaining the same seasickness excuse for Cecile and keeping up their happy faces.

That evening again they went to dinner, made apologies for Cecile, and ate some of that great chef's delicious food, sneaking a little into a container – to give to Cecile. The Boar appeared to be getting back to his usual calm self, but inside he was still deeply angry that he couldn't eat any more cujies. Instead, in an attempt to quench the fiery hunger, he ate even more food than they had ever seen him eat before. Plates and plates and plates. He ate until he felt sick and then ate some more.

After dinner Jack and Suzan went onto the top deck to watch the moon. The moon was large and hung low that night, faint and hazy, covered by drifting clouds of fog. Like an animal darting behind a hedge only to reappear again, moments later, on the other side.

After a while the children began to feel drowsy and decided to turn in for the night. They settled down into their comfortable bunk beds, snuggled under the covers and turned off the light.

Beneath their covers they chatted about some of their school friends and wondered what their friends might say, if they heard about their adventures. Gradually the words slowed and trailed off into silence.

Suddenly, in the middle of the night, abruptly, they were awoken from their dreams. Startled into consciousness they heard, and they felt, a large explosion. And that is all they remembered…

CHAPTER 43

A FAMILIAR FACE

Suzan and Jack awoke to a familiar face. A face they had not seen for a long time. Long untidy green hair hung down her back. And deep rich majestic green eyes bedazzled them. They gazed up from their beds to that warm and loving familiar face.

'Muuuuum… mum,' Suzan cried out, you're not going to believe the dream I've just had!'

Then Jack cried out: 'Mum! When did you arrive back from work? I've just had a crazy dream, all about pirates.'

'Don't worry children,' the green-eyed lady said. 'You'll feel better after some more sleep.'

With exhaustion both children drifted off again. But this time they had joy and contentment in their hearts. It must have all been a dream and even better, their mum was home. Just a dream!

'The Hound wasn't real and… and… nor was the Boar. All a dream... We're home… Mum's home… All just a dream,' Suzan muttered, as she drifted to sleep.

Later they awoke, for a few moments, feeling full of energy and excitement.

'Jack, mum's home. And I've just had a nightmare,' said Suzan.

'Yes, I had a nightmare too,' replied Jack. 'There was the most fearful man, his name was the Hound.'

'Yes, he was in my dream too. He was the most horrid man.'

As the candlelight flickered in their bedroom – or what they thought was their bedroom – slowly their mum's smile faded away and they fell asleep once more.

As the children slept, Cecile opened her eyes to a hazy candle lit room. She had a splitting headache and felt as if she had had too much to drink, but she had not drunk anything.

The last thing she remembered was being awakened, in the middle of the night, by some kind of explosion and angry shouting, but that was all. The rest was a blur, a hazy blank.

She looked around at her new surroundings, racking her brains to try to remember how she had arrived there. It wasn't the tiny cabin that she had fallen asleep in, on the Boar's ship. It was a larger room and made mostly of wood. It was difficult to make out. Though – as the candlelight flickered – there was something oddly familiar about the room, as if she had been there before, but she could not remember when, or why.

As Cecile searched her memories of countless adventures and stories, there was a sudden knock at the door. The old wooden cabin door gently creaked open and a strangely familiar face peered around. The lady had green majestic eyes and long, muddled messy green hair. She stepped into the cabin, softly and gracefully, and knelt beside the bed.

'Hello old friend,' she said, looking directly into Cecile's eyes, 'it's been a while since we last saw each other.' The lady's voice was soft and gentle and filled with kindness.

A flicker of recognition, swept through Cecile. 'Of course, I remember you. You helped the talking owl. That article I wrote, made me famous!'

'That *was* a wonderful adventure. I'm so pleased we were able to help that poor owl,' replied the green haired lady, smiling – her green majestic eyes sparkling. Suddenly her smile faded, and her face was full of concern and guilt. 'I'm really, really sorry that we tranquilised you, to bring you here.'

'WHAT? Why would you do that? And what is going on?' Cecile demanded, in a raised voice, momentarily outraged.

'I must explain,' replied the green haired lady, 'we thought you were part of the Boar's crew! Along with my children too! I gave orders for everyone to be tranquilised. It was a shock to see you and the children brought on board!' Her voice then lost some of its warmth and kindness and her tone became sharper as she said: 'What were you doing with my children? They went missing from a museum weeks ago. Why are they with you?'

Cecile reacted to the change in tone in the green haired lady's voice and she too was colder and sharper in her reply, blurting out: 'How dare you tranquilise me, why did you do that, Captain Green?'

Both ladies took a moment to calm down and rationally explain themselves to each other. They were indeed old friends and really wanted to believe that there was a perfectly good reason for the events.

Daisy - B

In a composed and more gentle voice Captain Green said, 'I think you should go first. I hope you can explain, because kidnapping is a serious offence, and friends or not friends, I will turn you over to the police, if you are lucky!'

'No, no, I didn't kidnap them,' Cecile burst out, 'I can explain. You know I wouldn't do a thing like that. I'll tell you what really happened, but it's an exceptionally long story…'

CHAPTER 44

AN OLD FRIEND

Captain Green pulled up a chair and beckoned Cecile to begin her story. Cecile told the long tale of how she had met the children and how they had saved her life. How they were searching for the legendary treasure of CC. She told her how the children had found the sextant and the book.

Captain Green wore an expression of surprise and disbelief, as she listened to the story that was unravelling in front of her. 'Reality is sometimes stranger than fiction!' she chuckled, as Cecile reached the middle of the tale.

Cecile nodded in agreement. 'As you know I've made my career from the strange and mysterious. But this *is* by far the strangest mystery that I've ever come across.'

Cecile continued, and as she spoke of their escape from the terrible man called the Hound, Captain Green remembered that her children had been muttering his name in their sleep a while earlier. *Now* she realised why.

She listened engrossed in the story of how Cecile and the children had sailed the yacht. She heard all about the damaged sail and how the Boar had saved them from starving and offered to take them to a port and the kind host he had appeared to be.

When Cecile reached the bit about the island of Cujies, tears trickled down both of their faces at the thought of the gluttonous Boar. Suddenly Cecile remembered her bag. She jumped out of her bed, frantically looking around for it.

'Are you looking for the strange, cute cujies that were in your bag? Don't worry, they're safe. I wondered where they'd come from.

'As you know I've made it my life to protect and defend animals. I've *never*, in *all* my travels, seen any creature like them before. They're in a comfortable, special area and are being cared for by my team,' reassured Captain Green, as she settled down into her chair and untensed, for she now knew that there was a good reason for her children to be with Cecile. In fact, she was really grateful to Cecile, for looking after the children. And she realised that, in fact, Cecile, Suzan and Jack had saved each other's lives. Later on, when the children were awake and feeling better, she would let them explain more details to her.

Captain Green was still rather bemused and surprised about the story of the long-lost treasure and how it related to the old story of the Mist. She had been led to believe that the story of the Mist was just a bit of a fun family tale, passed down from her great-great-grandparents, probably from *their* great-great-grandparents. She could remember her mother and father telling her the same story, when she was a girl. And her grandfather told it too. She had never imagined that there was any truth to it, or indeed that somewhere out there, there was a great treasure hidden.

Dragging herself away from thoughts of the Mist, Captain Green peered back at Cecile and suddenly realised that she had not really given her a full explanation of why she had been after the Boar and his crew. 'I guess I owe you a bit more of an explanation.'

Cecile looked expectantly at Captain Green: 'Could you tell me why we're on your ship and what happened?'

'I'm really sorry. I said earlier, I didn't know it was you, or my children. We had a one-off tip about a man, a heinous man. Wanted in fifty-two countries in the world, for *black market* animal smuggling. The Boar! He smuggles some of the rarest animals. Animals that are close to extinction. He smuggles them around the world, to high paying rich people who want to have them as a novelty. Did you ever look in the hold of his ship Cecile?'

'No, we didn't look, but I must admit, now come to think of it, we *did* hear some strange noises on that ship, especially when we were first on board, walking up the stairs, just a little way away from the engine room we could hear bashes, crashes, and cries, but never knew what they were. We usually had no reason to be in that bit of the ship. But on our journey with him, he seemed a kind man and so hospitable and a great host. His chef made us the most wonderful food. I didn't feel too suspicious. But it all makes sense now,' Cecile said, sadly. 'When we saw him on that island, eating all those kind and gentle little animals, we saw another side to him. I can see now that he has no respect for animals and their rights.'

Captain Green nodded her head. 'He might have manners and be a gentle host, but he is a king pin in underground black-market animal smuggling. Because of his animal trafficking, many rare species are close to extinction. They are poached and then sold to the Boar, who then transports and sells them.

'He has made his lifetime career on it and has single-handedly driven fifteen animals to extinction, due to popular demand as pets. Animals that do not adapt to domestication well and need to be in their natural habitat. Often rich people buy the animals as a novelty, but lack the knowledge and environment for them, so they die from incorrect feeding, or neglect.'

Cecile listened and as she listened, she dropped her head in shame. To think that she had been travelling with such a heinous man. A man who had done so much damage to the world.

Captain Green smiled from ear to ear. 'We've got him now!! His animal trafficking days are over,' she exclaimed elatedly. 'And because we have him, his whole network of thousands of people, all over the world, will be lifted. He's going to be handed to an anonymous contact we have – high up in the police force – who will personally see to it that he pays for his crimes.

'He'll be given a jail sentence so long that he won't get out. And his luxury eating days are over. He'll be on bread and water!! And *that's* if he cooperates and tells the police all the names of the people in his network – the smugglers and the poachers.

'The Boar is someone I've been hunting for most of my life. And finally, I've found him!' Captain Green finished, with a glint of triumph.

Cecile looked curious. 'Where is he now?'

Captain Green looked even more thrilled at Cecile's question. 'Don't worry, he's safely locked up in a large animal cage that we took from his ship! Eating bread and water! We thought we'd get him used to it – ready for prison. And we thought that he should have a taste of his own medicine; being locked up in an animal cage!'

The two talked for a little longer and were happy to be in each other's company again. Eventually Cecile lay back and drifted off to sleep again. Silence fell over the ship and the candles burnt down, until they flickered softly – like the last few rays of the sun's light as it flickers over the horizon, in the dusky sky, before the moon and the stars come out.

The two children, Cecile and Captain Green all slept contentedly, knowing that they were all safe. The ship cut its way through the waves and gently rocked under the moonlight. The crew kept them on course. On they sailed…

CHAPTER 45

WAS IT ALL A DREAM?

Next morning, the dawn broke, with great beams of light that bounced off the gentle waves as they bobbed in the distance. First in the middle, like a small pin-prick of light in a piece of fabric; then – moments later – the light tearing open the fabric and engulfing the vast ocean in a warm golden glow of light. The light bounced its way in through the old wooden cabin windows, where the children slept.

Slowly the children stirred, stretched and opened their eyes. Suddenly they could see – the room was *not* theirs. There was now no doubt about it, they were not home, they were on another ship. Sitting bolt upright, they both looked around, filled with confusion.

'Where are we?' asked Suzan.

'I really don't know, I thought mum was back. Where have we been? Are we on a pirate ship?' Jack said, screwing up his face in bewilderment. 'I don't know what *is* and what *isn't* a dream anymore.'

'Are we dreaming now?' asked Suzan, jumping out of bed and walking across the room to Jack. 'Pinch me, Jack, pinch me,' Suzan demanded, as she held out her arm… 'Ow, that hurt. No, we're definitely not dreaming, that's for sure. So where are we? The last thing that I remember is that we were on the Boar's ship.'

'Yes, that's right. That's the last thing that I remember too, so it couldn't be a dream. Do you remember the island with the Cujies, and the island with the Hound?'

'Yes,' replied Suzan sadly.

Both compared their memories and agreed that none of it could be a dream. They strode over to the window and looked out upon the open ocean. There was no indication and nothing to use as a clue to their location. Then they looked around the room for clues too, but there was nothing they could pin down – to tell them where, or *whose* ship they were on.

Suddenly, the door opened with a creak, and their mother walked in, her green eyes glowing with happiness.

'Good morning children. I hope you're feeling better now.'

'Yes, but… but what are you doing here, and where are we? Last time we heard from you; you were on a business trip in Sydney,' said Jack, confused.

'Sit down on the bed over here, children,' their mother said. 'I must tell you the truth. It's something I'm ashamed I've lied about to you. Now, you've seen me here, there's no going back.'

Both children sat down on the bed, one either side of their mother. They looked at her, as if she were half a familiar person and half a complete stranger. Both listened intently.

'Children, I'm really sorry I lied to you both. I've lied all your life. I don't feel good about it, but I did it for the bigger picture. Let me explain. You know that I told you that I was away year in and year out travelling on business. Well, you can see that I am not quite a business-lady.'

Suzan raised her eyebrows in surprise. 'What is it you do then, mum? Do tell us!'

Jack butted in, 'Yes, do tell us mum.'

Captain Green smiled. 'I am an animal activist…'

'What *is* that?' Suzan interrupted.

'It's been your father's passion and my passion, since even before you were born. In fact, we both met each other as animal activists. We've travelled around the world, protecting animals, and stopping them from being hurt, from being smuggled, or stolen. And that's what I do now.

'My crew and I sail around the world and represent animals. We're their protectors. We sail under a flag, a little like that story I always used to tell you both, the story about the Mist.

'Some people might call me a pirate. I'm definitely *not* a pirate who steals for greed or for my own pleasure, but I *sometimes* have to operate outside of the law of the world, because the people I have to deal with and protect the animals from, also act outside the law.

'Take the man who owned the ship you were sailing on, the Boar. He's the kingpin of a huge black market animal trafficking operation. He promotes poachers who kill or capture animals around the world, animals who are almost extinct.

'He then smuggles them to different countries, where they're sold to the highest bidder. And in doing so, he has created a whole industry that promotes animal trafficking and promotes pets that people can't really, truly look after, like novelties.

'The poor animals usually end up dying. And he's the boss, the pinnacle leader. People like him operate beyond the law. And because they operate beyond the law, the animals need someone to protect them. Someone to fight back. Someone who is not afraid to break the rules, to bring down great criminals like the Boar.

'Your father and I spent many years together travelling the seas, protecting and standing up for the animals, trees and nature. Being the voice that it didn't have. Together, we have stopped hundreds of thousands of animals from being hurt or killed,' their mum explained, passionately.

The children gazed at their mother in a new way. Both surprised that she wasn't a businesswoman, but also in awe of her passion and determination to protect the earth!

Captain Green gazed back and then continued: 'Your father and I met protecting nature. I've never told you this story, but it's about time I did...'

CHAPTER 46

ECO WARRIORS

Suzan and Jack waited eagerly, for their mother to begin her story.

'Come on mum, tell us,' urged Suzan, impatiently.

'I was a young teenager, about nineteen years old, when I met him for the first time,' their mother said, smiling a little. 'It was during a great protest that was in a large ancient woodland, in a county that had decided to cut down many of the trees and build a bypass road through. And it was one of my first demonstrations.

I had chained myself to a tree, as had other protesters. And in front of me, chained to a tree, was a tall handsome man. The man who was to become your father!

'It was our friendship that kept us going, throughout the long weeks that we stayed there. We almost starved ourselves and drank only water. We refused to unchain ourselves, as all the time that we were chained to the trees, they couldn't cut them down and build their road.

'Much wildlife would have been killed if they'd built the road there. We spent day and night talking about the world. The state of the world and how people treat the animals.

CA W-B

In our shared passion there was a great love too. And that is how I met your father.'

'He's never told us anything about how you met,' Suzan said indignantly.

'What happened next mum?' demanded Jack.

'After that we travelled the world together, protecting animals and trees and stopping cruel people from harming them. After quite a few years I became pregnant with you, Suzan, and a year or so later you came along too, Jack.

'We had to make an exceedingly difficult decision, for your father and I loved the life we had, standing up for animals. It was for us the only life. But we also agreed that it was not the life for a small child. Not the life for a little child to grow up in.

'We couldn't give you an education, or a stable home and we didn't want you to necessarily follow our ways, for some of the things we do could be seen as piracy. As against the law. Some of the methods that we use are extreme. But that is because we're fighting extreme, terrible people like the Boar.

'After a long, long time of discussing and debating, your father offered to stop his travels as an activist. He made the sacrifice to let me continue. He moved to the city and found a job to try to support you. He's done his best to keep this other life from you and to build an image of a responsible mother that would not sway you becoming like us.

'We wanted you to have an education, friends, a home and a *choice* of what to do. We didn't want you to be on the run, like me. I'm wanted around the world, *not* for hurting animals, but for the methods I've had to use to *protect* them and by many horrible people who want revenge, because I've put paid to their cruel ways, to their profit from innocent creatures. But I can't keep it from you anymore. I hope you're not disappointed in me, or in who I am, or that I lied to you,' she said, with solemn eyes.

Both children wept and hugged their mum. They said that they loved their mum, no matter what her job was, no matter what she did. And that they thought she was a brave and great person for protecting the animals, at a time – especially now – when some animals are more at risk than they have ever been in the history of humankind.

'I'm honoured to have such a strong mum,' Jack said, proudly.

'Me too,' nodded Suzan, 'I think you're an *eco-warrior*, saving trees and animals!'

Captain Green's face dropped, and her voice filled with sadness. 'I'm afraid I'll have to ask you to keep this all quiet, because my real name and identity is known by only a few people. Please call me Captain Green, in front of my crew and everyone else. I have to keep my true identity secret.

'We all have nicknames here, to keep our identities secret and to stop us from being caught. Some of us have had nicknames for so long, that we've even forgotten our real names! It's only when I set eyes on you, here on my ship, that the two worlds I've tried so very hard to keep apart suddenly collided!

'Now it's like a vase dropped on the floor. You can gather the pieces and stick it back together again, but it will never be the same again. I don't know what to do. Please, please keep the secret.'

Jack smiled. 'Of course we will mum, at any cost!'

Suzan nodded. Then her attention switched to another topic. 'So, father used to be like you? What was *his* nickname?'

271

'His nickname was *the Dragon,*' Captain Green replied.

The children realised just how much their father had given up, to give them a stable life.

'Now,' Captain Green said, inquisitively, 'It's your turn. I know you've been travelling with Cecile – incidentally, we once shared an adventure together. I'll tell you about it one day. Anyway, Cecile said that you saved her life and that you were hunting for treasure – from the story I used to tell you? What's that all about?'

Jack and Suzan took it in turns to retell the whole story in far more detail than Cecile had told it. Captain Green sat intently listening to every twist and turn, asking questions about every single detail.

Suddenly, Jack jumped up and from his bag that was sitting in the corner, he pulled the sextant, the old book of memoirs, and the almanac. He spread them all on the floor and their mum, Captain Green, spent a few hours with the children, looking at the memoirs, reading the stories. Jack showed her the letters that they had found at the islands.

Their mum could not believe it. She kept saying: '*Reality is stranger than fiction sometimes,*' quietly, almost to herself.

Finally, Jack showed her the last clue. 'We wanted to find the treasure, because we thought that you were working so hard, as a business lady, and we wanted the money so that you could come home and live with us as a family again.'

Their mother burst into tears. She was so touched that her children would go on such a perilous adventure, so that they could be together as a family.

Suzan perked up: 'I know that you probably want to send us back home to dad. So, we can go back to school and be normal. But look, we've escaped being hurt and have been at sea for a long time now.

'We've come so far and have overcome things that even adults were unable to overcome and solve. We want to know what's at the end of the trail. Even if there's no treasure, we *don't care*. But we just *must* know what's at the end of this.'

Their mother was curiously hooked by the details of the adventure they had experienced and the objects they had shown her. 'Well,' she said, 'it's difficult for me to tell you to go back to being *normal*, to go back to school and be good children, when I clearly haven't led a *normal* life either... Wait here children. I must just go and make a radio call...'

CHAPTER 47

DRAGON'S DESPAIR

Back in the children's grandfather's house in Dover, in a dark gloomy room with the curtains drawn despite it being daytime, sat the children's father. His head was in his hands, and he was in despair.

It had been months since the children had disappeared now, and the police still had no real leads. No one had heard anything of them, despite the fact that he and the police had used social media and many other channels of communication.

He was in total despair. He picked up the bottle of whiskey that he had bought the night before. He had tried to be really strong and to focus on finding them. He had kept telling himself that they would come back. But it had been months now since they had simply gone to the local museum and disappeared.

Tears trickled down his face. He sobbed and sobbed and sobbed. He could not stand it anymore and he had not slept for weeks. All he could think about was where they were, whether they were safe and what had happened that day of their disappearance.

Three times a day he had walked the same journey Suzan and Jack had walked, looking – in the hope that he might find some clue that had been overlooked. He had been in and around that museum hundreds of times, asking the same people the same questions, but nothing. Nothing at all.

All the police knew was that the children had been kidnapped and that there was probably a coach used. The police had asked for the CCTV video footage for that day, but unfortunately the security guard that day had fallen terribly ill and had spent most of the day in the toilet. And so had the person who looked after the video footage. And for some strange reason the footage was completely missing.

The police had drawn the conclusion that probably the kidnappers had planned the whole thing and stolen the video footage, to stop anyone from following their trail. Luckily, there were a few cameras in the streets around the museum. One had captured the children being bundled into the coach, in sacks. But that was all the police knew. The two assailants had been incredibly careful to wear hoods and keep their backs to the cameras.

They had the number plate of the coach, but it had later been found at the bottom of the dock – after a report, by some of the locals, that a coach had rolled off the side. When the divers had investigated, they found it completely empty and abandoned.

Unfortunately, the sea water had washed away any fingerprints and other forensic evidence. The police had to hand it to them, the kidnappers were particularly good at what they did. They obviously hadn't done it alone either. They had to have been connected to other people who had helped them.

When the children had been reported missing, the airports and ports had been notified. The police said they must have been smuggled out of the country, using a dark network of criminals. Otherwise, their passports would have been flagged.

The trail had gone cold a long time ago. Their father knew that but had tried to keep his head up. Deep down he blamed himself for not taking them to the museum and for not being there. He blamed himself for everything. Clearly it wasn't his fault, but he didn't know.

Finally, he had given up hope. He had been sitting on his own and hadn't been to work for days. He hadn't shaved or eaten. All he had done was sit in a chair crying. He pictured his children's faces as they left the door that day. His hands dropped down to the floor, like a rag doll, his head dropped to his chest. Without his children he was a broken, broken man.

Tears rolled down his cheeks like waterfalls over jutting out rocks. He was angry. Sad and deeply depressed. Silence buzzed at his ears, a lonely empty silence that had filled his house.

Suddenly something began to bug him, like a sound on his peripheral hearing. The very edge of audible recognition. It had been there a while, but he had not noticed it. Now, suddenly, he began to wonder what it was.

Reluctantly he dragged his empty self to stand and slowly lethargically stumbled around the room. He stepped out into the hall. It was louder now. What was it? It made him angry and irritated. It was an odd crackling sound. Familiar somehow. It was coming from his bedroom.

After a while he realised what it was and that it was not going to go away. Like someone repeatedly ringing his doorbell and refusing to stop. Like the world knocking at his door, to try to bring him out of his deep and dark state of mind.

He climbed the stairs in an angry state, annoyed at being disturbed. *I don't want to speak to anyone, just leave me alone,* he thought to himself, as he threw open the bedroom door. As he entered the room the crackling became louder.

He stomped over to a CB radio. For those of you who don't know what a CB radio is, it is a two-way radio that can be used to speak on. They were very popular before mobile phones!

The children had seen it several times, but didn't know what it was for, or why he had it. It was a very special one. It was always on – he was very, very particular about that. Resting on the desk, attached to it by a wire, was a microphone.

Turning a few dials, he tuned into a specific channel. The crackle turned into a voice that said: 'Chhhh…t. Green to poppa Bear, do you read me?' It repeated this over and over again. The voice was someone who was so dear to him. The sound of the voice broke through his state of sadness, it was the love of his life.

He wanted to answer, but what was he going to say to his wife? Standing there, in conflict between his love and his fear, he picked up the microphone and in a low soft voice said: 'Poppa Bear to Green I read you.'

There was a pause, as the lady on the other side realised that he had answered. Then the lady, who was of course Captain Green, said joyfully: 'Great news. I have the children here. They're safe and well. It's a long, long story. I can't tell you now. But they're safe!'

There was a pause while Suzan and Jack's father processed this. He was in shock, but the sheer happiness inside him, at hearing these words, was like a volcanic explosion. 'YES!' he shouted in a giant's voice. He was ecstatic and filled with happiness, that his children were safe.

'What happened? tell me a little, I must know!' He said hungry to find out the details.

And then Captain Green, in a strange, coded language that you and I would not understand, told him the main parts of the story.

He was shocked and surprised. 'I want to come out and be with you all.'

'Well, the children want to carry on with their adventure and I feel I owe it to them. They've been so brave. It could take you a couple of weeks to reach where our ship is. Best if Cecile, Suzan, Jack and I carry on, on the small sailing boat. Then you can join us a little later,' Captain Green suggested.

Suzan and Jack's father agreed. 'But make sure you keep them safe.'

'My crew will maintain contact with you and arrange your journey. As soon as you are with them, you'll be able to sail to meet us and then we can adventure together,' explained Captain Green.

They kissed each other goodbye and said how much they loved each other. Then the radio returned to the crackle. Quickly – without any time to lose – their father grabbed a suitcase from a wardrobe and threw an assortment of things into it.

CHAPTER 48

A WEEK LATER!

After her call with Dragon, Captain Green swiftly organized a strong sailing ship, just big enough for the four of them to continue their adventure. Within a week they had followed the last set of coordinates, which had led them to their final clue on a rough and rugged island. They had encountered several trials and narrow escapes, along the way, before Jack finally discovered the clue cunningly concealed in the strangest of places…

Eventually, the four figures wearily rowed back and clambered aboard their strong sailing ship. Suzan pulled the rowing boat by its rope and attached it around the back of the sailing ship, tying it to a large metal loop.

The sun lay low in the sky, as the four of them climbed down the narrow steps that led to the cabin below. A narrow gangway opened to two sets of bunk beds and a small lounge area further on.

The four of them slumped down onto the sofa, wearing a look of tiredness, yet satisfaction and triumph.

'Where to next then?' Cecile asked, whilst clutching her most treasured possession and companion, her notebook, tightly to her chest.

'Jack, would you do the honour?' his mum asked.

A grin appeared on Jack's face, as he slowly reached into the long inside pocket of his jacket and drew out a crumpled and ancient piece of parchment. He held the yellowed, rolled-up piece of paper, with great care and smoothly slid off the large wooden ring that kept it scrolled up.

Their eyes widened as he unrolled the note. And they gazed at that familiar swirly writing.

'Hmmm,' Jack said, to clear his throat and to add a little suspense. He paused and peered at the three faces – all engrossed, transfixed on him. He hesitated just for fun, to allow their suspense to boil, like a kettle left on. Suzan gave him a scowl, which seemed to do the trick. 'It says…

"Hello again my dear friends. If you are reading this, it means that you have survived the tasks and trials I have led you on, so far. It means you are strong, but more importantly you have kind and gentle hearts and you have resisted temptation. The next step of your journey will be the last."'

Jack scanned further down the page. 'There's a new set of coordinates here.' The three were about to jump up. Jack held up his hand. 'Wait, that isn't all of it. There's something else after the coordinates. There seems to be a riddle, it says: *"You must sail to the island that cannot be found. To find it you must stop looking!"* Hummm, how strange.'

'What's that supposed to mean?' asked Suzan, in a confused tone.

'I'm not sure, but I think we could set out for the coordinates and give the riddle some thought on route,' Captain Green suggested.

'*Yes*, let's go,' they agreed in unison.

Suzan jumped up excitedly and ran towards the top deck, followed by the other three.

'Raise the anchor!' Jack bellowed.

'Raising the anchor,' Suzan repeated, as she pulled up the heavy lump of iron, which clicked when it reached the top and locked into place.

The four had been at sea together for only a week or so, but had sailed almost constantly. They worked in perfect unison, like a well-oiled machine. Suzan sprinted around to the wheel and pulled off the leather strap that held it in place. Cecile raised the sails, and Jack pulled out the sextant, to begin taking readings and cross-referencing in the almanac.

Soon the ship was gently cutting through the calm waves that lapped around her, on course for the unknown. The sun slipped down below the horizon, with the last of its rays shimmering upon the surface of the mirror like ocean.

Suzan was exceptionally good at steering now; she kept the ship sailing true, which is no easy task. Sailing ships is not like driving cars, or even motorboats: the wind shifts, and currents constantly adjust the direction of the ship. But Suzan had become very sensitive to just how much to turn the wheel starboard or portside in order to right the course. She kept one eye firmly fixed on the compass and the other out to sea, constantly adjusting and readjusting.

Cecile sat at the rear of the ship, frantically writing notes. Since they had set off, she had avidly taken notes about their journey, their adventure, and had gathered enough material to write hundreds of articles about many different mysteries.

Jack took very frequent readings of stars and the moon, as he plotted their course. And Captain Green kept a lookout and also rustled up some food for them all, when they were hungry.

As the evening turned into the night, the star sprinkled sky and the wispy Milky Way shimmered like a silver scarf. Each took it in turns to rest, while the other three kept the ship sailing on course. For the first few hours Captain Green took a nap, then Jack, then Suzan and then Cecile.

At around three in the morning, Jack was on lookout duty and was peering around the starlit seas, when a strange silvery glimmer came from behind them. He spun round and reached for his telescope, however no sooner had he turned, than the flicker had disappeared. *That's strange, where's it gone? Guess I must just be imagining things,* thought Jack. *Perhaps I'm still sleepy. No, I can't be, there it is again.*

Lightning quick, he spun around and extended his telescope at the very place he had seen the glint, towards the back, just above the sea. But there was nothing there. He rubbed his eyes and again put it down to tiredness. He didn't see it again.

The rest of the night went by uneventfully, as did the following few days. On the fourth morning of their journey Jack plotted their course and announced, in an almost captain like voice: 'We should make landfall today. If my calculations are correct, we're about three hours away from the next island!' His words peppered up his motley crew and they found a sudden spurt of energy.

The four enjoyed a hearty breakfast and kept a sharp eye on the horizon. Three hours slipped by, but alas there was no island.

'It should be here. We're at the exact coordinates. I don't understand,' Jack said, with an air of confusion.

'Maybe we are in the wrong place?' Captain Green enquired.

'No, I've triple checked it. We're in the exact place,' Jack replied confidently.

'Well maybe the island sunk in the last hundred years, or whatever it was is simply no longer here. I once wrote about an island that appeared almost overnight. Landscapes can change over time,' Cecile suggested.

'Or maybe it's a shipwreck on the seabed, with the treasure in it,' Suzan said.

'No, we're in the Pacific Ocean, which is the deepest ocean with an average depth of four thousand metres,' Jack said, matter-of-factly.

'Where's that last note from CC? Let's take another look!' Suzan suggested.

Jack pulled it out of his coat pocket.

'Do you always carry it around with you Jack?' Suzan asked.

'Yeah, it never leaves my side sis! I even sleep with it in my pocket!' Jack said, with glee.

Suzan rolled her eyes. 'O… K, then.'

Jack rolled out the note, on a dry area of the deck and reread the riddle. 'It says: *"You must sail to the island that cannot be found. To find it you must stop looking!"* Hmmm.'

The four of them crinkled up their faces, as they pondered the words.

'How would we stop looking?' Suzan enquired.

'Maybe throw the coordinates and note away,' Captain Green tentatively suggested.

'*NOOOO*, you can't!' Jack blurted out in horror.

'Maybe we should stop sailing for a while and figure it out,' Cecile recommended.

'That's it! We should literally stop sailing! And stop looking,' Suzan said in excitement.

'So, sail to the exact location and then drop the sails, don't steer and stop looking? That would mean we might end up anywhere,' Jack exclaimed, in surprise.

'Hey kids, it's worth a go, right?' their mum said. 'And I reckon that Jack's good enough with that navigation device to find our way back even if we *do* become completely lost, so we don't have too much to lose by trying.'

They turned the ship around and headed back to the exact coordinates.

'OK drop the sails,' Suzan called, at the same time as letting go of the wheel.

CHAPTER 49

DRIFTING

The four of them stood on the centre of the deck. They felt a bit odd, not maintaining control and course of the ship. The stern of the ship gradually drifted around and then, almost as if it was on a rail, the ship started to move in one direction, as if it was being pulled. For the first time, in over a week and a half, the four of them sat down and rested.

They took in the sights of the rich deep blues that faded to the hazy horizon and the waves, as they lapped at the ship. Sure enough, they were travelling somewhere. The ship was completely drifting subject to the sea, yet it was drifting in a set direction, and it was gathering speed too. Soon they were cutting through the sea quite quickly. Amazement swept over the four, like a sudden sea fog.

'How are we even sailing without wind and where are we going?' Suzan asked, perplexed.

'Currents my dear,' Captain Green said softly. 'The seas are full of undersea currents, and we must be riding one!'

They sat back propped against the mast and other items on deck and watched the scenery with awe. For the first time, they were passengers on their own ship.

Suzan peered over the edge and gasped in amazement, as she saw a majestic dolphin surfing the current.

Moments later, it jumped clean out of the water, only to splash into the darkness and disappear and then to reappear again, on the surface.

Jack and the others rushed over to the edge, to peer over.

'Look!' Jack beamed, as he extended a finger to point. 'Wow is that a blue whale?' he asked, in utter disbelief, as a giant puff of water blew up into the sky, a way off in front of them.

They could just make out the whale's large, graceful body as it gently cruised through the water. And that wasn't all. The stretch of water the ship was drifting down was filled with fish, turtles and other marine life in abundance – all surfing the current.

_AW-B_

289

Daisy - B

290

It was strange, because the two children had sailed and travelled on this wild treasure hunt for a while now and they had seen countless amazing things, but had not had the moment, or the presence of mind to enjoy and be in awe of them. But now there was nothing to do but to sit back and enjoy the ride, gaze upon the sights, and wonder at the beautiful animals.

The ship drifted on and so did the day. As the sunset marked the end of the day, the stars crept across the sky and a phosphorescent display flashed and bounced around in the water like fireflies. They lay gazing at the stars, in utter awe.

Jack pointed out some of the constellations but didn't know them all.

'I can't believe there are so many stars,' Suzan said.

'More than all the grains of sand on every beach in the world,' Jack replied.

Cecile smiled. 'I remember some beautiful words, from the Bible. It says…

"Lift up your eyes and look to the heavens: Who created all these? He who brings out the starry host one by one and calls forth each of them by name. Because of his great power and mighty strength, not one of them is missing."'

A silence fell as the four allowed that idea to trickle down, through the chasms of their minds. They drifted off to sleep, in utter wonder at the beautiful world they lived in, whilst watching shooting stars like fireworks. And the ship drifted on, gently rocking them like babies in a pram.

The next day they awoke to the searing sun overhead. And they spent the day relaxing, as they watched the richness of the life around them.

Like the ship, the days drifted on, merging with the dimmed diamond-filled nights like a vivid dream. How long they drifted for, it was impossible to say, but eventually they awoke from a night's rest to see a strange mystery. One by one the dolphins, whales and other sea life all turned away from the current, leaving them drifting alone.

They watched as the last of the animals and fish disappeared into the darkness of the sea. Jack jumped to his feet and rushed to the bow of the ship, to marvel over the sudden change of course that the animals had made. He scanned the sea ahead. 'Look there's a shoal of jellyfish ahead, that must be why the animals and fish left the current.'

The other three came to join him at the front of the ship, to see the jellyfish. But as they drew closer, they looked away in horror.

'They're not jellyfish,' said Suzan... 'They're plastic bags.'

'Oh no, this is horrific. Look there's so many of them,' Cecile said, in a melancholy tone.

Soon, it wasn't just plastic bags. There were other things too: fishing nets, plastic bottles containers, and other pieces of floating plastic. Silence swept over them as they all hung their heads in dismay. The ship slowed. The further they went, the slower it became – until eventually, there was so much plastic, that the ship would not move anymore.

Jack scanned the horizon, with his telescope, and exclaimed: 'We're surrounded by plastic. It stretches as far as my eye can see, in every direction. Directly ahead I can just make out the tiny peak of an island, right in the middle of it all.'

Suzan took the telescope, to see what he meant. And sure enough, right in the middle of all of the plastic, she could make out a brown crop of land that jutted out. 'That's where we need to go. We need to take the dinghy and row through the plastic to get there,' Suzan said, with certainty.

The children looked at their mother for agreement.

'Hmm it looks a little dangerous. What if we become bound up with all the plastic?' Captain Green asked, with concern. She was distracted for a moment, as she turned her head away to survey the ship and the current situation. Then she turned back to her two children. 'Though I don't think we'll be much better stuck on this ship, bound up in all the plastic. Let's row over to the jut of land. But we should take a little food, warm clothes, and other supplies, just in case.'

Suzan and Jack had been waiting with expectant faces. Their faces exploded into smiles, as they sped below deck to gather some supplies and get ready. Ten minutes later they were all climbing down into the little dinghy and setting off towards the island outcrop.

It was slow going and tiring, rowing through so much plastic.

Cecile reached for her notebook. 'I need to do a piece on this.' Swiftly she wrote: *"This is a real and harrowing reminder of the damage that humans have done to the earth."*

'That's good wording and so true,' said Suzan angrily. 'What right have humans to just dump all their plastic rubbish out at sea?'

'Yes,' agreed Jack, 'it's horrid and it kills many beautiful sea animals, fish and birds. That's why all the dolphins and all the creatures and fish stopped swimming alongside our boat…'

No one spoke as they rowed. A solemn silence fell over them like a blanket. Inch by inch they grew closer, until – with a grating bump – the boat hit rock and lodged tight. Jack grabbed the rope that was attached to the dinghy and tied it round a rock on the shore.

They climbed off the boat, jumping onto the rocky surface of the small island. It was a dusty, deep reddish brown. Almost the colour of mahogany. The four of them secured their backpacks with food and provisions and tentatively walked inland. The reddish brown rock shot abruptly up into a sharp jagged mini mountain.

'I've seen this very same weird, shaped mountain before somewhere,' said Suzan, puzzled.

They trekked around the shard-like mountain, to a dusty track that led inland. The sun cast long shadows from the rocky terrain and the salty warm sea breeze brushed past them, ruffling their hair. Following the track took them to a small valley, or recess, at the centre of several jagged mountains.

'Look at those strange small brown and green hills, at the base of the mountain over there,' Suzan said, as she pointed.

'That's odd, it seems to be almost the only greenery on this outcrop,' Jack said.

'And look at the strange vegetation that's fluttering and swishing around in the breeze,' said their mum.

The four stood gazing. 'Something about that seems to strike me as odd. I can't put my finger on it though. It's as if it…,' Jack's words trailed off into a buzzing silence.

Everyone froze. Everyone kept absolutely quiet – so quiet that they became aware of the sound of the sea breeze, dancing around the jagged rocks, and the thumping of their elevated heart beats.

Cecile flinched and in a tiny timid, mouse like voice, whispered: 'It moved.'

'And again,' Suzan mouthed,' with almost no sound.

Suddenly two large eyes, the size of basketballs, fixed themselves on the four statue like figures.

'Don't move an inch,' Captain Green whispered, hardly moving her mouth.

CHAPTER 50

AN AGE-OLD GUARDIAN

Two large eyes continued to glare. Then a great echoey, booming laugh shook the outcrop.

Small stones and rocks rolled from the tops. The four turned and ran. But as they pelted over the rocky barren surface, with their hearts pounding, great thuds grew closer…

THUD, THUD, THUD, THUD. The sunshine seemed to disappear, and they were plunged into darkness by the towering shadow of whatever it was that had paced the island, in just a few steps. Squinting, the four froze mid run. Their eyes started to adjust to the darkness, just as when you turn off your bedroom light. Slowly details began to reach their hungry minds.

'HA HA HA HA,' echoed the great booming sound of laughter, as it shook the outcrop. Staring down at them was a giant!

His proportions and features were just like that of any person, yet he towered at ten times the height of the average human. The giant was old and grey, his face was like a great landscape, carved by the chisels of time. Furrows and trenches moved as he laughed.

AWB

297

His long and tatty hair fluttered in the wind like a great tree canopy of silver, and the torn sections of his old and sun-bleached clothes flapped in the breeze like flags. Yet his body was surprisingly muscular for someone so very, very old.

His arms and legs were filled with scars and blemishes, which oozed of age-old stories and battles and his posture told no lies as to his age, like a curved and ancient old tree.

The giant's eyebrows, like two great silver hedgehogs, arched in a fixed solemn expression. He looked angry, yet there was a touch of kindness behind those solemn eyes. *'WHO ARE YOU AND WHAT DO WANT HERE?'* the giant bellowed, his eyebrows and gaze still glued to them.

'Gulp,' Suzan and Jack said in unison.

'Err,' Captain Green mustered.

Cecile, the great mystery solver, just stood in utter shock. She thought she had seen just about everything, but a giant, well – she was dumbfounded, overcome by surprise, but also excitement. She had set out looking for proof of giants but had *never* thought she would be staring into the eyes of one.

Suzan managed to pluck up a little courage. 'Please don't hurt us. We were led here by CC's clues.'

'Now that's a name I haven't heard for *at least* two or three hundred years,' the giant boomed, a smile almost forming in the corner of his mouth. A ripple of emotion seemed to wash over the landscape of the giant's face, like a field of grain rippling in the wind. CC's name awoke and stirred powerful memories in the giant. And his eyes softened.

'You know of CC?' Suzan asked, her voice rather shaky.

'I do, but what makes you think you can turn up here and I'll suddenly believe your story?' The smile shifted to a frown and the tenderness to ice.

Suzan was scared yet determined. 'We've travelled thousands of miles, been kidnapped, been from island to island, almost died so many times, just to find another note from *CC,* leading us somewhere else. Like one long wild goose chase. All with the promise of treasure. And so far, the only treasure worth finding has been finding our mother and truly knowing her.' With tears trickling down Suzan's face she gazed up at her mother and turned to walk away. 'In fact, you know what. My mother is worth all the gold in the world, I don't care about treasure anymore. Let's go home everyone.'

Astounded, Jack looked at Suzan and mouthed: 'You can't talk to a giant like that, he'll crush you.'

The giant's eyes bounced between Jack, Suzan and their mother, until they finally settled on Suzan again. A great sunrise smile crept over the landscape of that solemn giant's face, for the first time in maybe a *long time*.

Jack and Cecile cowered as suddenly the giant crouched down and knelt in front of Suzan.

'Dear child, you're right, family is by far one of the greatest treasures we can ever have. We must never forget that.' The giant's tone was softer, as a great wet tear – the size of a bucket of water – splashed them all. 'Come you all and sit with me. Tell me your tale. I've room for one more yarn in my memory.' And without warning, the giant stood up and started to walk back towards the bottom of the mountain shard where he had originally been sitting.

Daisy-B

Suzan began to walk in that direction too, but a firm hand grabbed her. 'You're lucky he didn't grind us up and make us into bread!' her mother said with severity in her eyes.

'Sorry mum, but he seems nice. Let's go and chat to him. I really don't care about finding the treasure anymore. But when are you going to get the chance to meet a real giant and chat to him again?' She gave a cheeky smile.

'Well not for a few days!' retorted Jack with a chuckle.

The stomp across the island, that took the giant merely moments, took a little longer for the four of them! But soon they arrived at the base of the rock, where the giant was now sitting. The giant held a large handleless cup of hot tea and glanced down, pointing to four piping hot cups of some kind of tea.

Jack crouched near one of the cups. Peering up at the giant's bath-sized cup and then down to the human sized cup before him. 'Why do you have human sized cups?'

The giant laughed a great rumbly laugh. 'You think you're the first humans that I've met? I've watched your species grow and evolve and in days of old, before the metal birds took to the skies, I would often share a cup with a passing sea-leg. That is, the few who came here by accident, for most came to fight.' The last few words carried a solemn and sad tone.

His eyes glanced over some of his scars for a few moments, before they flashed back to the four humans.

'To be honest I've watched civilisations come and go and the depths that your race is capable of. Greed, gluttony, and anger have driven most to fall, one way or another.' His eyes glazed over, as if he was holding back a thousand tears. He turned his head to the side quickly, took a deep sigh, and when he looked back, he was smiling again. 'But those particular cups belonged to great friends of mine. But enough about me. When you've lived for close to a thousand years, your head swims with memories like the sea with fish. Suzan, your story, my dear?'

Suzan's face lit up, 'How did you know my name?'

The giant chuckled and continued to look expectantly at her. Suzan began, 'Well, it all started when we had to move away from our city…'

The giant listened intently, and not once did he break his gaze or attention in the whole story. It took Suzan quite a while to explain every detail and twist and turn of their journey.

The giant asked questions, nodded, and followed every detail with a plethora of emotion, which shifted the landscape of his face. Jack, like Suzan's assistant, pulled out various items, as they emerged in the story.

By the end of the story, the five were surrounded in items and letters. Jack went to taste his tea; strangely it was still very hot. He pulled back, as the hot liquid scolded his lips. The giant noticed, and before they could all move, he took a *giant* breath and a great gust of wind whistled around them, cooling the liquid.

Jack tried his tea again; it was just right. 'Hmmm, what is that?' he asked, as he rolled the liquid around his mouth in curiosity.

'That's a tea made from herbs from my garden,' he bellowed, while gesturing to a section of land that looked cultivated. There were many vegetables that they recognised, potatoes, carrots and onions, but there were also many items that they had never seen before.

'It's a type of herb that we used to grow in Aquasentia, my home. I managed to save a few seeds and grow it here. It's related to the herb you call mint.'

The four enjoyed their tea. It was warm and refreshing.

'Where is Aquasentia?' Cecil asked, with bulging eyes, her fingers already reaching for her notebook.

CHAPTER 51

A TEA PARTY

'What's this, a tea party?' The voice was smooth and calm. The man stood in front of them, his eyes narrowed, like a leopard ready to pounce. His moustache well-kept and waxed into sharp points. A fresh scar ran down the entire length of his face.

One of his eyes appeared a cloudy white, possibly blinded. And his sharp flamboyant rich jacket seemed to hang limply, over the area where his arm had once been.

He held a golden pistol, directly aimed at the giant's head. 'Why was I not invited?' he asked, one eye twitching, but voice still smooth and silky.

Suzan and Jack's faces drained of colour, as their wide eyes bulged with shock. Cecile and Captain Green looked the man up and down in puzzlement. The man's last question seemed to hang in the air, like an unpleasant smell.

'Well?' he pressed, with a slight hint of anger this time.

Jack and Suzan were horrified and struck dumb with fear. Silence blew around them.

Hound &
A.W.B

The giant let out a great roar of laughter, which seemed to fuel a great fire in the man. His eye twitched so rapidly now, that it was impossible to see whether it was open or closed. And his face twisted into rage. Yet he maintained composure over his aim and stance, as if he was no stranger at all to rage; as if he was the kind of man who thrived within it, like fire in a forest.

'Clearly you have trouble taking me seriously, big man!' And without warning he jolted his gun and aimed it at Jack. A loud *CRACK* sounded, echoing, and bouncing around the rock face.

By the time everyone had realized what had happened and gained control over their shock, Jack was lying clutching himself in agony. Suzan rushed over to him and held him.

'No, Noooooooooooo,' she cried out, as she tried to stop the bleeding.

'Sss sis…,' groaned Jack, as he drifted in and out of consciousness.

The man didn't even look at Jack, he just glared at the giant. 'Perhaps I'm not making myself clear enough here,' he said, wrestling with rage. 'Give me the *ultimate treasure*! *Now*.' Conquering his rage, his voice became smooth once more. 'I'm the Hound, the *greatest* treasure hunter who's ever lived.' He peered around as if waiting for an impressed and subservient response to his declaration.

AWB

The giant's warm and kind eyes turned to icy glares. His great strong hands picked up Suzan, Jack, Cecile and their mum, with the gentleness of a mother bear taking her cub in her mouth. He placed them gently down behind him.

'Clearly you don't want to do as you're told *you stupid giant*,' the Hound roared, rage now surging through his veins. 'I've travelled far and wide and …' His eyes gazed down at his empty sleeve and at the scars on his remaining hand, 'and… paid a price for this moment. Now give me the treasure: it's mine!!'

And, like a flood-gate giving way, he erupted. Lights flashed from the barrel, as cracks rang out. Crack after crack exploded from the automatic pistol, as the Hound gave way to his rage.

Suzan clutched Jack, shielding his ears from the sounds that made him twitch. Captain Green knelt at Jack's other side, crying. Only Cecile peered around the side of the giant and watched as the smoke from the gun drifted like a veil.

The Hound waited for the smoke to clear, muttering: 'I do love it when I have to take treasure by force.' His tone was ecstatic. But surprise suddenly swept over his face, for the giant continued to sit upright, like a mountain, unmoved and unscathed.

A stone-faced look came over the giant's face, and he narrowed his eyes. 'You're the worst of the human race! I've met thousands of men and women, over the centuries. Pirates, privateers, kings, treasure hunters, smugglers, robbers, and you're all the same. Each has their own justification and story, yet all have lost their hearts to greed. You're *nothing special*, little man. What can your treasure really buy you?' He gazed behind him, at

Suzan suddenly filled with compassion and concern for Jack. 'This girl has far more treasure than you can ever begin to imagine.' The giant continued.

The Hound let out a laugh. 'That stupid girl? She's a poor little runt. I had her kidnapped, along with her stupid brother.' He aimed his gun again at the giant's head. 'Let's not play games, just give me the treasure. The ultimate jewel, the ultimate treasure, which was the Mist's. And I can be on my way.'

'I cannot give you something that cannot be owned. And I cannot show you what you would not truly see. And I cannot let you be in awe of something that you would never truly appreciate. And I cannot let you hold that which cannot be held but must be cherished.

'You are a man who values treasure by its monetary worth, like many a pirate of old. This treasure would mean nothing to you. Yet it *is* the most beautiful jewel in the universe!' And with that, the giant picked up the Hound by his arm and tossed him like a ragdoll.

The Hound hurtled through the air, twisting and turning. And still he flew, as Cecile watched she saw him getting smaller and smaller until he was just a tiny dot, and still he hurtled through the air. Where he landed, and whether he sunk, or swam, well that is for another tale!

CHAPTER 52

WOUNDED

The giant's eyebrows closed together in a great face of concern, as he turned his head to inspect Jack. 'He'll be okay! Suzan, look at me.'

Suzan tore her eyes away from her brother for a moment and found herself looking into two ginormous, kind eyes.

'Listen Suzan. Jack's going to be okay. It's just his shoulder. But he has gone into shock and has lost blood. We need to act quickly. Run over there and pick the green herb that has red teardrops on its leaves. Be quick.'

Suzan jumped to her feet and tore over to the herbs growing nearby. She scanned the neatly kept beds, filled with different vegetables and herbs. She passed mint, thyme, and many that she had never seen before, until she came to a small patch with a clump of tall, dark green leaved plants that had tiny teardrop shaped red dots all over them.

She plucked a leaf and raced back over the dusty path towards the giant. Arriving in a panting mess, she handed him the herb leaf. He was already sitting by Jack and holding a giant pestle and mortar, which is a kind of bowl and crushing implement.

The giant gently peeled away the leaf sections either side of the stalk, and placed them into the mortar. He began mashing the leaf up with the pestle, until the leaf was a brownish, red mush. Tearing a small section of fabric from his clothing, he delicately placed the mush on Jack's wound and wrapped the fabric around it, to hold it all in place.

'The herb originally came from Aquasentia and has been used for thousands of years, to heal wounds. It draws out impurities, is an antiseptic and aids quick healing. It also helps with shock. CC always carried some, whilst battling the seas,' the giant said, as he gazed down at the small human sized cups that they had been drinking out of earlier – he seemed lost in a haze of memories.

'Ahhhhh. Ow. He shot me.' A rather groggy voice came from Jack, as his eyes slowly opened. The giant grinned and gently tapped him. 'Rest, Jack; don't try to stand yet. Let the wound seal. You were lucky that the bullet passed straight through. In the days of old, musket shots were far messier.'

Suzan rushed over to Jack. 'Are you ok? I thought you were dead!'

Jack opened his eyes again and a grin slowly appeared on his face. 'Of course I am, who else would you find to beat you at ... well everything.' He chuckled to himself until his shoulder stung.

'You wish!' Suzan replied.

The giant laughed, a great roar, as he listened to the two bantering.

'Jack must not sail for a day or so, while his shoulder heals. So, you're all welcome to stay with me.' The giant said, in a loud, rumbling tone.

'Are you sure you have space? I mean, you've done so much for us already, saving Jack's life,' Captain Green asked politely.

The giant's great silver-grey eyebrows lifted, and a kind smile rippled across his face, revealing several smile or laughter wrinkles. 'It's no trouble. I have a lot of space. It's at least two centuries since people last stayed here, but I've washed the sheets, so don't worry!' The giant joked.

Without warning, the giant stood up and very gently scooped Jack up. Cradling him in the palms of both hands, he slowly walked towards the base of the cliff. Suzan, Cecile and Captain Green jumped up and followed.

At the base of the cliff there was a giant wooden door. Its red wood blended in with the red rocks around. The door swung open to reveal a long corridor that appeared to be carved from the rock. The walls were lit by old oil lamps and the giant wandered slowly down a passage that led downhill. It curved and twisted and turned.

Occasionally they passed small alcoves and doors set into the rock. Eventually the passage opened into a large cavern; the ceiling had long stalactites that hung down, like natural chandeliers. Against the wall was a gigantic sofa, big enough for the giant to sit on. And next to it, a giant chair, that seemed to have a strange wooden structure built over the top.

The walls were lined with shelves, filled with old books; some great shelves holding books that were bigger than Cecile. On another wall hung an amazingly old pirate flag, it was so old it was in tatters, but they could just make out the faint lines of original markings against the black background. And on the other wall there sat two giant polished red wood doors. They both had old black forged iron hinges and handles. And right at the base of both doors, there were small human sized doors, almost like cat flaps! On the final wall there hung a strange selection of old items, items the four had never seen before.

The giant placed Jack on top of the strange wooden structure, over the giant chair. Suzan spotted a set of wooden stairs that led up to the structure.

'Hang on Suz, let me go first,' her mum said. She led Suzan and Cecile up the creaky old wooden stairs, round and round to the very top, where she found herself several storeys high on a sturdy platform, which had an ornate wooden banister all the way around.

In the centre where Jack lay, raised high on soft cushions, there were six ornate chairs. Cecile, Suzan and Captain Green sat in a semi-circle, near Jack.

314

'Welcome to my humble home! I don't think that I have told you my name. I am Elgor, the last caretaker,' the giant said, quite softly, but with an air of grandeur.

'Elgor, *You're Elgor*, like the label in our old family photo album,' said Suzan excitedly. 'When we first moved into our house, we found an old album and…. ah… now I remember where I've seen the strange shape mountain before. It's in a photo in the album.'

'So, CC managed to keep the photo and take it home safely. I'm so pleased,' beamed Elgor. 'Did you smell the sea?'

'Yes,' Jack called down, in rather a weak voice. 'It was – well, weird. Why does it smell like that?'

'The rocky pools near here have special qualities to them. Once an item is dipped in one, it helps to preserve it and the fresh smell of sea remains forever, as a reminder of the world's beauty,' replied Elgor, still beaming.

CHAPTER 53

SWAGGER OF
A PIRATE

Settled on the strange structure high above the giant's chair, the four were in a state of excitement, keen to ask him questions.

'You said you were the caretaker. What are you the caretaker of?' asked Cecile, with her notebook open and her pencil poised.

The giant sat back in his chair, pushed the grey hair back out of his face and whispered, 'I'm the caretaker of many things!'

Cecile hovered her hand above the page, searching for words to write, then shook her head and looked back up at the giant. 'How long have you lived here?'

'I've lived here for almost a thousand of your human years,' came the booming reply.

Cecile scribbled notes this time, slightly more satisfied to have some intriguing information.   'And where are your people?'

The giant's eyes glazed over in tears and his eyebrows met in the middle, like a giant silver mountain. This time, the reply came in a slow melodic tone. 'Most of my civilisation died out long ago. Those left sailed all the way south to make a new life and home in the barren icy land you call Antarctica.'

Cecile looked saddened by the news, but still scribbled her notes. 'And why did you stay back?'

The giant drew a great breath in and let out a huge sigh that blew Cecile's hair all over the place. 'I stayed back, to be the caretaker. My wife and children left,' he mumbled, sadly.

Cecile was about to fire off her next question, in reporter fashion, when the giant spoke again: 'I'll show you some of the things that I take care of tomorrow. When Jack's stronger. It's a long journey,'

The large cavern fell silent as the giant's words filtered down, through the four human minds.

'No more questions today. I'm an old man now and the days seem so long without my …' His words grew quieter and quieter and trailed off. Till great rumbling snores echoed around the room. He had fallen asleep. Suzan gazed around the room at the books, and assorted items.

Then one by one they all dozed off. It had been a long and very eventful day.

The next morning, they awoke to find the giant gone and one of the large doors wide open. Suzan ran down the steps, to take a look. She peered around the great door, which was thicker than her, to see a large corridor that had several other doors leading from it. The nearest door was open, and Suzan could hear soft humming. Curious, she drew closer.

The giant was dusting and cleaning the room as he gently hummed: 'Yo ho ho… yo ho ho ho.'

Suzan cleared her throat politely, to avoid startling him. When he turned, she saw a beautifully furnished room. Rugs hung on the walls, and there were six human beds, each one carved delicately from a red wood. Swirls twisted their way across the head and baseboards. And in the corner of the room sat a green-topped writing desk, identical to the one that they had discovered in the old tree on the island of the cujies.

Hanging on a wooden mannequin, there was a longish dark blue top, matching tight trousers rather like thick tights, and a tricorn hat. A sword hung on a hook nearby. The hilt had a large emerald on the pommel and gemstones on the cross-guard. The scabbard was a thick dark blue leather; with an ornate gold carved locket and chape – the top and bottom parts of the scabbard.

Suzan's mouth dropped open in shock to see a real pirate outfit, in the giant's cave. 'I thought you didn't like pirates.'

Daisy-B

319

The giant knelt at her feet and looked down into her eyes. In a soft whisper he said, 'I don't, but not *all* pirates are alike. Once I was honoured to meet a pirate who had a kind and gentle heart.' A grin eclipsed Elgor's face.

Suzan looked confused. 'How could a pirate be respected and any good at dominating the seas if they were kind and gentle?' Suzan asked, in a bemused tone.

'Oh, I kid you not. This pirate was feared, and one of the greatest that ever there was. But she was so clever she never had to kill, or fight. She was one of the richest too, but always shared her spoils with the poor and homeless. Anonymously of course; she had to maintain a reputation!' Elgor whispered.

'But what about that sword?' Suzan glanced at the sword and imagined how many people it had *run through*.

Elgor gestured, towards the sword. 'Take a look for yourself.'

Tentatively Suzan strolled over to the sword and carefully drew it. The blade was beautifully ornate, like that of a king, or queen's sword. Yet there was no edge on the blade. And the tip was round.

'She never needed to kill! She was far too cunning,' the giant said with awe. 'From the worst of humanity, she was the best. And we were the best of friends.'

A tear trickled down the giant's face like the first drop of rain in the desert. 'But human lives are so fleeting and fast, compared to giants. She lived hers to the full. Brash, but just, kind, and honourable. She sailed those seven seas a hero, and retired a wise old lady.

'She had a long and eventful life. Yet it seems like the blink of an eye to me.' More tears streamed down the old giant's face. 'She was my best friend, and even caretaker for many a year.' The giant peered around the room at the items and then put his head in his hands and sobbed.

Suzan reached up and cuddled his great hand. Soon she was covered in wet giant tears. She started to shiver.

The giant looked up, peering through his hazy eyes, at the small shivering child. He wiped his eyes. 'Sorry, I've drowned you with my tears. Have a look in that trunk over there. There are some things to change into.

The giant left the room, and pulled the door to, while Suzan rummaged and changed. She squelched across the floor dripping wet and soggy and opened the old trunk. The lid opened with squeaky, reluctant hinges. A musty old smell that seemed familiar to Suzan drifted out. She pulled out some clothing. It was all very old but seemed to be well kept.

There was a cream cotton tunic, with a pair of rough trousers. Though they were too long, she managed to put them on and rolled up the sleeves and trouser legs. There was a knock at the door.

'It's okay I am changed and dry now,' Suzan called.

The giant stepped in and inspected Suzan. 'You look good in her clothing!' He said with a grin 'A tiny bit big for you though!'

'Who was this great pirate?'

'Ah, she had many a name, some called her the Mist, others CC, but I always called her *Sa Swen*, which is a giant word meaning *sister of gentle heart*.

Suzan's mouth was open completely, as she realized that not only was the giant's friend the Mist, but that the Mist was a *girl*! *One of the greatest pirates ever, was a girl? Well of course!* Suzan thought to herself. 'You said that she was a caretaker? What did you mean?' Suzan asked.

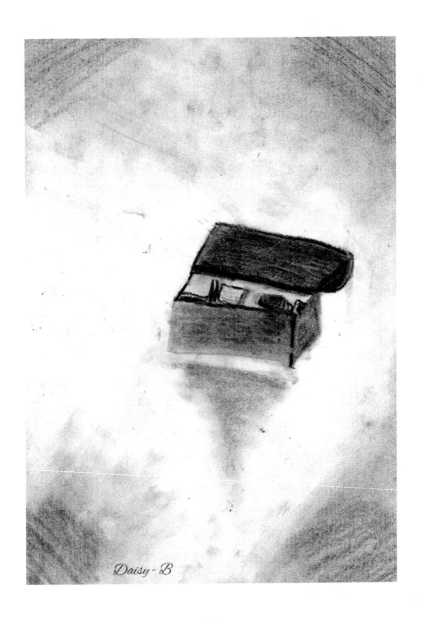

Daisy - B

'Ah, well we were friends for a long time, and she took care of everything here, while I swam south to see my family. That's before the plastic wasteland you humans created. She was one of the only people I've ever trusted to do my job while I was away. I entrusted her with everything!' The giant said with respect and admiration.

'What, this cave?' Suzan asked with a puzzled look.

'And much more. You have much to learn and see little one. Follow me with your family and Cecile and I will show you,' he said with a warm and gentle smile. He stepped back out into the corridor, with Suzan following behind, trying to keep up.

Back in the living area of his cave the other three were wide awake and taking in their surroundings. So much had happened the day before and they were still processing it all.

'Where's Suz?' Jack asked.

Captain Green looked around with concern. 'I… I… I don't know. I'm going to look for her,' she said, jumping up and starting down the long wooden ladder.

Just then Elgor boldly stepped in, followed by Suzan in her new, well … very old, but new to Suzan, attire.

'Wow, cool swagger sis!' Jack exclaimed.

'A grin from ear to ear appeared on her face. 'They used to belong to CC – to the Mist!' She said with pride.

Everyone's jaw dropped. Cecile's notepad was already in her hand and her pencil poised.

'CC's clothes. Wow that's awesome sis!' Jack said.

'Elgor was friends with *her* for many years and has lots of *her* things.' Suzan explained.

'Did you say *her*?' Jack asked, as he raised an eyebrow.

'Yes, one of the greatest pirates to ever live, *of course* CC – the Mist – *was a girl*!' Suzan replied with a smug look. She peered up at Elgor, for confirmation.

'HA HA HA,' the giant's booming laugh sounded. 'CC certainly was a woman, one of the greatest I've ever met too. And one of my dearest friends.'

There was a large hubbub of conversation as Jack, Suzan, their mum and Cecile, all excitedly discussed CC, and Suzan explained what had happened. Elgor slipped silently away.

CHAPTER 54

THE GREAT JOURNEY TO AQUASENTIA

Suddenly the door swung open and Elgor appeared, with a gigantic tray of food. 'My friends, I've prepared some breakfast. It's all fresh from my garden. Eat like giants, for the journey today will be long and perilous.' His voice sounded mysterious.

Cecile's brows furrowed. 'Where are we going?'

A grin cascaded across Elgor's face. 'To Aquasentia of course!' He boomed back.

Cecile jumped up and down, hardly able to keep composed, like a small girl excited. Then she stopped and with a concerned face, asked: 'But I thought it was destroyed?'

The giant slowly shook his head. 'No! Eat up and then we will leave. Oh, and bring warm clothes. Do you have spares with you? There's plenty of human clothes in the trunk if you need them. Suzan, you know where they are.' Suzan nodded.

Soon the five of them sat, heartily gobbling down the delicious homemade vegetable soup, bread and fresh fruit. A word was hardly exchanged, as they were all so excited.

When Elgor observed that they had finished, he stood and swung a small sack over his back.

'Follow me,' he ordered, and without further word, he strolled off slowly, through the door to the right. It led into another hewn rock tunnel that was lit by lamps.

Once the five of them were through the door, Elgor reached out and closed it behind them. They heard a loud click as the door locked. 'I always keep the door locked!' he said in a matter-of-fact tone. 'Now Jack, the journey is long. I will carry you in my pocket later on if your shoulder hurts.'

Jack grinned. 'Not everyone can say they've been offered a ride in a giant's pocket!'

Elgor walked extremely slowly, almost shuffling, so that the four small humans could keep up with him. The orange lamp light cast soft shadows around the tunnel. The uneven walls were covered in marks, from great giant tools that had once hewn the stone.

When they had walked for ten minutes the tunnel began to go uphill.

'I thought that we were going down?' said Cecile, with her notebook and pen glued to her hand.

'No, Cecile. We're travelling to a part of the island that's very special.'

Finally, the stone tunnel opened out into a giant cave. The cave was also lit by lamps but was so vast that the light's hazy orange fingers could hardly reach the corners and the roof.

Glittering in the dim light, right at the centre of the cave there was a crystal-clear blue lagoon. As they walked across the vast cave towards it, the sound of their footsteps bounced off the walls and echoed around the room, as if a vast army was approaching.

Jack peered over the edge of the lagoon, into the glistening water, his eyes probing, to try to find the bottom. Yet though the pool was extremely clear, it was also extremely deep. Too deep to make out anything.

'If any of you would like to change your minds about coming, now is the chance. The journey is dangerous, but the only way to reach Aquasentia.' The giant said with concern, while looking at each person's face one by one, for confirmation.

'Kids, are you sure you want to come along?' asked Captain Green. 'I'd feel better if you both stayed here.'

'*What?*' Suzan, exclaimed. 'We've travelled far and wide, and been in real danger so many times, why should we give in to fear now!?'

Jack went to open his mouth, but changed his mind, as Suzan had already summed up his thoughts too.

'I know kids, and I won't stop you, if you're determined to go. But as your…'

She looked round instinctively and continued, 'as your Mum,' she whispered, 'I'm always concerned for your wellbeing.'

Jack and Suzan threw their arms around her, giving a reassuring cuddle.

The giant looked again at their faces, awaiting each and every nod of approval. 'Step this way then,' he boomed, as he led them to a strange great wooden arm – suspended over the lagoon. The wood was as thick as an ancient tree. On one side of the gnarly, swirly grained red wood, there were levers and a huge wheel. The wheel resembled an old ship's wheel, but must have belonged to a giant ship, given its size.

Hundreds of metres of strange rope had been wound around the wheel. On the other end, suspended over the lake, was a strange transparent bubble.

The giant pulled back one of the levers and the beam, complete with the bubble, swung smoothly over to the water bank. Cecile tapped the clear ball, and a high-pitched sound resonated around the cave. She took more notes, in her overflowing notepad.

The giant's great hand stretched out and with two gentle and delicate fingers he opened a tiny human sized handle on the side of the ball. A concealed door slid open and the four saw that inside there were old wooden seats, makeshift seatbelts, and a sturdy wooden hand railing.

'Get in and make yourself comfortable. That middle seat is where *Sa Swen* always used to sit,' the giant said, with a fond smile.

Suzan made a dash for CC's seat and sat down. 'It's very comfortable, actually,' she said, then looked at Jack, 'Oh, by the way *Sa Swen* is the giant name, Elgor gave *CC!*' She said, with a smile.

'I see you told us that *after* you bagsied that seat!' Jack said, with a smile, but also a hint of disappointment.

'Yes, but you can sit here on the way back!' Suzan replied, with a kind grin.

Cecile took the seat that had a table next to it, so she could take yet more notes. And Captain Green took the seat between Jack and Suzan.

'Is it ok to go in the water with this?' Cecile asked, after a flurry of written notes.

'Of course,' replied Elgor, 'it's made of *Calana* which is a material developed by my ancestors. It's stronger than steel, floats like a feather and is watertight. And the rope doubles up as tubing, to give you fresh air. But hold on and wrap up warm. It will be very cold going down.'

Soon, they found themselves sealed into the bubble and being gently swung over to the centre of the pool. Then all of a sudden, there was a great splash, which covered the ball in gallons of water.

When the water had run off the ball, they peered out to see the old giant gracefully treading water next to the ball, right in the centre of the pool. He took a deep breath, took hold of a rope tassel that was hanging from the bottom of the ball, and dived below.

Suddenly there was a jerk, and the ball began to submerge, being dragged by the tassel. The echoes of the cave abruptly disappeared, as they looked up at the light trickling into the mouth of the pool and watched its orange glow dim.

CHAPTER 55

KINGDOM
OF OLD

The clear blue water was broken only by the occasional bubble, as it floated to the surface to escape. They watched the bubbles wobble their way up like jellyfish. Soon the orange glow above was almost gone. It was silent and peaceful.

Still, they descended into the blackness of the water, until they felt that they were no longer sure which way was up, and which way was down. They could have been anywhere. The only reminder was the chill that began to fill the ball. Jack put on his sweater. The others swiftly searched for their warm things.

Completely disorientated, they lost track of time completely. How long they rode that eerie capsule it was difficult to tell. But all of a sudden, a light sparkled and blazed. The giant had some kind of torch he had just turned on, and the beam, like a tunnel, cut its way through the blackness.

At first, they could see only speckles of particles that were floating in the sea. Then all of a sudden, the light hit a vast yellowy rectangular stone, then another and another.

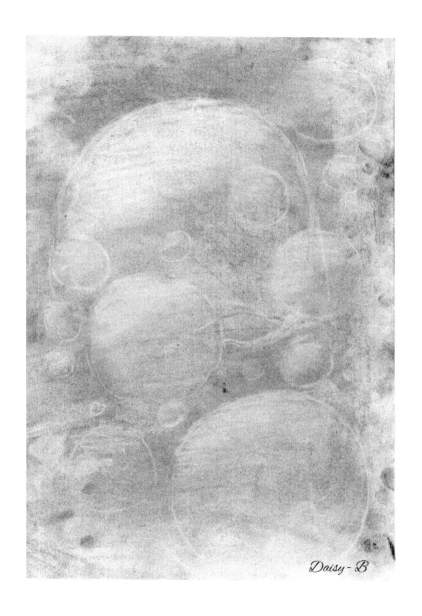

Daisy - B

'What are they?' Cecile asked.

'Look over there, there's an arch, it's an ancient city,' Jack said, with vigour.

Great angular buildings rose out of the seabed. Towers, halls, houses, castles – all exquisitely built out of a yellow stone. They could make out streets too, lined with great herringbone blocks.

The streets meandered around and between the buildings. Their tiny bubble was dwarfed alongside the immense city. Like a shrimp swimming around the contour of a whale.

Though the great city had rested there at the bottom of the sea and the currents had eroded and softened the edges, it still had an elegance to it. The way the blockwork had been laid for each building, the curves of the great arches; it was all very simple in design but had been built by loving hands.

Soon the streets converged to a great wall, which seemed to stretch on around a central area. Elgor turned his head to look back at them, and a great grin appeared. He winked and then turned away, to carefully pull the bubble through the nearest great arch.

On the other side of the arch the buildings were vastly different. Great spires and towers rose out of the base, almost like a termite's nest. Made of a strange crystal, the surface was smooth and gleamed in the torch light, like a thousand mirrors. Some reflected light bounced around from building to building, and some caught inside the crystal – revealing glimpses of great halls.

Unlike the surrounding stone city, the strange crystal looked untouched, and unscathed by the centuries of elements. As they were pulled around the first great series of towers, they came to a large tunnel entrance, also made of crystal. Passing through the tunnel, they watched their reflections flickering on the surface of the shiny crystal and saw the light pick out shades and tones of the world inside the tower.

Suddenly the tunnel curved abruptly uphill. Four astounded faces were fixed on Elgor's bubbles, as they rippled up – only to disappear on what looked like a surface. Soon, they saw Elgor stop swimming and place his foot on a step, then another and moments later he was climbing steps, that seemed to lead out of the water.

Once close to the top the crystal bubble became buoyant and bounced to the surface. The giant pulled them closer and then clasped the door handle with his cumbersome fingers.

'NOOOOO! We'll drown!' Jack called out, in panic.

The giant hesitated, then smiled. 'You're perfectly safe.' They heard his muffled voice seep through the bubble.

As the door of the bubble hissed open, the four peered out. The air smelt old and musty but seemed safe to breathe. The giant held his hand out and one by one they stepped onto it. One by one, he lifted them safely onto solid ground.

While she waited for her turn, Suzan peered into darkness, straining her eyes to see her surroundings, but the darkness swamped almost everything. Her imagination filled in the vast gaps.

'This way', the giant whispered, and shone the torch into the room. Great glass like sparkling ceilings undulated and flowed up, way up above them and then stretched down to the floor, making no separation between wall and ceiling.

The floor was made of a white crisp marble with floral carvings and inlaid with darker marble and rare minerals from all parts of the world. The whole building was like a great jewel, reflecting and refracting light and colour, sparkling in the darkness of the ocean depths.

Elgor reached a crystal pillar that seemed to be hollow and stretched far up into what looked like the next floors. He turned a small silver dial and suddenly a bright light whooshed up the pillar, illuminating the whole room. 'Come this way.'

Cecile was mesmerised by the twinkling surfaces of the crystal. 'Is this the ultimate jewel?' she asked, pencil poised.

'HA HA HA HA!' The giant boomed with laughter. 'This? No this is merely where our kings and queens of old once lived. But because it was so well constructed, it's strong and still standing.

'It was built out of one of the rarest and once most prized elements to giants, calena. It's as clear as diamond, and as strong too. Luckily so, as it manages to withstand the great pressure of the water above. Though it wasn't designed that way.

'This city once was part of an island above the waves. And the pool we arrived in was used to dive for fish and pearls,' the giant explained. 'Follow me, we must journey through the kingdom of old, to a place far more important.'

CHAPTER 56

GREED

Obediently the four followed the giant, as they gazed at each other in confusion. They walked through great chambers all built from the shimmering calena.

The first was a great banquet hall, with a giant table made of a black polished marble. Great murals danced across the surface, all finely depicted by inlay of metals, stones, minerals and other rare materials. Giant chairs lined each side, each with twisting and swirling carved backrests, with once-fine red leather cushioning.

Strange eating implements were laid out, beside a series of flat platters. And all the colours and patterns could be observed a thousand times over, in the backdrop of the calena walls and ceiling.

Passing through the room without stopping, they came to a corridor where the calena walls had been moulded into hooks for images to hang. In golden frames, hung faded images of giant kings and queens. Suzan stopped to stare at the giant royalty of old.

'Time waits for no man, or woman. Even the greatest kingdom can be swept away in time, and the treasures of the richest lose their sheen,' the giant said, with a soft reflective tone.

They continued walking, each room or corridor was like a street to them.

'Now I know how toddlers see the world!' Suzan said, as she peered up the legs of a chair that, just to sit on, would be like climbing a tree. The chair was part of a semicircle that surrounded two humungous thrones. One slightly smaller than the other. Encrusted in jewels and carved from blocks of solid gold, their yellowy warm glow shimmered wherever Suzan looked.

'Is that solid gold?' Jack asked, with a slight glint in his eye.

'Jack, take heed,' replied Elgor, his voice suddenly stern and cold, 'you'll see many items sought after as riches here, but none will bring you anything except greed, misery and loneliness. And a path to become someone like the Hound.'

'My brother isn't anything like the Hound, he isn't bad,' Suzan said, with a little fire in her eyes, defending her brother.

Captain Green knelt down in front of Suzan and Jack. Her eyes met theirs. 'Do you think people like the Hound were born bad? No, he was once a kind and happy child. It's his pursuit of treasure that has, step by step, changed him – given him a cold heart and eyes only for gold. And somewhere in all that, he's lost himself. Don't be so certain Suzan, the things that separate people are merely their pursuits.'

Elgor extended his great arm and gently patted Jack on the head. 'Are you tired yet, Jack? You tell me if you would like to ride in my pocket.'

Jack nodded. 'Maybe later would be good.'

'What happened to your people and this kingdom?' Cecile asked tentatively.

'Follow me,' Elgor requested.

They hiked across several other rooms, all filled with equally opulent items, until they came to a truly gigantic room where the calena on the walls had been sculpted into shelves.

Peering up, Suzan could see old remains of thousands of books. Elgor stopped in the centre of the room and peered down at a great floor map, made from mosaic. Tiny minute pieces of minerals and stones had been delicately used to depict a map of a large island. Excitedly, Jack and Suzan walked around the outside of it.

'Hang on, that little section looks familiar. Where have we seen that before?' Jack asked, astutely.

'That's right Jack. You've been there! It's the island that we met on. It was once part of a larger island – this one! We referred to it all as Aquasentia. It was home to my people for many epochs and it saw many rulers and governments,' Elgor explained.

The four of them listened intently, transfixed by the story.

'So, what happened to it?' Cecile asked, with twinkling eyes. She had found the answer to the mystery that she had chased all her life!

'Ah, well it's a long story. But it would be better to show you.' Elgor strode across the room, followed by the four who took considerably longer.

He took them through yet more corridors and rooms – stopping outside a doorway that seemed completely out of place. It was a simple red wooden door, made of hand cut panels that still revealed marks of the primitive tools used to cut and shape it. It hung in a great wooden curved frame, on hefty black iron hinges.

On the left was a huge, black, iron handle. Its top

glistened in the light, from so many years of hands touching it.

'This was the oldest room on the island and one of the first buildings my people made on Aquasentia.' Elgor twisted the great handle and the door softly and smoothly swung open.

It was pitch black inside. But Elgor took out a large match and lit several old lamps along the wall. As they stood just inside the door, he pointed to a small pool of water. 'That's one of the main reasons that my people originally settled on this island, a long, long time ago. Back in that time, the whole island was covered by the most majestic red oak trees. A rich lush woodland that stretched from tip to toe.

'My people discovered the island on passing, but soon found the woodland to be a great resource to build their houses, to hunt for food and they decided to settle there. In those days they were respectful and only took what they needed...' Elgor paused and drew a huge breath, before continuing...

'Then deep in the heart of the woodland, they discovered this pool. It was allegedly said to reveal the greatest treasure, if you gazed into it with a pure heart, unclouded by temptation. And legend has it, that the first giants saw the greatest treasure in its shimmering waters, every time they looked.

'Soon they built a small town and built this building, to house the pool. But as time went on, the giants cut more and more of the trees down to expand their town. And then the first king stepped forward and took on the role of leading them. He seemed fair and kind. But, as the town grew further, so did their needs and desires. Bit by bit the giants who gazed into the pool, saw the riches of their desire, and not the greatest treasure. They became distracted by what they had seen and desired to own it all.

'Eventually, they went on great conquests and collected the objects and riches they'd seen. Only to return, gaze in the pool, and see even more treasure. And each king who gazed into those waters desired greater riches than the last.

'Little by little everyone focused on riches and forgot about the true treasure. The *hungry* desire to own *more* and *more riches* led to conquests, trade, and wars. Yet none were able to quench that infinite thirst.

'The last king was so filled with greed, he cut down the last of the trees to build great ships and he became a ferocious pirate. And those who would not follow his lust for gold, were banished from the city.' Elgor paused to draw another huge breath.

'What happened next?' asked Suzan impatiently.

Elgor looked sad. 'We lived with very little, growing vegetables and taking care of nature – outcasts – completely banished. While trip by trip, the great pirate brought back opulence from around the world, in giant sized quantities, beyond your wildest dreams. The city became one giant treasure trove. Bursting at the seams.

'One day the island began to crumble under the weight of all the treasure. The giants grabbed what they could and fled, just as the last parts of the island collapsed into the sea. They sailed off and faded into legend.

'The only part that remained was the small part that you met me on. It was the part the outcasts and I called home. That is until a few centuries ago, when the last of my kind sailed south to make a new home.

'Now I stand watching out over the sea, the caretaker of these things. Alone!' Elgor looked away, to hide the great tears he had tried to hold back.

CHAPTER 57

DON'T TOUCH THE WATER

Suzan, Jack and Captain Green had been so captivated by Elgor telling his tale, that they had almost forgotten they were at the bottom of the ocean, in an ancient city.

The orange from the old lamps flickered and danced around the surfaces of the stone floor tiles, which were worn and broken with age.

Unlike the rich calena rooms, with their musky smell of old air, the inside of the giant wooden hut smelt of rich aged wood.

'Elgor, is that really the pool from your story?' Cecile asked, peering over towards it.

'One and the same,' Elgor confirmed.

'Does it still work?' Cecile asked, with her pencil poised.

'Why don't you see for yourself?' Elgor said, in a slow inviting voice.

Cecile smiled in delight as she tucked her precious notebook away into her pocket and slowly and cautiously approached the worn, sculpted, old stones, which surrounded the pool. The dull echo of her footsteps, whispered round the giant wooden structure.

Elgor strode over too, followed by the other three, overfilled with curiosity. Cecile stepped tentatively up to the edge of the large stone side and stared into the pool.

The water flickered and shimmered with golds, silvers, blues and greens. At first, she saw her own reflection, tinted by the mysterious, ancient liquid. Gazing deeply, she allowed the colours and glints to wash over her.

Her peripheral vision of the room slipped away, till there was nothing but the colours and swirls of the water. Her reflection shifted and turned like a cloud constantly in flux.

The murmuring of Suzan and Jack, as they watched her, faded. And still the mesmerising waters lured her gaze, further and deeper, until she saw letters and sentences of articles flash before her. And then a golden award for best journalist, then two, then a whole mantelpiece filled with trophies and awards for journalism.

She reached out her hand, to touch the trophies. She thirsted for them, she hungered. *Just a little further,* she thought, *then they're mine. If only I can just stretch a little further.*

'*DON'T* TOUCH THE *WATER,*' A great booming voice came like a thunderclap, shattering the tranquility of the night.

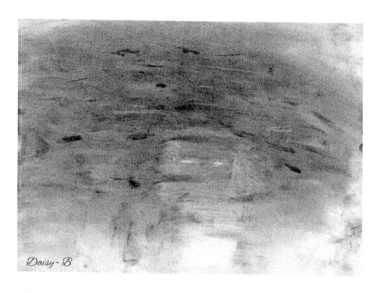

Daisy - B

Cecile sharply looked away and came to. She found herself on the floor, crouched really close to the pool, with her fingers inches from it.

Elgor's eyes were wide and filled with concern, staring directly at Cecile. 'Never, ever touch the water,' he repeated, in a softer tone.

Cecile rose to her feet and staggered back.

'I'm sorry, I should have warned you first: to *not* touch the waters. For some, the desire to have what they see, can be so great that they become lost in the pool and try to grab it. Just like one of the kings of ages, who saw something he wanted so much; he dived in, and the moment he touched the pool's liquid, he evaporated. Or so legend says. But, needless to say, we don't want to test *that* legend.' Elgor looked around for Cecile, to find her in a dark corner sitting on the floor muttering, quite beside herself.

He knelt in front of her, took out a small vial of green liquid, removed the cork and moved it to and fro under her nose, in a gentle fashion. The scent seemed to be very pungent and instantly pulled Cecile out of her hazy state, back to her usual bright and alert self. She walked back to the group and stood, watching.

'What did you see? Was it the ultimate treasure?' Jack asked.

'N N No, I didn't, I saw my desire to become a world-renowned reporter and to win awards,' Cecile said, in an ashamed tone.

'Would anyone else like to gaze?' Elgor asked.

'Yes, me!' Jack said with excitement. He straightened his back, pushed out his chest and strode forwards towards the pool. Swirls and colours enchanted his gaze, until his reflection morphed and contorted.

A flash of him standing on a pirate ship, as a captain, sped before him. He closed his eyes and stilled his mind. When he opened them again, he saw a treasure chest filled with loot. The golden shine, like hands reaching to him and beckoning him.

Again, he closed his eyes and stilled his mind. When he opened them, he saw a flash of blue and green and then he saw his mother, father and Suzan's smiling faces. Filled with love, he broke his gaze, turned, and ran to give his mum a huge hug.

The pool had reminded him of the family he treasured so much.

'It seems Jack here managed to control his heart's fleeting desires, enough to move beyond that desire. Well done, Jack! If you had held out a little longer, you might have seen something else,' Elgor said, in admiration.

'For a moment, I saw something, but just a fleeting flash of blues and greens.'

'Very good Jack, you were almost there.' Elgor glanced towards Suzan and Captain Green. 'Anyone else like to try?'

Suzan stepped forward. 'Why not!' She stepped up to the pool and looked deeply into its waters. The colours and tones shifted and swirled, her reflection distorted, and she found herself gazing at her mother and the desire to be with her always. She closed her eyes and stilled her mind, cast out all thoughts and slowly opened her eyes.

Before her was the most beautiful twinkling thing she had ever seen, beyond all riches, all words and imagination. Swirly blues glistened, rich greens and flecks of white.

An exquisite gem, floating in the velvety blackness. She was mesmerized by it. In awe of its beauty, yet she had no desire to take it, or own it. She knew it could not be owned, yet just gazing upon it was enough. It flickered and then disappeared. She found herself looking back towards the others. Four set of eyes were looking at her.

'You saw it, didn't you child? I *know* that look, yet I've seldom seen it!' the giant said gently.

'That is the most beautiful thing I've ever seen,' Suzan whispered. 'A gemstone, unique in every way, filled with so much prettiness, but I had no desire to own it, just to *protect it.*'

Elgor smiled fondly. 'Well done child. You saw it, but not completely. If you gaze for longer, you will see more.'

Jack stepped up to the pool. 'I want another turn. I want to see this legendary jewel!' He let the colours soak into his eyes again. He stilled his mind and drifted, until he saw a flash of a pirate ship. He closed his eyes awhile. Then came the gold. Again, he closed his eyes.

Next, he saw his family and gazed upon them for a moment, before closing his eyes once more. Suddenly, opening his eyes, he saw that blue-green jewel, set like a gem in the velvet of blackness. It shone and stirred his heart, tears of awe rolled down his face, as the shimmering object came closer, and he could make out more of the endless depths of its beauty. Something seemed familiar, yet he knew not what. It flickered then was gone, in a blink of his eye.

'You saw it too!' Elgor said with joy in his eye. 'It's very normal to cry. I cried for days when I first gazed upon its layers of intricate beauty. And I was filled with that urge to protect and cherish it. But there is more. Suzan, try again. See if you can see its true richness.'

Suzan smiled and stepped towards the edge. She let her mind and gaze become lost in the glittering colours of the pool and once more she stilled her heart, every time it fluttered. Until she was looking at that blue-green jewel again. She kept her mind clear and looked ever deeper, tears trickled down her face, and with every moment, she saw another intricate detail of unimaginable beauty.

Deeper her mind went, closer and closer. It felt familiar, vast, and exponentially ornate, yet infinitely fragile. Awe, respect and love washed over her. She felt like a visitor, allowed the precious chance to be somewhere truly special. Like being invited into the grandest palace ever made. Closer still it came. Textures and colours drew her in further, each detail a jewel. Like a jewel made of jewels.

Suddenly it was so close that her sense of familiarity took over. She knew it, yet had never seen it with such eyes. Glistening waters, rustling forests, swirling clouds, and sailing birds came into clarity. As the realisation struck her, she looked away, and she was back in the room, with the giant gently smiling at her.

'I…I saw, the most beautiful place. A palace,' Suzan stammered, tears still flowing from her eyes.

'Well done, Suzan, now you know what it is too,' Elgor said fondly.

'What is it?' The others asked in unison.

Daisy - B

The giant stood with them one by one and helped them to still their minds for long enough to see a glimpse of it. None saw it quite as long and clearly as Suzan, but all wondered on its beauty.

'It is indeed a palace, but it cannot be owned, and must be cherished, and though it is vast, it is fragile, so we must cherish and protect this jewel. This beautiful jewel – this beautiful planet.' Elgor said softly.

CHAPTER 58

THE PRICE
OF
FREEDOM

Suddenly Elgor seemed to look and feel his great age. He sat on a great rock nearby. His arms hung limply at his side and the carved craters of age on his face furrowed in the orange lamp light.

'Elgor what's wrong?' Suzan asked, running over and wrapping her arms around his ankle.

'Suzan, I'm tired and old. I've sat on this rock, protecting its secrets, riches, and history, for far too long. The years have left me weary. And I've not seen my family for centuries. It's a great warmth, to meet you all. For it's been so long since I had visitors here.'

Suzan peered up at the giant's huge, kind, tired eyes.

'Why don't you go and visit them?' She said with soft concern.

'I can't leave this place unattended,' he said softly.

Jack smiled. '*But* the treasure is not actually *here* Elgor, it's *everywhere* and to cherish and protect it, we must be out there. Like ...' Jack paused, in realisation, as he looked at his mum. 'Like my mum, stopping people from damaging the animals and the earth.'

Elgor peered into Jack's meaningful eyes. 'You're right Jack, because you've seen the true treasures and values in life, but most have not and they would go to any lengths to get their hands on the riches, that the giant kings of ages have gathered down here. And others to excavate the history of my people, to prove that giants were once around, and then humans would be fuelled to search for them, leaving no rock unturned in this world. No, it's better to stand guarding this place forever.'

'What if...' Jack started and then stopped, realizing that what he was about to say was too extreme.

The giant's expectant eyes shone. 'Go on Jack what were you going to say?'

Jack composed his thoughts, trying to word his idea in a delicate way, but there was no way to sugar coat his idea. It *was* extreme. 'One day, you won't be able to guard this place anymore Elgor. You'll be too old. What if ...' Jack looked down, his voice now a quiet mumble. 'What if... if you destroy the city of treasure.'

Elgor's face moved through a plethora of expressions, like a landscape remoulding itself. 'You would have me destroy my people's city, for the sake of ensuring giants go on, unknown to humans. For my freedom to see my family. Hmmmmmmmmmmm.'

His great pondering sounds echoed around the walls of the room and the city, like the sounds of the once bustling streets, long ago. 'You would sacrifice the untold riches and history, for the love of family?' Elgor gazed around at the four expectant faces.

'Your people's history would live on, through the stories you told with other giants. And the real riches would still be there, your family, freedom, and the ultimate jewel. Maybe you could even play a part, secretly, in protecting this jewel,' Suzan said, excitedly.

'HMMMMMMMMMMM,' Elgor's great echo bounced around the walls, of that great ancient city again. 'For people so small – children – you sure can change giant minds!' Elgor gave them a warm smile. 'You're right, holding onto this place has stopped me from enjoying the true riches in life. I agr…' his sentence trailed off, his mouth dropping into a frown. 'No. I can't go, sorry,' he uttered, sternly.

Captain Green had been standing back in awe, watching her children change the mind of a stubborn giant. Swiftly she stepped forward. 'Elgor, what's wrong, what stops you?'

The giant sighed a humungous sigh and hung his head. 'I've often thought about leaving and destroying the city, but I can't leave anymore, even if I did wish to.'

The four faces looked on in perplexment.

Elgor continued, 'You see, I haven't been able to leave in a while, since your kind filled the sea with plastic. It all ends up here, swept over by the currents. See, I couldn't leave even if I wanted to. I tried once you know, and just got bound up in it all. I only went a few hundred meters and had to turn back. It tangles fish, animals, and anything that comes near. A whole continent of it floating. Vast and an almost impossible task to clear.'

The four hung their heads in shame of what countless generations of humans had done to their beautiful planet. A silence washed over them, like a great wave. Ashamed and speechless, the four stood looking at Elgor, for what seemed an awkward eternity.

351

Suddenly Captain Green stepped forward, with a newfound fire in her eyes. Straight and tall she stood. 'Then we will clean it up!'

Elgor's eyebrows wrinkled and furrowed in utter disbelief. And it was not just him: Jack, Suzan and Cecile, were all staring at Captain Green, in complete scepticism.

'Mum, do you realize how many tons are in the oceans around here?' Jack asked. Without waiting for an answer, he continued, 'There's approximately eighty thousand tons of plastic. It's an impossible task.'

But Captain Green's resolve remained etched into every inch of her face. Her green hair gently bristling in the breeze. 'If you think it's impossible, you've already lost. Look around you! These giants built a great kingdom from riches around the world. How many civilisations and pirates have done the impossible for treasure? How many companies have created and achieved the impossible, for the sake of innovation!? And how many people have braved the impossible for love? No, it's *not* impossible!'

The giant and the three humans stood transfixed by Captain Green's passion and determination.

'I agree mum, that it's a cause worthy of determination, but how will you actually clean-up about eighty thousand tons of plastic?'

'The same way that people have moved or built mountains, piece by piece! And with as many hearts as we can rile up!' Her words echoed around the city, like a thousand voices. She stepped toward Elgor. 'Are you willing to destroy this place?' Her questioning stare was serious, almost deadly.

Elgor looked around at the room, and through the doorway at the magnificent city. 'You're right this is just stuff. Life is out there! And my people, well they're here.'

He put his ancient, wrinkly hand over his heart and smiled. A smile of total contentment. 'It's time to go home! I'm ready!'

'Then our work begins!' Captain Green said. She turned to Cecile, who was standing at the back, with her pencil moving so quickly that it was in danger of catching light! 'Cecile, I must ask something of you too. For Elgor to be free, he must not be seen, or known about. Giants must be creatures of legend and fairy tale. Cecile, I know this is the mystery that you've chased all your life, but …' Captain Green looked down, and her words trailed off.

'I know what I must do!' Cecile said with a stern face. She took out her notebooks, and placed them on a rock, doused them in oil from one of the ancient lamps and touched the flame to the oil. It burst into flames sending orange and red embers, floating around like sails.

Everyone stepped away as the flames danced over the surface like the last echoes of the people and stories within. Soon the flames died down and flakes of black ash fluttered around the room, like butterflies.

Daisy - B

Daisy - B

355

Cecile smiled a strange, rather sad smile. 'Some things are better off remaining as a mystery. Elgor, when this place has gone, your people can truly remain the creatures of legends and fairy tales, and the truth can be lost to the mists of time.

'It's safer that way. Sometimes the truth is stranger than fiction, but other times, it is better left as fiction!! Elgor you must go south and be with your people, to live undisturbed in safety.'

Elgor wept at Cecile's gesture and Captain Green's determination.

'Right people... and giants! We have work to do and people to contact!' Captain Green said with a glint of fire in her rich green eyes.

CHAPTER 59

IT BEGINS

A small alarm went off onboard Captain Greens majestic ship, the *Emerald*, as it gently cut through the calm waters of a distant sea. The crew leapt into action.

'Fox, you know what to do!' said Eagle, a valuable member of Captain Green's crew.

Fox, an equally valuable crew member, rushed down towards the captain's cabin. Carefully she entered and closed the door behind her. She opened a large cupboard door that led into a tiny, concealed room.

The minute room was clad with wood from floor to ceiling and had a single desk with a simple wooden chair. Pinned to the walls were many scraps of paper: each one had a codename for a person or place and then a series of random looking letters and numbers. Set in the middle of the desk there was a large radio transmitter – buzzing frantically and flashing a series of lights.

'Hu, it's Captain Green!' Fox said in surprise. She picked up the handset, turned some dials, until a low-pitched muffled fuzz came over the speaker – *CG T... LD FFFFZZZZZ*. Fox slowly turned a dial to tune into the frequency.

'CG to *Emerald*, do you read me?' the muffled voice called.

'Emerald here, we read you CG!' replied Fox. There was a pause...

'Emerald, we need your help. Prepare to receive instructions,' the voice commanded.

'Copy you CG, standing by for instructions.' Fox reached under the desk and turned on a device resembling a printer, but a printer with some *heavy* modifications. It whirred into action, spitting out pages of illegible letters. As Fox was studying the printed pages, trying to decode the first few lines, the radio burst into life again...

'Emer... is that you Fox? Has Dragon arrived safely?'

'Copy, Dragon has arrived safe and sound,' Fox confirmed.

'We'll need his help too, show him the instructions. He'll know what to do! Over.'

'Copy that CG. Over and out,' Fox replied. The lights on the radio device flickered and went off, and the sound returned to a dull fuzz.

Fox turned the dials down, picked up the papers, stepped out and securely closed the door. She rushed out of the cabin and knocked urgently on a door along the corridor. It swung open and there was *Dragon* – Suzan and Jack's father.

'Do you have news from Captain Green and ...' he paused as he composed his words, 'the two children.' His tone was anxious.

'Yes, this just came in on the secure line,' Fox said as she handed Dragon the pages the printer had spat out.

'But I can't make out the code she has used, it isn't one of the usual ones,' Fox said, in a perplexed tone.

Dragon glanced over the first few lines. '*HA HA HA,*' he bellowed out. 'Green does like her cyphers! This is an old form of cypher, that we used to use all the time in my day!' His eyes twinkled with fond memories. 'Right, gather Tawny and Eagle and meet me in the captain's cabin in two minutes, and I'll take a look at her instructions.'

Two minutes later the four of them were sitting around the pages, with three faces all expectantly looking at Dragon to read and decipher the instructions. Dragon picked up the pile of pages and walked away from the expectant faces, towards a small fire hearth.

He placed the pages on the blackened metal grate and reached into his top pocket to pull out a silver item. He turned the small rectangular item over and over in his fingers, as if it stirred distant and fond memories.

Finally, in front of three shocked faces, he flipped the object lid open, ignited the lighter – bringing it down to the paper, which burst into flames with a *whooopf* and just as quickly simmered into glowing embers. The instructions were gone.

'What in the world are you doing, Dragon? That was the instructions, directly from our captain,' Eagle said in a stern and surprised tone.

'Relax Eagle. I have already read them. We must sail to the edge of where our captain is, to help her. Our mission is shrouded in secrecy and your captain asks that you ask no questions with this mission. She needs your help, but asks you to do only as she requests, no more and no less. She has trusted me with a few details, but not much more than you know. Do we have an accord?' Dragon asked, in a powerful and determined tone.

Eagle, Tawny and Fox looked at each other to confirm their agreement, then all turned to Dragon and nodded their heads.

'Good answer! Let's set sail immediately, and not waste time.' Dragon handed a scrap of paper to each of the three. Then without another word exchanged, the four rallied the crew and set sail double time!

Daisy - B

CHAPTER 60

RISK AND RUMBLE

Seventy-two hours later the *Emerald* dropped anchor on the edge of the plastic continent. A small, but extremely strong, rowing boat plopped into the water. Alone at the oars, Dragon carefully rowed through the tangled plastic, to the giant's tiny outcrop.

Eagerly awaiting his arrival, Suzan and Jack were looking out, towards the plastic covered sea. Eventually Dragon's small boat came into view.

'There he is, there he is…there's dad,' called Jack excitedly. 'He's all by himself.'

'Course he is,' remarked Suzan, 'the *Emerald's* crew can't know about Elgor.'

As the rowing boat crept closer, the children began to wave frantically. Jack started to jump up and down, trying to get a better view. 'Look, he's waving back.'

No sooner had the small rowing boat touched the beach, than Dragon jumped out to hug his wife and children. Tears streaked down his face – the joy of seeing them was overwhelming.

Captain Green broke away and peered into his eyes. 'You must keep everything that you see here a secret and never speak of it, not to the crew, not to friends, or even to us after today. I need to show you someone.' She led Dragon across the island to the giant's cave.

When Dragon set eyes on the great ancient towering giant, his jaw dropped, and he could hardly believe his eyes. The children told him of their adventures, with their mum and Cecile adding details, here and there. The giant happily stayed with them, only too pleased to re-listen to all the tales and to hear again how they had discovered his island.

When they reached the end of the story, with the giant city and the pool, Captain Green's eyes turned from reflection to anticipation. 'Dragon, we must ask a great task of you. And something that you've not done for many years,' Captain Green said, with a twinkle in her eye. 'I must ask you to help Elgor to destroy the city.'

'What? But why?' Dragon asked, in utter disgust.

'It's the only way that Elgor can leave here, meet his family again and destroy all proof of his race. I don't ask this of you lightly. But if anyone can destroy a giant city with explosives, you can,' his wife said, with a wink and smile that lifted one side of her mouth.

Dragon gazed up at the towering giant sitting near them. Elgor gently nodded his head and softly smiled.

'OK, I'll do it,' Dragon agreed.

'There's much explosive material we can use down there. It was gathered by my people many years ago when they were pirates, but if we rig it well, it will work. Follow me and I'll take you to Aquasentia and tell you more about the city, and my plan,' Elgor commanded.

Dragon stood up and followed Elgor.

'Don't forget to signal and *be careful*,' Captain Green shouted after them.

363

'Just *how* are you going to clear that plastic, mum?' Suzan asked.

'Piece by piece, just like moving a mountain. Well, that and we need as many people as we can muster to help,' she replied, with a smile. 'Cecile, I need you to take some photos of the plastic and write a story to reach as many people as possible. I've one or two favours to call in…' She looked at the sceptical expression on Suzan's face. 'OK, perhaps a *few more* than that, in fact, I might have to call in favours from millions of people.'

'But what are we doing now, while we wait for all these favours?' asked Jack.

'You'll see Jack. We're all going to be busy.'

'Right, to the *Emerald*,' commanded Captain Green, as she stood up. Soon they were picking their way through the plastic in the small rowing boat. They arrived on board the *Emerald*, to a hubbub of welcomes and conversations. However, every man and woman on that ship, kept their promise to ask no questions about the mission.

The captain stood on the deck of the ship, as it gently swayed and sloshed up and down in the swampy plastic-filled waters. 'Right team, I need every one of you to help me. You all have roles to play in one of the biggest clean ups… well ever.

Snout, I would like you to immediately put out word on every channel, number, platform, social media, and wavelength, that Captain Green is calling in her debts. And needs a no questions favour. And tell them to pass it on,' she said to a short wiry man who stood at the back of the small circle.

'Yes, Cap,' Snout replied, in a quiet voice. He flicked his long scraggly hair out of his eyes as he went to turn, then paused. 'Do you mean *everyone*?' Snout asked, in a whisper like voice.

'Everyone, Snout. Tell them all!' his captain replied.

Snout turned and ran off towards the decks bellow.

'Eagle, I need you to lead security. No one comes onto the island. That is of upmost importance. No matter what happens.'

'Security! Oh, I love security duty,' Eagle said with a great smile from ear to ear. 'Yes, cap. You can rely on me; I'll protect the island. Right, you five with me.' The towering great stocky man flexed and turned on his heel, stamping his foot in a military gesture and marched off, followed by five crew members.

'Fox, I'd like you to be on nature duty, any tangled animals and fish need to be cut free and any injured need to be taken care of. Choose your team and open up the lower decks.' Fox nodded, chose her team, and headed off below deck.

'Tawny, I'd like you to lead and guide the great masses of ships that arrive. And they *will* arrive! Help them to work as one team and correlate their movements and tasks.'

'Yes, cap,' Tawny replied and walked off.

'Suzan, have you and Jack ever been up in a crow's nest?' their mum asked, with a grin on her face.

Suzan and Jack glanced at each other in excitement.

'No m… err Captain!' Suzan replied, almost saying the *m* word.

'Let's go!' their mum said. She started climbing a ladder that reached right up into the rigging, and beyond even the sails, to a large round wooden platform surrounded by railings.

Jack and Suzan smirked, and both jostled each other to be the first up.

'Jack, you don't stand a chance of winning this climb,' Suzan said with a glint of determination. She shot up the rigging, like a monkey in a tree.

Jack hustled, hand over hand, as he heaved himself up; his chest was on fire from the exertion. Alas, every time he grew close to Suzan's ankles, she sped up further.

Moments later two panting children yanked themselves that last metre, onto the crow's nest. It was far larger when they reached the top. Easily big enough for the two kids and their secret mum.

'You both took your time,' their mum said with a smile!

'Sorry Captain Green,' Suzan grinned.

They stood, cradled by the nest, leaning on the railings and looking out over the vast expanse of plastic-filled water between them and the tiny island. Their mum took out a telescope and pointed it at a small outcrop of rocks on the island. 'Now we wait for your father and Elgor to do their task and give us the signal that they're safe.'

Just then there was a low, but auspicious rumble that crept up on them, getting louder. The sea around the tiny outcrop began to bubble and writhe, like a great cooking pot on the boil.

Water violently pulsed and spewed over the edges of the island. Rocks on the island shook and crumbled, leaving a great dust cloud that drifted and fogged the area.

The ship, though far from the island, began to bob at first – then to rock more eagerly, until the intensity of the rippling and energetic waves jolted and buffeted viciously.

Eventually, the ship slowly settled back to a gentle sway. The three of them fixed their stare on the island, eyes trying to break through the haze of dust; their mum, eagerly awaiting the signal.

They waited, and waited, but nothing came. They knew that the rubble must have been the city exploding – hundreds of metres below the sea. Did Elgor and Dragon get out in time? Or did something go terribly wrong?

CHAPTER 61

CRYSTAL WATERS

Still no signal from Dragon. Minutes turned to hours. Cold and windswept, Jack, Suzan and Captain Green probed the island. Even after the dust had settled and the orange dust was replaced by the fiery fingers of the sunset, the three lone figures stood expectantly.

As the first of the stars came out, Suzan was the first to see a small sign. Then Jack and their mum. A flash, then two. Then a series of short and long flashes.

'Morse code,' Jack exclaimed.

'*Yes*,' exclaimed their mum, 'it appears from their message, they're safe now, but your father was injured, and they've only just arrived at the cave of outcasts. We're not to worry.' Their mum smiled, as she decoded the dots and dashes little by little. Raising a large torch, she sent a series of flashes back.

Elgor replied, with a final series of bright flashes.

'What did you send mum?' Jack asked.

'I asked if father is ok and needs a medic. Elgor said he's ok, and we mustn't worry,' their mum explained.

'Right let's get to sleep, tomorrow is going to be a busy day!'

They climbed down and by the time they had all crawled into their warm beds, everyone on the ship was fast asleep. All except one, that is.

In her cabin, under the soft glow of a computer screen in an otherwise black room, Cecile sat. 'All the articles and stories I've ever written have prepared me for this moment,' she muttered aloud to herself. 'Yet for the first time ever, I'm writing to protect a mystery, not to solve it! And what's more, to clear this terrible pollution that humans have created and neglected. The stakes are high.'

Daisy - B

She could feel it, welling within her. The ideas bubbling and simmering inside. Her fingers tapped nervously on the laptop edge. The white empty page stared back at her, expectantly.

Suddenly her eyes narrowed, her back straightened, and her fingers exploded into a great frantic surge of typing, trying to keep up with the speed and intensity of her thoughts, emotions and ideas. The tapping and beating of those keys continued deep, deep into the night.

Long after the first rays of light stretched across the open sea, two tired eyes closed peacefully and restfully, satisfied and contented. Cecile's laptop screen flashed the word *sent*, dimmed, and then blackened. The hard drive whined quietly down and finally silence stretched across the ship.

A tired Captain Green turned over in the warmth of her covers. Her dream was just too delicious to stop now, yet something was echoing at the back of her mind. Something disturbing that blissful dream. She ignored it at first, but as the sound became louder, it echoed around the rooms within her mind, and pulled her out of her dream – like a parent pulling a child out of a sweetshop.

She awoke, eyes wide open, bolt upright in her bed. It was not the dream, there was a great booming low-pitched rumble *booooo*, a pause, then *booooooo* again. 'YES! I know that horn anywhere!' She shouted, as she jumped out of bed, not bothering to change. Only stopping to put on some slippers, on route to her cabin door.

She arrived on deck just in time, as a gargantuan tanker pulled close to their ship. It was like a great skyscraper compared to a tiny house.

A bright and cheerful lady peered over the edge of the railings, high above their ship. 'Ahoy there, *Emerald*, we came as quickly as we could. Oh, I see you've dressed for the occasion Green,' she noted with a chuckle.

Green glanced at herself; she was wearing fluffy pyjamas, with an image of a heart around the earth on the chest. The legs and arms of the pjs were too long and hung loosely, way past her limbs. Her hair was a great ball of matted green mess. It looked as though she was wearing a green, rolling desert plant on her head.

'Thank you for coming. Did you pass it on?'

A rich and joyous smile came from the lady far above. 'Only to a few thousand ships!!'

Both of them chuckled.

'Right, where do you want me to begin?' the lady asked.

'Tawny, can you let the *Nature Warrior* and crew know where you would like them?'

Tawny nodded. 'Sure will. Right on it.'

The giant ship had hardly moved off, when Captain Green noticed another ship closing in, and another. And so it began, as ship after ship arrived. First friends and people akin to saving nature and the earth, and then their friends and contacts.

Next, were people who had read Cecile's moving article online, then their friends... In fact, Cecile's article went *totally viral*. Until word spread around the world. Word that it was time to act. Time to clean up the oceans and put right what we had put wrong.

Even with thousands and thousands of ships though, it was just like moving a mountain, stone by stone. It took time, and perseverance. How long passed, is difficult to say, months, years...

Finally, bit by bit, those ships took away that plastic and saved the animals who were tangled. Until, one day, the last few ships left with the last few holds full. And a rich sea surrounded the island, just as it had been before, centuries ago.

As the sun set on that final day, six people stood alone on the beach. One considerably taller than the rest. Captain Green, Dragon, Suzan and Jack, side by side, holding hands. Cecile, happy and calm – notebook and pencil silent and still.

Elgor, tears streaming down his face. Not just at the thought of his freedom, but at the thought of so many people all working together, not for money, or greed, but to put right one of many damaged places on that planet. At the thought of two brave children, a reporter, and at the thought of the determination of one lady, to move a mountain – against impossible odds.

'Look at that sunset,' Jack exclaimed. The five humans looked round, to gaze at the beautiful and majestic richness of the reds and oranges, dancing on the crystal-clear waters.

When they looked back, they were alone. Elgor was gone. They glanced out across the waters, scanning for him. But there was not a trace. Just then, far off in the distance, they saw a great gush of water, and the graceful curves of a whale as it surfaced then disappeared.

Daisy - B

THE END

Almost...

EPILOGUE

It had been many weeks since bidding farewell to their mountainous friend. Their journey home had been full of joy and banter on board the Emerald, watching their secret parents in their element. Suzan and Jack had mucked in with the crew, learning and enjoying their roles on the great sailing ship. Those memories, though vivid and colourful, seemed like a distant dream now.

On the surface they had slipped briskly back to their old way of life, yet there was something that had changed forever in the children. The secret adventures, and more importantly the truth surrounding their mother – the great Captain Green – was now a rippling excitement, bubbling below the surface.

There was a sense of peace and completion that had settled on their family. They were happy knowing the truth, and no longer having to make up stories with each other.

The hardest thing had been going back to school, for the two children were famous now, not for fighting pirates, or for meeting giants, or even for discovering great treasure, for those were the best kept secrets! No, they were famous for having been kidnapped. This was where the truth of their long absence stopped, and the fiction of their cover story began. The cover story, which they had to repeat – on a daily basis – to their inquisitive friends and teachers.

Oh, how they itched to tell their friends the true story, but no! Exposing their mother's secret identity, and

Elgor's existence, was not worth it, no matter how dumbfounded and flabbergasted it would make the faces of their friends. But, when they could be sure they were alone, and in the secret of whispers – in the safety of their room – they would speak and laugh about their adventures and ponder on what their mum was doing, and where Elgor was now. When the surging excitement bubbled to the surface, they could allow their vivid minds and memories to take the centre stage.

On one such rainy Saturday morning, when the sky was drab and grey, the weather mattered not to the two children who sat in a particularly vivid discussion of their mother's adventures.

Jack turned the last postcard over in his hand. 'Fun that mum still sends us these!' he said, glancing at the picture of New York city.

'I guess it helps her keep up the façade of being a businessperson, but also allows her to send us the real messages in plain sight of anyone. What did her last one say again?' Suzan asked.

'Let me read it for you sis!' Jack said, turning the post card over in his hands carefully and glancing at the back. 'It says: "*Hi children, hope you are enjoying school. Just been to New York for a business meeting with a big company. Tried the food here, the portions were big!*" and then it says…' Jack said in his best and clearest voice, pausing for a moment with a grin on his face. 'Ouch!' he exclaimed, after receiving a rather vivacious jab on the arm, from a scowling Suzan.

'You know I meant read the coded message!'

'Oh, sorry Captain Impatient! Ok. So let me see,' Jack replied, as he studied the simple message and began to decode it – just as his mum and dad had taught them, back on the Emerald.

'She says that they have just caught a large group of illegal loggers – taking trees from one of the most beautiful forests, and shut down two illegal animal test labs. And that she's planning a trip for us three to join her in the next holidays. Oh, and she will write again in a couple of weeks.'

'And we've had that card since a couple of weeks ago and it's Saturday today. You remember she said they'll always arrive on Saturdays, but she wouldn't explain how she managed to ensure that,' said Suzan.

'What time is it sis?' Jack asked, excited at the prospect of the next postcard that morning.

"Six AM,' Susan declared.

They both glanced at each other, and then at the doorway to their room. In well-practiced moves, each of them slowly and sneakily tried to stand and be closer to the doorway,

'Last one downstairs is the Boar's next lunch,' Suzan yelled.

Both sped downstairs at top speed. There was jostling and bumping as they tried to hustle their way to the front door.

'That was foul play,' declared Jack, as Suzan nudged her way past him.

'Sorry, but by hook or by crook I'll be there before you, Captain Slow!'

Both settled down, with their eyes peeled on the letterbox, waiting in great anticipation.

'I wonder where she is now?' Suzan muttered, without taking her eyes off the letterbox, for even the briefest of moments.

Thirty minutes or so later, footsteps drew closer to the front door, and the letterbox groaned, a tired and reluctant sigh, as something rustled through it and fell, with a small thud, to the soft floor below. Bewildered, Suzan and Jack glanced down, as the soft thud had certainly not come from a light postcard.

There on the mat was a brown paper parcel, with an odd array of stamps – from faraway lands. They eyed the parcel suspiciously.

'Dad probably ordered something online,' Jack said.

'No, Jack. Look at the names on it. It's addressed to us.'

Jack picked up the parcel, and put it to his ear, then felt it, to see if he could work out what was inside. 'Do you think it's safe to open it Suz?''

Suzan took a look. On close inspection, she saw a familiar name on the back, scribbled in swirly letters. 'Look it says *"Cecile"* on the back. Let's open it!'

Tentatively they tore open the brown paper parcel, to reveal a book… 'It's called…

The Legend of the Ultimate Treasure.'

Suzan read, as she flipped the book over to read the back. 'But this is… It's all about…' she said, with a furrowed brow, handing the book to Jack.

'What the… Ok, so she's changed everyone's names, but it's the whole story! Is she mad?' Jack exclaimed, looking quite disgruntled.

'Hang on, there's something inside.' Gently Suzan opened the book and pulled out a postcard. 'It says…

"To Suzan and Jack, here is my latest fantasy work of fiction! Yours, Cecile"'

'How odd. Sis, let me take a look. Hmmm, very clever,' Jack exclaimed, tracing his fingers over the pattern on the front of the postcard. 'Recognise this?' Jack grinned.

Suzan's face twisted into a look of astonishment. 'It's mum's picto-cypher!' Suzan exclaimed.

'Suz, we should ...' Jack muttered, gesturing towards the stairs with his eyes.

'Yep, let's.'

Both went upstairs, shut their bedroom door, and huddled together quietly. Jack took a piece of paper and began to decode the cypher.

Jack read it out in a whisper. 'It says…

"To Jack and Suzan. It really does seem like the truth is stranger than fiction! I have spent my life chasing things thought of as fiction, to prove them as truth. But suddenly I find myself with a truth, that must only ever be seen as fiction! So, what better place to hide the truth than in fiction! Your friend Cecile."'

Why is plastic a problem? *

The plastic can tangle creatures like sea turtles, whales, fish, and seabirds. And impacts coral reefs and many other animals and habitats. As it breaks down into microparticles, it becomes ingested by the sea life. And sadly, plastic lasts for hundreds of years, so it can continue to damage and kill sea life well into the future.

When the problem is so big, it can be difficult to think that we can help, but just like the great Captain Green, we can move mountains stone by stone!

Join Suzan and Jack and be part of the fight to reduce plastic in our rivers and oceans.

Single use plastics are one of the main areas that create ocean pollution. An example of this is a plastic bottle, which is used once and then thrown away.

Every time you avoid single use plastic, you are fighting the fight!

Here are some ideas! *

Plastic bottles
Avoid plastic bottles and carry a glass or stainless-steel water bottle which you can refill with tap water.

Plastic toothbrushes
Choose a bamboo one, which is biodegradable, fast growing, sustainable and does not need the use of pesticides. Many are available with plant-based bristles too.

Plastic cups
Avoid these and carry your own reusable cup, which most good cafes will fill for you.

Paper cups

But they are paper right, so they are fine? No, sadly *many* of the paper cups available have a thin plastic liner. Take your own reusable non-plastic cup and ask to fill it!

Plastic straws
Avoid them, and insist on only using a paper one, or bring your own reusable stainless-steel one!

Plastic bags
Carry reusable bags, made from sustainable fibres. Many will fold into a tiny item to fit in your pocket.

Plastic takeaway containers
Avoid these! Some good takeaway places allow you to take your own container and might even give a discount!

Plastic shampoo containers
Avoid these – use shampoo bars instead or buy from one of the companies who refill your original bottle each time.

Plastic soap dispensers
Avoid these – use soap bars or buy from one of the companies who refill your original bottle each time.

Cotton buds
Avoid the ones that are made from plastic and choose paper-based ones instead.

Plastic Cutlery
Avoid it and carry safe reusable cutlery.

Food packaging
This is a tough one, but there are solutions! There is an up-and-coming movement of shops that have food in bulk and allow you take your own reusable containers! If you live close enough to one, take your own containers and say no to plastic wrapped food.

What about all the plastic litter in our towns, villages and cities? *

Lots of the plastic dropped in our towns, can end up into the rivers, and then washed into the ocean. You can get involved with local groups that clean up the discarded rubbish or take a rubbish bag on a walk and pick up plastic. Every item you pick up is one less item that could damage our oceans, or the local wildlife. Always make sure you protect and clean your hands for this though!

Upcycle

By even just doing one of the above you are making a difference. But... we are so reliant on plastic that inevitably we will still have some single use plastic in our house. But the great news is that instead of throwing away a piece of packaging, you can be creative and *upcycle* it! There are tons of ideas online and in books, to make useful items from packaging.

Recycle

And finally if you can't *upcycle* it then *recycle* it!

*Information available in the public domain.

About the Authors and illustrators

Alexander Way-B is dyslexic. He has a background in art and design, studied ceramics and glass at university, has travelled extensively, worked in Japan, France and England and cares deeply for the planet and conservation. *The Legend of the Ultimate Treasure* is his first book for children.

Daisy-B is a young, but avid reader. She can always be found with her head in a book, writing her own stories, or creating pirate games of her own! She plays the piano, loves art and had much fun drawing some of the illustrations for this book.

ACKNOWLEDGEMENTS

Beta Readers
I would like to thank the following Beta readers, for taking time to read the book and for their constructive, kind, and supportive comments:
Rev Andy Bawtree
Thomas Dalton
Lisa Berry
Lesley Manton
Nettie Brannon
Daisy-B (age 10)

Publisher – I would like to thank my publisher, Louannvee and in particular Nettie for all her time and attention spent turning this novel into a presentable, and more importantly, readable book. Could not have done it without you!

Font – The fantastic font on the front cover and chapter titles is called *Booter*. It was created by Graham Meade. A big thank you to him for allowing us to use it. He has designed some very beautiful fonts.

Graphic design advice – A big thank you to Alexandre Mombrun, an exceptionally talented graphic designer, for all his professional advice and support.

Links to Dover and France – Whilst this book has its roots in Dover and France, all characters within the story are totally fictitious.

The little pathway: *Barton Path*, with its pretty river and *Happy River Mural* do exist and are enjoyed by many.
The description, of the old museum building and its staff - is purely fictitious. At present, Dover Museum is housed in a bright, modern building, complete with many interesting exhibits.

There *is* a place called *Argenteuil*, not too far from Paris, but the description leading up to and including the discovery of the huge tree, with its giant acorns, is purely fictitious!

Sadly, the famous French Chef: Pierre G. H. Francoeur, said to have trained the Boar's chef, is purely fictitious, though it should be acknowledged that there are many wonderful chefs in Paris!

Giants – And, needless to say giants are, of course, creatures of complete and utter fantasy, far removed from reality and the truth…

Quotations – The Bible quotation, in chapter 49, is from Isaiah 40:26.*

Links to pollution in the sea – although the description of the island, surrounded by plastic, is fictitious, sadly there are many areas of the oceans that are full of pollution. *The Great Pacific Garbage Patch* – for example – is a huge mass of discarded plastic and fishing gear, discovered in 1997 by CAPT. CHARLES MOORE. It has roughly eighty-thousand tons of rubbish and has been said to be about three times the size of France. *

*Information available in the public domain.

If you've enjoyed sharing Suzan
and Jack's adventures in

The Legend of the
Ultimate Treasure

Please write a review
Thankyou

www.louannveepublishing.co.uk

Printed in Great Britain
by Amazon

82672339R00233